THE MEN
CAN'T BE SAVED

THE MEN CAN'T BE SAVED

A Novel

BEN PURKERT

OVERLOOK PRESS, NEW YORK

ABRAMS The Art of Books
195 Broadway, New York, NY 10007
abramsbooks.com

For V

He was a man . . . he heard the sound of no voice but his own.

—Vivian Gornick

If it doesn't sell, it isn't creative.

—David Ogilvy

Part One

1.

I'm tempted to lie, of course. I'm tempted to tell you that I fully anticipated it would go viral. Or at least had an intuition. An inkling that what I'd written was destined for—and surely deserving of— what would follow.

In case you don't remember the ad, I'll refresh your memory. A shirtless old guy is holding an ax. And he's walking through a forest, stepping over rocks and ferns, until he arrives at a particular tree. It's not the tallest one around, but there's something about it. He draws close, then touches his hand to the bark like it's the face of a long-lost friend. A tender scene. Romantic, almost. But he's got a job to do. Simple as that.

We never actually see chopping. We only see him, with his surprisingly firm pecs and glistening torso, loading his haul into his pickup, then heading home to his adoring wife. When she greets him on the front porch with a flirty smile and an ice-cold beer, he sighs with total contentment. He's truly living the life.

And you figure that's it, that's the ad. It's another beer commercial, big deal. But you've been set up. This old guy, with his perfect body and his perfect beverage and his perfect wife, is sitting on a dirty secret: there's a steaming hot dump in his pants. Thankfully, with Smackdale All-Absorb Incontinence Men's Underwear, no need to sweat it. Heavy-duty protection—day in, day out! Go bigger. Go bolder. (Pause.) *Everyday Briefs for the Everyday Hero.*

People initially took it for parody. It was a skit, they figured, not a real ad for a real product. How thrillingly disorienting when they learned otherwise, as if the bounds of their reality had been stretched. The ad hit a million views in one week, seven million the next. The spike in sales was similarly exponential. In one fiscal quarter, Smackdale moved more adult diapers than the entire year prior, more than the company's puny offshore manufacturing arm could sustain. And while it's true that I didn't write the *whole* ad—just the tagline in fact—those six words were the campaign's crown jewel. I dare say that, without my tagline, the ad would've fizzled out in obscurity. *Inspired*, the client called it.

I brushed aside the praise, more or less. After all, the client was an authority on underwear, not the creative arts. Then advertising award season rolled around. I wasn't invited to the ceremonies—seating was reserved for executives, no junior copywriters permitted on the premises—but one week later, I tore through my office mail to discover a four-pound glimmering rhombus of Swarovski crystal. And there I was—*SETH TARANOFF*, italics and all caps—engraved along the base. I couldn't brush aside this recognition as easily. When I ran my index finger back and forth along the engraving, it felt deep.

My colleagues took notice. Who was this prodigy spinning shit accounts into gold? The other copywriters grew especially clingy. *Seth, can we bounce ideas off you?* Rather than dignify their pleading with a reply, I'd turn and motion for them to follow me down the corridor, dragging them breathless as I carried out tasks. Had they managed to keep up, I might've offered a few pearls of wisdom as a consolation prize. I always lost them after a lap.

Along the way, I'd drop in on the designers, specifically Josie. Just a year or so over thirty, she was already considered an industry veteran. Her desk was perpetually in disarray, piled high with papers. *Buy shelves*, I'd say. *Buy them for me*, she'd hit back. Her voice had

an alluring elasticity that snapped my ears to attention. Whenever I'd
find her hunched before the glare of her monitor, I'd sneak up from
behind to deliver a playful jolt to her chair. It was our little game,
and an easy one at that; her eyes tended to lock on her screen, so I
could approach undetected. But there was no winning with her, or at
least no concession of victory. Even when her shoulders jumped and
an audible gasp escaped her lips, she'd claim I failed in my attempt
to surprise. *Next time*, she'd say, and nothing more.

As I'd stroll back toward my desk, I'd pass the partners' offices
and hear my name summoned from behind frosted glass. Less clingy,
perhaps, than my fellow writers, though supplicants all the same:
Hey, can I get your eyes on this? or *I'd love to pick your brain!* They'd
only ever request use of my component parts—my eyes, my brain—as
if they implicitly understood themselves unworthy of the whole.

Diego, our chief creative director, invited me daily into his expansive office. It had the look of a well-curated art museum's gift shop:
framed charcoal sketches and loose onyx bookends and a hand-
carved teak figurine sliced out of some rain forest's heart. (A dozen
rhombuses along his window, most of which, I never failed to note,
had collected a decade's worth of dust.) Sitting opposite him, I'd
curl up in his egg-shaped chair like an unborn hatchling and, in fits
of boredom, fantasize about punching through its fiberglass shell. It
wasn't that Diego was boring but that he strained so hard to appear
not boring. He often referenced working as an apprentice to a famous
East Village sculptor—*But that*, he'd say with a wistful air, stroking
his bald and imperfectly round head, *was in a prior life.* I never asked
him about it, never permitted him any life but this one.

Seth, he'd begin, *where are we going?*

I got what he meant. He was asking about the future of our industry, or maybe our agency specifically. Founded as an advertising shop,
RazorBeat was undergoing a big transition: our focus was turning to

brands now, not ads. But what might tomorrow hold? And the day after? Oracle that I was, I offered some sincere guesses, but mostly I stirred random nouns and verbs into the air. He'd nod, stare out his window, and rub his temples raw from deep contemplation.

Diego *freaking loved*—I'm borrowing his phrasing—my confidence. It didn't matter if a meeting went well or bombed; it was critical to maintain one's swagger. He'd staffed me on all his accounts, so he had a front-row seat when my presentations weren't well received. Sometimes he'd lose his nerve. He'd deploy one of his trusty clichés in a panicked fit. Perhaps we could find common ground? Perhaps we could meet in the middle? I refused to be displaced. And really, I held firm for his sake. I had to set an example for him to follow. He was my boss in name only. He had, by nature, an apprentice's disposition.

It was obvious from the moment I started working at RazorBeat that Diego had feelings for me. It was all right there in plain sight: when he paid compliments on my new haircut; when he urged me to invest in a pair of pants that hugged the thigh; when he begged that I give him the name of my personal trainer and then, upon learning I didn't have one, erupted in a shrill pip of disbelief. I let all this go, of course. He saw me, in his words, as *The Future of RazorBeat*. It needed to stay that way.

Then one morning he called me into his office and explained he had a proposal. *Specialization*, he said. He was outfitted in his typical fashion of subtraction: clear rimless glasses, wristwatch sans numerals, black V-neck tee with no overshirt. He kept both elbows high at his sides, hands knotted under his chin. Ordinarily he was given to fidgeting, but not now. Even his eyes sat stiff in their sockets.

Specialize? But I already was a specialist! Taglines were my domain. My copywriting colleagues possessed other so-called expertise. They spent their days toiling on dense blocks of web content, an impenetrable architecture of product details and disclaimers. I did the blueprint; they did the bricklaying.

He said I was thinking *too horizontally*. Recalling the breakout success of Smackdale, he suggested I concentrate on the men's health sector, *a booming vertical with untapped potential*. And, if I was agreeable, he had the perfect client. Though technically this new account wasn't his. Another RazorBeat partner was managing it.

I stared at Diego as if from an arctic distance. *A booming vertical with untapped potential?* Who was he kidding? It wasn't just the offensiveness of the suggestion itself, but that he was so blatantly straining to sell me on it. It seemed foolish from a business perspective. Diego and I, while not ideally suited to each other, had good chemistry in presentations. We were an effective duo, recent hiccups aside. So why pair me with someone else?

I popped out of his egg and left without a word, slamming the door shut behind me. I vowed the silent treatment for days, weeks possibly. That same afternoon I blocked him on RazorChat, deleted our standing catch-up from my calendar, and swore to myself I'd never set foot in his office again. Or at least not with him in it—only with Josie, and only late at night, long after everyone else had left, cleaning crew included, so there was nobody but us.

* * *

"Don't be a baby," Josie said, as we walked to Omni Café for lunch.

When I protested, she spun toward me. In the midday sun, her face was all freckles. She took my arm and wrung it hard: "You should learn to *listen*."

"Yeah? To who?"

"The adults," she said, then steered us inside.

Just a few blocks from RazorBeat, Omni was one of those quintessential New York establishments, a cheap melting pot of international lunch fare: kimchi, pierogi, jerk chicken wraps, pork quesadillas, pho. Josie navigated the islands of steaming trays and plastic sneeze guards with no hesitation—how sharp her maneuvering, how shredded the air once she passed through it.

At RazorBeat, everyone was sleeping with somebody else. "RazorBreed," we called it, though such relationships were never reproductive. Josie and I began hooking up shortly after Smackdale, so we'd been going strong for a good while. We'd been staffed together only once, and only for a short time, which was fortunate. It gave us a helpful bit of distance, a tidy void across which to air frustrations.

"It's so obvious what Diego's doing."

"Oh?" She took up a serving spoon and broke into a mash of baked ziti.

Diego, I said, was no fool. He was restricting my client roster because he felt threatened. It was an attempt to slow my professional growth, to keep me in check. In our industry, even the senior partners were looking over their shoulders.

She piled on a few yucca fries, then tossed her hot lunch onto the scale. "Maybe he's looking out for you? You ever consider that?"

I shook her off, though I did sometimes worry about potential burnout. It was hard to put work out of my mind; I'd pass strangers on the street and compose taglines for them. Not for fun, but by necessity—they looked naked otherwise.

"And besides," she said, "what's wrong with specializing?"

"Men's health?" I replied, sorting through Omni's extensive selection of protein bars. "It's an insult."

She dug into her canvas handbag for a credit card, inspected it, then pulled out another. "You have better luck with those clients."

"Well, I'm not sure that luck is really responsible for—"

"That account from last year. Crack whatever?" She ran a scribble across her receipt. "You did a good job," she said, rounding off a slight edge in her tone. "Very charming. Very cute."

"*Smackdale*," I corrected. "And it was just a few months ago."

"The old-guy diaper thing?" she said, leading us out and back onto the sidewalk. "Definitely last year."

I figured I knew the source of her confusion: the ad had earned a Best of 2013 award, despite first airing in early 2014. Given this technicality, I'd asked Diego if I might find myself in contention for 2014 awards as well. He promised to make an inquiry.

In any case, Josie had no time for my complaining. She had her hands full at work with Lexus. Just when she thought she was finished refreshing the automaker's logo, she now had to redo the kerning. Those five characters in "Lexus" were, in the client's view, too crammed together. It was imperative that the brand's typography convey spaciousness and—

"Seth?" She paused at the curb. "Are you even listening?"

I assured her I was. I'd given little nods of affirmation, hadn't I?

"Incredible." Her eyes fluttered under the raw sting of the sun. "You're still not over Lexus, are you?"

I insisted I was very much over it, though there was nothing I felt I needed to get over. During the pitch, I'd simply told the client the truth. Their brand appealed to nobody. Or almost nobody. Maybe suburbanites like my mother—the kind of person who'd lament that her sedan compared unfavorably with others in the JCC parking lot. But when it came to cosmopolitan-minded consumers, Lexus meant nothing. Too old. Too stale. I tore the cellophane off the conference room pastry platter, liberated a bear claw, and was gone. The next day, Diego informed me that the client had requested a new writer, since she hadn't *vibed* with my contributions. Case in point, I thought. Too old, too stale.

Josie and I continued walking through the midtown bustle, a hot mess of car horns and food trucks and tour groups craning their necks to see how high everything stretched.

"Tell Diego," she said, after a block of silence between us.

"Tell him what?"

"This new client. I'll take it."

Since when, I asked, was she a copywriter?

She took a few more hurried steps, then stopped short and broke into her lunch for a fry. "Men are *really* simple, Seth." Her words, crisp with salt, cut clean off the tongue. After her nibble, she grabbed my arm again, her grip gentler this time. "You're the simplest damn thing in the world."

Before I could reply, she zipped into the RazorBeat lobby. She was running late for a meeting.

I had an open few hours, so I decided to clear my head at Java Envi, my favorite spot to sip an espresso while drafting taglines in my notebook. Most copywriters swore by their ergonomic keyboards, but I relished the physical act of writing by hand, the mechanics of setting words in one's head, then dispatching them with the thin churn of a wrist. It sometimes proved agonizing. I'd bleed ink out of all my ballpoints, scribble myself in circles. But I trusted in the struggle. It got results, didn't it?

If I ever needed a boost, I'd rewatch the Smackdale ad and peruse the YouTube comments. The overwhelming majority were glowing, though some trolls questioned the use of that phrase *Everyday Hero*. There was nothing heroic, they sniped, about chopping down a tree. What these critics failed to comprehend was the symbolism. It was an ad about toppling stereotypes! Who says an elderly gentleman in no-leak underwear can't serve as a sex symbol? Why must incontinence be a source of shame? I took the internet cretins to task and, using a pseudonym, explained what should've been obvious. When really heated, I dispensed with the fake name altogether. Once or twice, I even identified myself as the mastermind behind the tagline. If anyone understood its message, if anyone knew what *Everyday Hero* meant, clearly, I wrote, it was me.

Diego hadn't planned to staff me on Smackdale. He wanted

someone more seasoned, more suited to the demographic. But all the senior copywriters turned up their noses. It thrilled me to consider the depths of their regret. If only they'd been the ones to transform this total unknown into a household name! If only! When my colleagues watched TV in the dank recesses of their private lives, they surely anticipated Smackdale commercials with dread. I imagined them shielding their eyes and ears as my tagline ripped through the halls of their split-level homes, rattling their faded furnishings, knocking picture frames off their yellowing walls.

There was great upside to taking on underdog clients. Launching a little-known brand into the spotlight—*that* was real impact. That was making a difference. Really, wasn't Josie wasting her time on Lexus? Why indenture yourself to a name the whole world already knows? Where's the glory in that?

Sipping my espresso, I felt a new possibility surfacing. Maybe I'd misread Diego's intent. Maybe this wasn't a demotion; it was the trial before a promotion. He'd thrown me on a trash account once before, and I triumphed. He was betting I could do it again.

I downed the rest, slid a tip to my barista, and shot back up to RazorBeat. Diego was on the phone in his office. It didn't stop me.

"Seth," he said, after tapping the mute button. "Maybe I owe you an apology."

"It's fine."

"I didn't mean to suggest—I mean, please don't—"

"Seriously, forget it. We're fine."

"We are?" He shriveled into a thin smile.

"And maybe you're right," I said. "About specializing."

He scratched wordlessly at his scalp. He'd frequently fall silent in the middle of our exchanges, as if pausing to chart out a path across rocky terrain. "We still value you here. I still value—"

"The new client," I said. "Who is it?"

* * *

Whenever I write a tagline, I follow a process. I begin by listing out
practically every word in the English language. If a word has only one
meaning, I discard it. "Refrigerator," for example. I can't use that. If
a word has multiple meanings, but one of them is slang for "penis"
in Mandarin (which, I'm afraid, is not an infrequent occurrence), I
must discard that too. If a word has multiple meanings, none penis
related, I save it. I treasure it. I pair it with other such words. I experiment with all pairings, all permutations, until *eureka*—the skies are
parted, the code is cracked, the gospel is written, and all those double
and triple and quadruple meanings are multiplying exponentially.
A great tagline is more infestation than persuasion. It swarms the
mind like a plague of locusts. It means and means and never stops.

I'm proud to say my approach was entirely self-taught. I max-
imized my output by minimizing distractions: market research,
getting to know the client, blah blah blah. The less I absorbed, the
better. Isn't this true for all creative geniuses? Monet was half blind.
Beethoven was mostly deaf. I was completely ignorant.

Whenever Diego staffed me on a new account, I rushed to start
drafting taglines, and this time was no different. I mentioned the
assignment to Josie later that same day, just before midnight. She was
waiting for me in his office. Stretching across his wide window was
midtown Manhattan's lit-up skyline, its antennae tipped red with pulse.

"Well, look at you," she said. "The man who'll cure cancer!"

Prostate cancer, to be exact. The new client was a prostate cancer
nonprofit.

"Diego must have more faith in you than I thought."

"It's not his account," I said. "It's Moon's."

"Oh." Her smirk fell away.

I explained that I'd come around on the whole thing. Clearly, Diego
was assigning me this client with an eye toward my advancement.

Partnership, probably. Josie was periodically yawning while investigating her split ends.

"So you're gonna work with Moon? Really?"

He was one of the only partners I hadn't met, one of the few who hadn't called upon my services and genuflected thereafter at my altar. He was often out of the office, hustling for more clients. Whenever I did pass him in the corridor, it was fleeting; he had a habit of attracting dense flocks of interns, like a garbage barge blanketed in seagulls.

"Why? What's the issue?"

She sat on Diego's desk at an angle, her legs crossed and dangling off the side. A suggestive pose, if inadvertently so. This was something I found attractive about her: how intentions rarely announced themselves, daring me to draw near and trace them. But I was mainly attracted to her energy. She moved with pace at all times; even at rest, something was briskly ticking away inside her. With her intensity, she seemed to me an extension of the agency itself. Talking with Josie was like talking with RazorBeat, kissing Josie was like kissing RazorBeat, fucking—well, you get the picture.

"Moon's even worse than you," she said.

I feigned being insulted. Was I really so bad?

She blinked herself upright. "You're a gentleman compared to him."

"What've you heard?" To my knowledge, she hadn't worked with him. "Did he, like, do something to you?"

While I double-checked the door's lock, she reached for Diego's teak figurine. It was a nude woman abstractly conceived—no limbs, no hands, no nipples on the breasts. Josie flipped it over, searching for a signature. "How much is this worth, you think?"

"No idea."

She kept turning it over and over, the tiger bangles on her wrist clattering. "Rough guess?"

"It's Diego's, so probably a lot."

"Yeah," she muttered. "*A lot* a lot."

I stepped to the window and drew the shades. There was nobody left in our office—I was sure of that—though I did worry about people looking in. Given the late hour, it seemed unlikely. Our office abutted other offices; anyone who saw us was probably doing the same thing we were. Though most corporate cultures weren't like ours. We were in the habit of servicing multiple clients at once; it taught us to be promiscuous. I was a prude, relative to my colleagues, since most were cheating on significant others. I'd never met Josie's boyfriend, but I knew he existed.

What would it be like, I wondered, to date Josie? We'd never discussed the subject of her boyfriend, but the details she volunteered piqued my curiosity: a Marxist with a music career who wore safety pins in all his clothes, tiny holes poking through everything. She made clear they had no future together, so I found myself almost endeared to this poor sap from afar. As long as she was with him, she was available, or would be in a matter of weeks, months at most.

When I finished closing the shades, she was still busy with the nude figurine, inspecting it under the glow of Diego's desk lamp. One step, two steps, an easy grab.

"Hey!" she squealed. "Not yours."

"Not yours either," I taunted, dangling the prize out of reach.

I hoped for a swipe, a slap, a little fire. But she showed no interest in playing along. She'd already dragged her gaze toward another valuable on the shelf, appraising it with a scowl.

"Now back to Moon," I said. "Tell me what you know."

"Let's just do this, Seth." Her fingers bothered the square buttons of her shirt until it fell, crumpled, to Diego's desk. "I need to get back to work."

* * *

I focused exclusively on Prostate for weeks. I'd spend long hours at Java Envi drafting taglines in my notebook, then return to my desk to cull through my many worthy contenders. Things were going well. Swimmingly, in fact.

I still hadn't met Moon, but I'd feed him detailed updates on my progress. He didn't reply. Not once. It started to infuriate me. Here I was, slaving away on *his* account, and he didn't have the basic courtesy to email back? Finally, when he did respond, the message was blank except for a hyperlink. It was titled **IMPORTANT RESEARCH**.

Those two words alone set me off. What was he implying? That my work wasn't sufficiently informed? As soon as I clicked, I went from annoyed to aghast: he'd sent me a seventeen-minute video labeled "DIY Prostate Exam." More pornographic than educational in nature, it featured a dubious medical expert bending over a cocktail ottoman and inserting a lubricated index finger—sans glove because of a stated latex allergy—into his own rectum, explaining what to feel for and why. I shut the browser window before anyone else could see.

I wasn't sure what was more shocking: that a partner sent me such a thing or that RazorBlocker failed to intercept it. I swiftly deleted it from my inbox and mind. I wasn't in the mood for jokes, if that's what this was. And it was, wasn't it? A joke?

Moon was traveling a lot, so email was our only means of communication. I endeavored to puzzle him out in his absence, scrutinizing his profile on the agency website. Most partners had professional black-and-white portraits, but Moon's headshot was a soft-focus selfie; he wore a tomato-red polo and a grin that split open his face. I saved the high-res version to my desktop—so I could analyze it at length—and charged onward, well into the wee hours.

Colleagues urged me to go home. They alluded to scientific studies about creativity and sleep cycles. I held firm. Night, I insisted, helped me focus. Sure, there were distractions: the mosquito-like buzzing of globe lights suspended from the ceiling, the erratic gargling of AC units, the irritable stirring of screensavers. But I loved staying late. The office transformed after dark. It assumed the austere chill of a holy temple.

And then there was Josie. When I was sure everyone else had left for the day, I'd RazorChat her, and, when obliging, she'd hit pause on her work to indulge in some light recreation. Poor Diego didn't have any idea of what took place in his office—on his desk, in his desk chair, and, for added spice, in his egg. After, it was like nothing happened. She'd button herself up and march back to her desk. Later in the night, if her chat icon dimmed gray, I'd pad down the corridor to find her slumped and snoring at her keyboard. It would've been cruel to scare her. Instead, I'd stand close, clear my throat, and read out loud—not to wake her, just a whisper—my latest taglines-in-progress. Good practice for client presentations. And intimate, in a way. Like postcoital conversation. Like cuddling.

I took these opportunities to say other stuff too. I paid compliments or posed rhetorical questions or tendered vague confessions. I confessed, for example, that sometimes—not often—I felt uncertain about my abilities. No, never as a copywriter, but as a future exec. Still, I knew I'd measure up, when the time came. Strong leadership style, though not heartless. I'd keep a box of tissues on my corner-office desk. It would signal tolerance for vulnerability.

In Josie's snoring presence, I'd sometimes touch on even more personal matters. Her boyfriend, for one. It nagged at me that I was party to, or a willing participant in, her infidelity. But hey, I wasn't the only one behaving badly. *A gentleman compared to him*, that's what she called me. Next to Moon, I belonged on a pedestal.

It was 2:00 A.M. when, after much internal deliberation, I emailed him my final proposed tagline for Prostate. Even Josie had packed up for the night, but I felt no desire to head home. My apartment fridge promised only moldy leftovers; I'd find greater nourishment in RazorBeat's complimentary snack drawer. After a few sodium-heavy handfuls, I returned to my desk, though not before stopping by Moon's office.

I wasn't exactly sure why I wanted to see it. In any case, the door was locked. When I stood on my tiptoes, I could just barely look in through a top strip of window, though the darkness made it hard to discern how he'd furnished the space or to even size up its square footage. I kept straining, even hopping a little, but the only thing I could see was my face in the reflection.

I was finally about to pack up when I decided to watch the Smackdale ad, just one more time. I was already quite familiar with the exhilarating high of seeing my tagline on-screen, so I focused my attention on the lead actor's performance. Masterful, really, how he muscles through scenes with such composure. Then, at the end of the ad, he looks into the camera and does the unthinkable. He winks. A playful gesture, but he's not breaking the fourth wall for laughs. He's selling to the audience. He's selling that he sees what they see; that he feels what they feel; that he's, effectively, one of them.

We're all everyday heroes, he's saying. With a wink.

2.

"The thing is, clients are addicts—soon enough, their nostrils burn out. Then we start dealing them shit, I'm talking about *actual* shit, straight out of our asses. They still take it! Let's be honest, and I'm not talking about you, Seth, but our work sucks dead donkey dick. No offense. Not your fault, not RazorBeat's fault. All agencies are basically the same. Hey, maybe you're interviewing? Maybe headhunters are banging down your door, selling you on some boutique shop in Dumbo? Treadmill desks, foosball tables, fuckable interns. But ask yourself, why are they bending over backward? It's because they're desperate! They'd kill to be RazorBeat. They'd kill, just like that."

I set down my beer on the airport bar's countertop. Moon indeed looked like his headshot, though his features appeared coarser in person. He wore his blond hair in an uncombed sweep. His nose jutted out with immodesty. As he spoke, his mouth opened wide around each word before smacking shut. In sum, he was large and loud. And yet even as he boomed, his face had a pinched quality, like someone had given it a good squeeze before letting go.

Moon was tapping away at his laptop. He stopped to sip his bourbon, then spun the screen around to face me. "This it?"

I scanned the title slide—"Prostate Cancer Research Group: Tagline Presentation"—and nodded. The file, I declared proudly, was ready for upload. He swooped his index finger to the return key, then enlisted it to dig excess wax out of his ear.

At twenty-nine, Robert McCloone was just three years older than me, though he held an impressive distinction: the youngest RazorBeater ever to make partner. From what I pieced together, Moon, as everyone called him, possessed a single talent: infectious freneticism. Upper management had taken note of his attention deficit disorder and diagnosed it as promising; he had the kind of motor that, if harnessed, could power a long and fruitful career. It was all bullshit, of course. He had nothing to offer the agency, nothing of real value. He was simply adept at toggling back and forth between multiple accounts, and the speed of this toggling gave the false impression he was managing an overwhelming number of accounts at once, a bounty of unspeakable proportions. It was absurd that he'd risen so quickly up the ranks, but it couldn't be helped. Every agency has its share of Moons.

As we waited for our connection to be announced, I told him I was excited. Prostate, I believed, could go big.

He said nothing in response. Then he turned over his bourbon with a few slow-paced swirls. "Nonprofits are the worst clients. True or false?"

There was a presentation to focus on. I wasn't inclined to play games.

"*True*," he answered. "And you wanna know why?"

I figured I knew what he'd say, something about philanthropic clients demanding discounts, charities wanting charity, etc.

He set down his glass hard on its coaster. "It's because those people are fucking miserable! And honestly, can you blame them? Imagine your day job was raising money for cancer research. You tell yourself you're changing the world, doing the Lord's work, whatever. Then you shoot an ad with a terminal case. Maybe you meet her kids, eat her tuna casserole, see her suffering up close. I mean, you really get

to know her. When it's over, you even call from time to time, just to
keep in touch. And the ad turns out great, a real tearjerker. But then
what happens? It goes live, and nobody gives!"

I looked away just to dodge the sharp end of his gaze, listening
for our boarding call.

"Sure, the big donors come through, as always. But the general
public, they don't blink. And pretty soon, you know what? You check
out. Too fucking hard." He sipped again. "And you stop calling that
poor lady, because really, what can you say?"

What was his point, exactly? It was difficult to imagine any organization more worthy of RazorBeat's services than one fighting cancer.
If the nonprofit was struggling with fundraising, we could help. A
great tagline was the key.

Silence pooled between us, so I splashed right on through.
"Nonprofits do good work."

He yawned. At me.

"What I mean," I said firmly, "is they make an impact."

"No guarantee. Not even fifty-fifty! My brother used to work for
HopeVision."

"HopeVision?"

"They're a redistributor, basically. They ask people to donate
their glasses, then hand them out to poor people with the same prescription. Nice, right? And they trek all around the globe, even the
most bumblefuck villages. That's how some granny in Uganda ends
up with a pair of Warby Parker hipster frames. But remember, these
people are *dirt* poor. Never seen glasses, let alone worn them. They
open their eyes and freak out. They're hugging everyone, because
everything's in focus. A whole new world! Incredible ad, incredible
publicity. So what's the problem?" Moon dipped closer. His hair was
so blond, it looked raw. "After one day with the glasses, they bury
them. Literally bury in the ground. Too scary."

I turned my focus to the terminal's automated walkways. Well-dressed businessmen passed with the smooth run of a new razor.

"Imagine you're living in Uganda, and you're married fifty years to some bastard, and he's a blurry piece of shit. Then, for the first time, you really see him. Warts, wrinkles, all of it. But hey, you'd still love him anyway. You could deal, right? Then you see *yourself* in the mirror. Well, that's murder! You dump the glasses in the ground and never look back."

I resisted the impulse to venture off to the gate alone. Fine, HopeVision was a failure. So what?

"Failure? You kidding? Raised almost a hundred million last year! They play that ad and everybody empties their pockets. The operation keeps expanding."

I still wasn't sure what his point was, if there was one. I insisted it was time to head to our gate. I was going to give the presentation, with or without him.

He yanked his computer charger out of the wall socket, its teeth dragging on floor tile. "It makes you wonder," he said, reeling it in slow, looping the slack around his forearm. "All those eyeglasses." He paused at his last loop and dreamed for a moment. "Who's gonna dig them up?"

* * *

Our Prostate clients, Lawrence and Gage, called down to the lobby to say they were running late. Rather than endure small talk with Moon in the interim, I stepped out into the oppressive Tulsa heat. I needed to make a phone call.

I wasn't the sort of person who calls his mother often, but business trips made for a good occasion to do so. I'd tell her my whereabouts, and she'd happily enlighten me regarding the size of the area's Jewish population. While I didn't particularly care how many fellow Jews

I might expect to encounter in, say, the greater Tulsa region, it gave us something to talk about. It was convenient that we were such a widely scattered people; thanks to diaspora, I was never too far from my own.

I tried on my cell but couldn't reach her. I was about to try again when Moon came out and waved me inside. They were ready for us.

Our khaki-clad clients offered a cheery greeting and led us through a corn maze of cubicles. We arrived at a conference room where a platter of cinnamon buns glistened on the table. It was understood that we weren't to eat them, that their mere visual presence was meant to satiate us fully.

The more senior of the two, Lawrence kicked things off. "Boys," he said, setting his flip phone to the side, "let's get to it."

I'd never presented with Moon before, but I had a good sense of how the hour would unfold: the partner spouts banalities about the weather, sports, etc., then clicks through a dry slideshow of research findings. He lays the strategic foundation, so to speak, but the *real* strategic goal is boring the client to tears. Then, when it's time for the creative, the room is hungry to say yes to anything. Such is the brilliance of The Reveal.

I never felt nervous during presentations. I was, however, highly attuned to the stakes at hand. Regardless of what Moon said, this was an important client doing important work. The prostate meant more than some ordinary product. It wasn't lost on me that I contained one myself.

There were other stakes too, of course. Had I been less certain of my impending promotion to partner, I might've felt it more acutely, the immense pressure to secure yet another career-defining win, another rhombus lovingly packaged atop a bed of Styrofoam peanuts. I could envision the agency-wide email announcement and what would follow. The copywriting department would shower me in bitter fistfuls of confetti. I'd fend off Diego's giddy advances during work hours, then join Josie in an evening of celebration. Maybe the two of us would go out for drinks, like a real couple. Maybe we'd dine somewhere without need of sneeze guards. And, soon enough, I'd have my own office for us to fool around in, though we'd likely still avail ourselves of Diego's on occasion—less for adventure's sake than a stroll down memory lane. In any case, the championship belt would be notched: RazorBeat's *new* youngest partner ever.

Moon was nearing the end of his spiel when I noticed something disconcerting: Lawrence and Gage didn't appear bored in the slightest. They were *laughing*. Moon had charmed them and thus botched his only job.

"Well," Lawrence said, "we can't wait to hear it."

Gage swiveled toward me, doubling the anticipation. Moon also swiveled, though with less verve, since he knew what was coming.

I should pause here to explain that every copywriter does The Reveal in their own way and, most importantly, at their own pace. Some drag out the suspense; others pounce fast for a clean kill. I belonged, proudly, to the first set. Prior to The Reveal, I'd recline in my chair and leave my mouth ajar for a pregnant pause. I liked giving clients the impression I was formulating the tagline at that instant or, better yet, that it was a spontaneous creation of mystical origin, the words spoon-fed to me by some higher power.

"Prostate Cancer Research Group," I declared, with a carnival barker's rising inflection. "*More Might for the Fight.*"

Lawrence scratched once at his chin, then nudged his eyeglasses up the steep slope of his nose. "It rhymes." He looked at Gage. "Does it have to rhyme?"

"Rhymes are good," Moon said. "More memorable."

Lawrence offered me a queasy expression. "And why 'might'?" He pushed out a chuckle. "It's sort of a funny word."

"I'm sorry?"

"Too wishy-washy. You *might* do something, you *might* not."

"Yeah, I agree," Gage said. "Sounds kinda weak."

I shot a blistering stare at Lawrence's subordinate, but his eyes were aimed low. He was tending to his mechanical pencil; it had malfunctioned, choking on its thin stores of graphite.

I placed my hands calmly on a cold stretch of table. "'Might,'" I asserted, "means strength, in this context. The very opposite of weakness."

"Oh, like a noun," Lawrence said. "Like 'fight.'"

"'Fight' is a verb, I think?" Gage looked up at me. "Isn't it?"

I considered reaching for the stale cinnamon buns so as to arm myself with projectiles. How could I reason with these imbeciles? How could I explain that every word had been handpicked on the very basis of its multiplicity? That I'd composed a tagline of such penetrating genius that it shattered all distinctions between parts of speech!

Lawrence exhaled and scratched again at the dimple in his chin. "Boys, I do appreciate the effort. But this slogan isn't it."

Moon offered something between a sigh and a grunt. Then, in the next instant, he tapped a happy knuckle on the tabletop. "I hear you, Larry."

I felt the quick and unmistakable sting of friendly fire. *Larry.* Was my own colleague taking sides against me? After *he* was the one who sabotaged our presentation?

"How about we serve up a couple more options?" Moon was talking to me but looking at the clients. "What do you say, Seth?"

Even at his worst, Diego never undermined me like this. I contemplated taking out my notebook and reading off some alternatives, but I knew that would only make me appear weak. More might for the fight, *that* was what was needed.

"No," I announced. "I'm sorry, but no."

I hoped the forcefulness of my denial would shake them out of their obstructionism. It was a move I'd pulled in the past to mixed effect, though on this occasion, it hardly registered. Lawrence was already thinking ahead to the next round.

"Try focusing on the science," he went on. "Give them a peek into what we're doing here in Tulsa. Genuine breakthroughs! You know about IQBlade360? You do, right?"

Moon was busy checking his phone. He shook his head no.

"Well, it started downstairs in our lab. There's no blade, of course. It's smart radiation." His voice fluttered in a sudden updraft of enthusiasm. "Each beam is like a GPS-guided missile. It actually *knows* where it's going. It's the game changer we've been waiting for, it really is."

Lawrence gave the conference room ceiling a dark stare.

"Men are dying. Thirty thousand each year. Two hundred thousand cases diagnosed annually." He stopped to let the numbers sink in. "That's basically half of Tulsa, right there."

"Tulsa," Moon muttered, "isn't all that big."

I kept trying to make eye contact with Moon to assess the damage—he had to have known I'd stand up for my work, that I'd defend it fervently, as any self-respecting creative should—but there was no getting through to him. His attention flitted with no anchor; he'd run his eyes over our client, then back to his phone, then the wall, then its window. The more Lawrence dragged on, the more antsy Moon looked. He'd begun inching his chair back from the table.

"Boys, it's been a silent epidemic for too long. I want an ad campaign that tells our story. That's the key right there. An inspiring story." Lawrence was appealing to Moon with this logic. Then he turned, so his eyes met mine and held there. "And if the tagline rhymes," he continued, "it rhymes."

I sensed Lawrence was softening his stance. This was my last chance to make my case, to persuade him that my tagline would do everything he needed and that he needed to trust me. I did Smackdale, for God's sake!

I was just about to speak when Moon cleared his throat. It was a deep and resonant sound, the tuning of a heavy instrument in the bowels of an orchestra pit. He ran a slow hand back through his hair, the strands tensing tall before collapsing in its wake. "An ad campaign, Larry? That's what you want? Hire an ad agency. Quit fucking wasting our time."

For all my shows of bravado, I'd never spoken to a client like this before. Never even considered that such language could ever find its way out of the mouth of any RazorBeat employee in a presentation context. Like all agencies, we pretended to push around our clients, but that's all it was, pretend. We play-slapped them because they begged to be play-slapped. This was different. This went beyond.

Lawrence looked physically unwell in the wake of the attack. He tried a few times to muster a response, then turned to Gage in a plea for support. His minion proved no help: he kept his head low while disassembling his pencil, bit by bit.

Moon remained glued in position. Then he doubled down. "We do *branding*, Larry. Big-picture stuff. That's what we"—he made a sweeping gesture that spanned just the two of us—"are all about." Then he gave a big smile, the same one from his profile picture on RazorBeat's website, the one that sliced wide through one end of his face to the other.

The meeting was over. There was nothing more to say, nothing more to do, except norms required we give and receive handshakes. I was so disoriented that I tried to shake Moon's hand. A horrendous faux pas. He stared at my open palm until it disappeared.

* * *

Tulsa's top steak house was closed for a private party, so Moon opted for McDonald's instead. "Fuck it," he said, swerving us into the lot.

The table felt sticky to the touch, and the lighting overhead cast a chemical-white gleam. A Ronald cardboard cutout on the wall announced we could win a million dollars or, better yet, we might already be winners and not know it.

Moon was still fuming, a mix of snarl and smirk. "You believe that jerkoff? Lecturing us like that?" He popped a McNugget into his mouth.

I was fuming too, but not at Lawrence. Upon entering McDonald's, I'd ducked into the bathroom so I could shoot an email to Diego. He had to know: this fiasco was Moon's fault, not mine. If only he'd had my back, if he'd given me any support whatsoever, I could've sold in the tagline, no problem. And yet, despite all this, part of me admired how he handled himself. It was an impressive show of force, like a hurricane punching the atrium roof off a mall. No, that's not the right simile. A hurricane is hollow at its center, whereas Moon seemed of solider and sturdier composition.

"So," I said, poking at a scrap of iceberg with my plastic fork. "How do we win back their trust?"

"Their trust?" Moon was mid-chew. He took a moment, then revved himself back up. "Those fucks don't even know what branding is! Couldn't smell it a mile away."

It was true that they weren't sophisticated. But if they didn't grasp the distinction between branding and advertising, it was Moon's job to explain it! Elementary stuff: ad campaigns come and go, but a brand is forever. It's DNA. It's who you are and always will be and really can't help being, even if you try.

I explained to him that, while I usually resisted such compromises, I'd go along with his original suggestion. I'd generate more taglines for Lawrence to consider.

"Don't bother."

"Really, I don't mind—"

"Not worth it," he said. "We're cutting bait."

As I picked at my salad, Moon kept plowing through his meal. A few rowdy teens took the table next to ours, but he remained unfazed by their presence. It was striking how dense he seemed at the surface, how the world just bounced off him.

I ignored Moon's comment and began quietly brainstorming some alternatives worth presenting. But it was clear he wasn't done.

"See, I warned you about nonprofits! He's bitching about inspiring folks. Want to guess why no one's giving?" He dragged out his pause between bites. "Ninety percent survival rate! You're a grizzled fuck and the doctor says you've got prostate cancer—what do you say? Thank you, Lord Jesus, sweet holy Moses; praise be to Allah!

"It's a joke," he said. "It's nothing."

The wooden trash receptacle near us was engraved with the trademark golden arches and the McDonald's tagline *i'm lovin' it*. One of the most recognizable taglines in the world, and one of the most daring. It's risky to speak in the customer's voice because it often causes offense. Really, who was McDonald's attempting to ventriloquize here? Someone with no command of capitalization? Someone too cool to care? The teens next to us had settled down.

"The thing is," Moon continued, "it's all a zero-sum game."

I tried to excuse myself for another bathroom trip—had Diego written back yet?—but he just kept going.

"Those poor shits in Uganda, you know what they actually need? Mosquito nets. We could rent helicopters, drop nets on their asses, cut the malaria rate right in half. But no. Not *innovative* enough. Not like . . . IQBlade360."

I nodded like I agreed, but I didn't agree. I typically had no problem telling partners why they were wrong; in Moon's case, I wasn't sure where to begin.

Before swallowing his last McNugget, he stopped and held it for a few moments in the light. "You know what this is?"

"It's a nugget," I muttered.

He brought it closer to my face. He was daring me to chomp. "It's a *gold* nugget," he corrected. "It's edible gold. Affordable gold." He dipped it in ketchup, bit into it hard, then wiped his mouth on his forearm. He stared admiringly at the half of McNugget that remained. "Whoever named this," he said, his eyes widening, "was a genius."

After lunch, he got us on an earlier flight. We raced to the airport, windows open, the wind tugging hard at our faces, testing how they held. I stared silently out at the passing landscape with its interminable run of single-story office complexes. I'd once asked Josie where she was from, and she said only that her hometown was flat and boring, nowhere special. When I asked a second time, she abbreviated. Just *nowhere*.

RazorBeat partners had the option of flying first class, but most, Diego included, chose to sit alongside their subordinates in the name of team building. Moon, however, claimed his throne without compunction. When I passed him en route to coach, he was sprawled in deep sleep, his chin tucked to his chest, with his hands in his lap and feet inching close to the aisle. They were very large, his hands and feet—a generous serving of extremity. I stopped and stared for a moment, mentally comparing them against my own, until the flight attendant nudged me along with a firm smile.

I took the middle seat between two old ladies and held quiet as the plane accelerated up and over the cloud cover. I was sure at least one of them would strike up a conversation, and frankly I looked forward to it; I'd push past the usual pleasantries and begin talking about my line of work, how I was employed at one of New York's top branding agencies and was involved—if not directly—in a highly specialized area of cancer research, and it all was highly complex, highly technical, and what about them, whose lives were they saving?

I grabbed as many snacks from the food cart as permitted. McDonald's left me with nothing but wilted roughage in my gut and a murmuring voice in my head: *i'm lovin' it. i'm lovin' it.*

I tried to forget about the tagline, but I kept returning to it, some nagging urge to dissect its composition. I fixated on the choice of verb tense. If you're *lovin'* something, that's a fulfilling experience. But if you *love* something, it's not as satisfying. You can love a meal and still be hungry after.

I sometimes wondered what would happen if I told Josie I loved her. I didn't actually love her, of course, but how would she respond? Would something flare or fizzle in her eyes? Or maybe nothing would happen. Maybe she wouldn't even blink.

I'd only ever told one girl I loved her, which hadn't exactly gone well. In fairness, I hadn't wanted to say it. She was my college girl-friend of three months—we lived down the hall from each other on the top floor of our freshman dorm—and she was constantly telling me she loved me. The thing was, it was clear she didn't. Not really. She was just saying the words in the hope I'd say them back. And it went on like this for a long time, her slipping *I love you* into every conversation, stabbing it like a blunt weapon into me, repeatedly, such that I might bleed out the phrase she wanted, until I had no choice but to surrender. And no, I didn't love her, but I did like her. I liked her a lot, in fact. But then a funny thing happened. The minute I said the words, she grew angry with me. She didn't like *how* I said them. She said it was obvious I hadn't meant them at all and that it was cruel to say those words to someone and not mean them. When I pointed out the irony, that *she* had started this little insincere game in the first place, she turned speechless with rage. But she must not have remained speechless for very long, because soon everyone in our dorm had heard I was a monster and worth avoiding at all costs, until I could walk down all five dormitory flights and not hear a single hello.

The plane bumped us through a run of turbulence. After the clouds parted, the old lady on my left gestured toward her window with a frail wrist. I craned but, from my vantage point, could see only sky. *Look harder*, her wrist said. *I'm trying*, my eyes said. (*i'm lovin' it*, McVoice said.) I figured she spied something a few thousand feet below. A church steeple of note? An architectural gem of a bridge? But she wasn't aiming at anything on the ground. She was pointing at the sunset.

It looked like every other sunset I'd seen. Beautiful, repetitive. The standard slate of colors swirling and looping back on themselves— peach to pink to peach—as if lacking originality, singing the same old songs, thinking the same old thoughts. I couldn't help looking down on the sky. It had no imagination. It was going nowhere.

She urged again, aloud this time, but I had seen enough.

3.

I decided we'd be sitting for lunch, and I'd be paying. For once, there'd be no Omni, no stomach-turning smell that came with it.

"Fine," Josie said, hunched at her monitor. "So where?"

Despite working at RazorBeat for well over a year, I knew few sit-down lunch spots. "Thai Palace?"

"You're taking me to a palace." She spun back from her work to hook me with her attention. "I'm so honored."

We braved the midtown swelter and took a booth by the restaurant's decorative waterfall. After we ordered, Josie left to go to the bathroom. I used those spare moments to review my notebook's latest entries. While the events in Tulsa had shaken me at first, I felt invigorated in the days following. When I explained to Diego what happened, he sounded unconcerned, perhaps a little preoccupied with other matters. As for Moon, I implored him to give me one more shot with the client. He answered, simply, that I was on my own. I interpreted this as a green light.

From the new batch, I'd settled on my three top choices:

Improving Science for Men.
Better Science for Men.
Science in Service of Men.

Any of these would win Lawrence over, I was sure. And maybe, though it pained me to say so, he'd been right. *More Might for the Fight* was too slick, too flippant. Moon could downplay its seriousness if he wanted, but cancer is still cancer.

When Josie returned, I noted a change in her appearance. Her hair was up in a donut bun, exposing the pleasing slope of her shoulders.

"Hey," I said. "Can I get your take on something?"

I'd invited her here for one reason: validation. It boosted my confidence to read my taglines to her while she was sleeping; awake, I figured, would work just as well. I shared the three options and asked for her favorite.

"What do you mean?" I said, when she declined. "Just pick!"

"I'm a designer. Words aren't my thing."

I told her I simply wanted her opinion. As a friend.

"Honestly?" She ran a forefinger along the underside of the bun, checking that it was still holding, that nothing had come loose. "They all sound the same."

She tried rounding into a more encouraging posture. Something about believing I could do better, how she believed I had it in me. I wasn't interested in long-winded beliefs. It was a multiple-choice question.

"If they all sound the same," I said finally, "that's perfect."

"Perfect?"

"Yes. It means I'm closing in on the right one."

She laughed out loud, then pulled up short. Her eyes took a second to blink themselves clear. "I have never met anyone so incapable of handling criticism."

I insisted she was wrong about me. I appreciated criticism, provided it was constructive.

"Must be exhausting," she said. She was leaning back in her chair and rocking slightly, testing how much its rear legs could bear. Then the line of her voice, typically taut, went soft. "You can't live your entire life like this, Seth."

I could feel the waterfall's mist on my face. "Like what?"

She shifted her weight forward. Her face was close to mine, like she was leaning in to whisper, except she wasn't. "I've known lots of fragile people, and they all pull the same shit. They blame their problems on everyone else. But the most fragile ones, the ones who've been fragile their whole lives, they stop eventually. And you know why?"

Where on earth was our waiter?

"Because, after a while," she said, "there's no one left to blame. They've pushed everyone the fuck away." Josie sat up straight and set back her shoulders. Then she swept a hand along her skirt, just to run out the creases, had there been any.

I couldn't let her comments go unchallenged. How was it *fragile*, I asked, to stand by my work? Perhaps, if anything, I was too loyal. My biggest strength was my biggest weakness.

The full weight of her hair loomed heavy above her forehead. "Your biggest weakness," she corrected, "is that you're weak." She delivered these words with stoic indifference, like they'd long ago hardened into fact.

I met Josie's stare and felt, for the first time, that I saw her for what she was. At night, in the poorly lit expanse of Diego's office, certain blemishes passed without scrutiny; but not here, not now. I was wearing my HopeVision glasses. I was seeing in painful clarity.

I was quick to snap my wooden chopsticks at the joint when the waiter set down our plates. Josie requested a fork.

I went in for a bite. "Your boyfriend," I said. "How's he doing?"

"Travis? Fine. He just wrapped up a West Coast tour." She dug her freshly delivered utensil into a mountain of sticky rice. "Actually, you might meet him soon."

I rested my chopsticks parallel at the rim of my plate. "Oh? Why's that?"

She looked up from her dish. "He's interviewing this week."

I let the news sink in, watched the mountain topple into itself. The waiter was back again, now with a tumbler of Thai iced tea. I hadn't remembered Josie ordering it. She offered me the first sip, though I wanted none of it.

"Interviewing for what job, exactly?"

Bringing the tea to her lips, she stretched out a pause. Then she smiled her eyes into dark slivers. "Copywriter."

I began smoothing my chopsticks with a restless fervor, rubbing each up and down the length of its mate. With sufficient friction, I'd produce sparks, possibly set the Palace ablaze. I asked her if Travis had agency experience.

"Zero!" she said. "Like you, when you started." The first week I joined RazorBeat, Josie was one of the only designers who didn't introduce herself. She later told me she saw no need. She thought it unlikely I'd survive.

"What about his politics?"

"His . . . politics?"

"You said he's a Marxist." Seeking employ at a profit-hungry enterprise like RazorBeat? What, pray tell, would Karl say?

"Seth, honey, you shouldn't feel threatened."

I assured her I didn't feel that way. Not in the least.

"And besides," she added, "he won't work at RazorBeat for long, just until he goes back on tour." She gave her iced tea a swirl, then let the condensed milk separate out again. "It's about the money."

It took me a moment before I understood: the agency's recruitment bonus. HR provided financial incentives for referrals. If Travis were to secure a full-time job, she'd pocket a thousand dollars.

As Josie lifted her glass for another sip, her tiger bangles tumbled wrist to forearm. I was focused on her every move, but she was looking away, toward the tiny waterfall.

I mounted a final challenge: I called Travis a hypocrite. "A true Marxist," I explained, "wouldn't care about money at all."

"Exactly," she said, toying with her bangles, catching them under the glow of Thai Palace's chandelier. "It's *my* money."

* * *

I needed a long vacation. By which I mean HR needed me to take one. I hadn't ever missed a day of work, so now I was forced to use my weeks or lose them. I told HR I'd valiantly sacrifice, but they objected. What if, they said, others felt pressure to forfeit *their* vacation time? It could snowball! RazorCulture could suffer! In hindsight, I should've pushed back harder. I submitted the PTO request through gritted teeth.

My modest bank account balance was going to hamper any vacation plans, so I asked my parents if they'd consider pitching in. Before I could enumerate all the character-building benefits of traveling abroad, my mom's enthusiasm leaped out from the phone. She had the perfect solution, she said, and it wouldn't cost a dime. Birthright.

I had no interest in going to Israel. Growing up, I'd been made to enroll in Jewish sports leagues, attend Jewish band camp, participate in every Jewish or Jewish-adjacent activity that my suburban Maryland neighborhood offered. I'd had my fill, in other words. But my mom had a point. Financially, it made sense.

I feigned ignorance during the application process to appear a more appealing candidate for indoctrination. (*Rosh Hashanah? Never heard of it. Shabbat? Not a clue.*) It worked like magic. As the trip neared, a little excitement took root. I fell prey to erotic fantasies set at the Dead Sea, replete with sunbathing, mud drizzling, titillating trysts of buoyancy.

When I told Moon about my upcoming vacation, I assured him I'd keep working on Prostate the whole time. I was nearing a breakthrough; I could feel it. He shrugged, then asked if I knew whether the communal snack drawer had been refilled and, if so, with which snacks specifically—the salt and vinegar chips, or those jalapeño ranch fuckers that nearly ended his life?

When I told Diego more or less the same thing, that I planned to work during the trip, he took a more scolding posture. "Give yourself a mental break. What can't wait until you're back?"

Prostate, I reminded.

"Small potatoes!" he said, barely looking up from his desk. "We'll find someone to cover."

I wasn't sure how to explain that Moon had taken a back seat, so really the account had become my pet project. And besides, which other copywriter would suffice? No, nobody was up to the task. I insisted the project stay mine and mine alone.

"By the way," I added. "We have enough copywriters."

Diego faced me now, his chin tilted high. He placed his rimless glasses on his desk and stared at me through breezeless air.

"I'm just saying there's no need to hire more." I straightened with stern affirmation. "The team is solid. As is."

A smile strained him. He nodded it away. "Seth," he began, after setting his glasses back in place, "I'd like to impart a wee bit of wisdom, a little something I've learned in the course of my many trips around the sun."

I'd never before heard him lecture. Or rather the transitive form: I'd never heard him lecture me.

"People," he continued, "are very *beautiful*, very *complex* creatures. But in many ways, we're no different from computers. Even brilliant creatives, like you and me. From time to time"—he extended an open hand to his laptop—"it's important to reboot. You'd be surprised," he added thoughtfully, "how much it can fix."

He smiled again, less strain in his teeth. Then he spun away toward his window and adjusted the shades, letting in a sudden flood of light. I stood by, silent and illuminated, as he checked email on his phone.

My attention lingered not on his words but on his window. Why, I wondered, weren't his shades open in the first place? It wasn't like him to leave them drawn so late in the day. I confronted a frightful possibility: Had I been careless during one of the prior nights and forgotten to open them back up?

As he thumbed at his screen, I scrutinized the calm of his face for a flicker of suspicion. Did he open the shades to send me a message, to signal what he knew? It suddenly hit home how reckless Josie and I were being. We were only fooling around, sure, but we were risking our future at the agency. Though my future, I reminded myself, was its own entity. It had nothing to do with hers.

Diego's mind was on his phone. Its glare rippled across his sloping brow.

"Hey." I gestured to his teak figurine. It sat on the middle shelf to his right. "I like that thing a lot."

He peeled himself away from whatever held his attention.

"Where'd you get it? A gift from a client?"

He shook his head no.

"That East Village sculptor? Is that who made it?"

"Not quite," he said. "I could never afford one of his." He swiveled and, with a curator's care, scooped it up from the base. "I nabbed this at auction years ago. Probably a good decade before you were born." He held it up to the window's light, where it found an added gleam.

"Can I have it?"

The sunlight was beating hard against Diego's bald head. I could see the outline of where hair might've sprouted, had he let it, and where there was simply no hope.

I shot off some random explanation for why I liked it so much, something about the form, the style, whatever. "So," I said, pushing my hard stare on him, practically through him. "Can I have it?"

It already belonged to me anyway. I'd marked my territory, and that included his office and everything in it. Maintaining eye contact with him, I summoned my upper body into a subtle flex, and my modest musculature complied as best it could, testing my shirt at a few seams, stretching toward intimidation. Hadn't Diego often referred to me as *The Future of RazorBeat*? Well, gaze upon me then! The Future, in the flesh.

He dragged his forefinger down and around the figurine's waist, slowly, as if taking some important measurement or weighing some important thought. Then he swiveled away from the window and back toward the shelf.

"Sadly, my dear," he replied, "it's one of a kind."

* * *

My mom phoned out of the blue later that week, which left me conflicted, caught between my usual choices. Was I one of those doting sons who rearranges his schedule to make time for an impromptu lunch? Or one who's too important, declining the invitation? Which son was I?

"Just a quick bite," I told her, splitting the difference.

Thai Palace had only one table open, the same one I'd shared with Josie.

"I don't know how you do it," my mom said.

She began adjusting her shirt's collar with its thin ruffle. I wasn't sure if a thread had pulled or if this was—I hesitate to use the phrase—*the fashion.*

"Do what?"

"This city! New York is so . . . not me." She started inundating me with updates from home. I asked about my dad.

"I'm texting with him now." She held up her cracked screen. "He sends his love."

My dad never accompanied my mom on these short shopping-filled trips. It was a chance to spend a night apart before the two dragged themselves back together with a dull but persistent magnetism.

"Tell me, how's work?" She opened her menu and tipped her gaze downward. "Are you busy?"

My mom worked in a related field, though our jobs were very different. She was a media salesperson for a local TV network back home, nothing like being on the creative side. *I* created taglines. What had she ever made except me? I did appreciate that she took pride in my achievements. When Smackdale aired, she forwarded it to all her friends. A few took offense. Surely, *they* weren't incontinent, if that's what she was implying.

I assured her I was very busy, but not too busy for Birthright. At the mere mention, I figured she'd plotz with joy.

"Are you sure you still want to go?" She squinted. "I mean, do you think it's a good time? Right now?"

"Mom, this trip was *your* idea!"

"That craziness with the rockets? And the settlements?" She put aside her menu.

"Relax," I replied, reaching for my own menu. "I won't be near all that."

"You won't be far! It's a tiny speck of a country."

"What about pad see ew with beef? To share?"

"Seth." Her eyes bore into me. They were my eyes, only dimmer.

"Fine, forget it. I don't need to go to Israel." I paused for a pass of introspection. "I don't need to visit Israel ever, in fact."

She once again adjusted the collar of her shirt, pinching it out from her neck. "I'm just talking, that's all I'm doing, just talking. Oh, I don't know. I'll give you a list of phone numbers. An old sorority sister joined a kibbutz. Pomelos! Have you ever tasted—I mean, this was a while back, so I haven't spoken to her lately. Probably not in, gosh, thirty years? Is that really possible? I'm sorry, one more minute, we've barely looked. Thank you. They're pushy here, huh? And she—"

"Mom."

"Or what about Mishaal?" She brightened. "I bet he'd love to hear from you."

"Seriously? Mishaal?" I took out my phone. "You should let that one go." It had been over a decade since Mishaal lived in our house. How old was he when we took him in? Eleven? Twelve? He'd moved back to Lebanon just a few days before the two of us were set to start high school, if memory served. Anyway, it didn't matter. It's not like we had anything to discuss, and Israel and Lebanon weren't exactly on friendly terms. What did my mom think, we'd catch up over tea at the border, perhaps in a UN patrol tower? Who knew if he even still lived there?

As lunch wore on, my mom's voice calmed. Once our plates were cleared, she reached into her pocketbook and handed me a folded piece of paper. It was a copy of the Kaddish, and would I take it to the Western Wall on her behalf? She didn't specify which of our various deceased relatives I was supposed to memorialize, so I could only assume all of them.

I was putting away the Kaddish when a Moon email lit up my phone. He wasn't its author, though. He was forwarding it. It had come in from Lawrence.

* * *

Moon wasn't in his office, so I checked our conference rooms. Each was designed after a New York City landmark and bore a tenuous likeness to its namesake: Statue of Liberty featured a torchlike wall sconce; Guggenheim sported a round white table; Memorial (originally Twin Towers) housed two columns. I thought about giving up my search and replying to Moon over email, but I opted for persistence; it was preferable to discuss Prostate-related matters in person.

Lawrence's note begged for an immediate response. Not explicitly, of course—the tone was, if anything, distant. He thanked Moon and me (he didn't mention me by name, just made reference to "the writer") for coming to Tulsa. He felt bad that things had gotten "acremonious [sic]" and hoped there was no ill will. Nevertheless, he'd contracted with a new agency. He was sure we'd understand.

There was no doubt in my mind that our Oklahoma friend was bluffing. If he'd signed with another agency, why hadn't he dropped the name? No, we still had a shot. One meeting, that's all I needed.

I kept searching the office for Moon when I saw someone I recognized. I'd never seen him before, though I still knew with certainty who I was looking at. He was pacing our lobby, periodically pausing to run a hand back through his dyed-black slash of hair. He looked young, younger than I'd expected. If his clothes typically glimmered with safety pins, he'd removed them as a formality.

I'd always known that Josie had a life outside the office and that that life was populated with people I hadn't met, but it was still bizarre to see this stranger in our midst. So this was Travis, this stiff and oddly angular wisp of a person, reminiscent of a toy wooden soldier. I wondered if she'd found him this way or whittled him down over time.

I decided to intervene before Josie or anyone else showed up. As I approached, Travis presented me his hand to shake.

"I'm supposed to ask for X. Is that . . . you?"

Xavier always conducted the first-round interview before handing the candidate off to one of his lackeys. I looked at the nearby HR desks and was relieved to find all were empty. Had to be RazorBeatz, our HR-sponsored monthly wine-and-cheese reception at a Chelsea art gallery with live music. (It was meant to boost the morale of our mentally spent workforce, but only HR went. The rest of us were, well, too spent.)

I glanced at our largest conference room, Central Park, and saw through a crack in the door that Josie was in a Lexus meeting. Perfect. I hurried Travis into Memorial.

"So," I said, motioning him to sit opposite me. "How'd you learn about us?"

He fumbled while producing his résumé from his briefcase, accidentally ripping the corner with his contact info. His home address fell in his lap. "I was referred."

He began spelling out Josie's full name, until I said it wasn't necessary.

"And what has she told you about RazorBeat?"

The slash left only one eye visible. "Nice work environment." He stopped to scratch at a pocked section of cheek. "Nice people."

"Yes! The nicest. We're one big happy family, really." I took up his résumé, digested some bullet points, then swept it to the side. "But we also work hard. *Impossibly* hard. Maybe," I postulated, with a dose of concern, "Josie failed to communicate that?"

The toy soldier was in trouble. He grew eager to emphasize his work ethic, his drive, his devotion. He'd clearly rehearsed this answer with Josie. His phrases even carried a touch of her construction.

I tapped my knuckle cheerfully on the table, just as I'd seen Moon do in Tulsa. "Let's try a little test."

"A test?"

"I'm going to give you a fictional client, and you're going to write them a new tagline."

His visible eye widened.

I told him not to worry, that it was a rudimentary assignment. I'd even do him a favor: instead of some big capitalist corporation, I'd start him small. "How about . . . a nonprofit specializing in prostate cancer research." I tore a fresh piece of loose-leaf from my notebook and rolled him a pen. "Any questions?"

He looked at me and said nothing. Blankness sheened his face. Then he grabbed hold of the pen and, after dismissing the slash with a quick sweep behind his ear, scribbled in bursts. He'd hunch up in a rush of cursive, then ease, then hunch again. If it was true that he possessed any musical talent, I could detect some hint in the alternating rhythm of his posture. After a few minutes, I ordered him to drop the pen. His time was up.

He cleared his throat and hunched further to bring his messy handwriting into focus. "How about *Treatment Is Everything?*"

Appallingly ambiguous, egregiously imprecise—I had to admit it was a pretty good tagline. Still, I shook my head. "Not inspiring."

"*Our Treatment Can Help.* Or maybe *We Treat All People*—"

"This isn't about *all* people, remember? Just those with prostate cancer."

He stalled, his lips pursing around a new possibility. It was obvious he hadn't written this one, and it was only coming to him now. "What about *We Treat Men Better.*"

The look of his face changed in that moment. There emerged a heightened resoluteness to the lines that met at his clean-shaven chin, a sharper intensity surrounding his eyes and how they held focus. He'd done well for himself. He'd played my silly game and, he believed, beaten me at it. Then, in the next breath, his confidence faltered, some nerve in him fizzling out at its end. He sighed, slumped his head back in frustration, and gazed up at Memorial's ceiling. "Still not inspiring, I guess."

I assured him it wasn't terrible. Not great, no, but I'd heard worse. I jotted a note to myself and paid him a token smile.

Once I declared that the test portion of our interview was over, he tried to steer the conversation toward unrelated qualifications. I grew bored. I stretched my neck—left, right—and studied the details of Memorial, specifically the two columns. Why hadn't they been removed out of respect? Or were they structurally significant?

I sensed Travis was eager to leave—he'd already assumed defeat at the hands of late capitalism—but this only bolstered my desire to prolong his agony. I led him on a roundabout tour of RazorBeat's departments, enumerating the nuances of their functions, peppering in back slaps on the way. On our loop through the kitchen, I pointed out the snack drawer, then hurried him along before he could sample its delights. As we walked, some guilt began calcifying inside me, hard as a bone spur. I persevered.

Lastly, we strolled past Central Park. To my relief, the meeting was still going on, though I wasn't as pleased when I heard what was transpiring. From the sound of it, Josie wasn't just presenting; she was *leading*. It was impossible to hear what she was saying to the Lexus client, only that her words had snapped the whole room into approving silence, Diego included. I hadn't realized initially that he was in there too, only when he piped up briefly, interjecting a couple of words before handing her back the reins. She charged ahead in full command. She sounded triumphant.

I pumped a final handshake out of Travis with an added bite of force. I curtly expressed hope that our paths would cross in the future, promised to be in touch, and all the rest. Then, with the elevator doors closing, I felt compelled to offer a more personalized sendoff. "Josie loves me," I said. And down he went.

4.

Treating Men to Better Science.
The Science of Treating Men Better.
The Science of Treating Men.

I took a break from my notebook to stare out the bus window. As we drove higher through the hills of Haifa, the landscape greened. I got a glimpse of the Mediterranean whenever the bus turned wide. The midday sun was catching waves at their crest.

Yael sat beside me, her semiautomatic in her lap. Its barrel nodded with the hard rhythm of the road.

"What's that?" she asked, tying back her wavy crop of hair. "A diary?"

I explained it was nothing like that, that it was real work. Since the start of the trip, I'd resolved not to check email, but that didn't stop me from composing taglines.

She pointed at my handwriting. "Really looks like a diary."

"It's not." I gestured toward her gun: "But I don't want to argue."

Four Israeli soldiers were assigned to us, but the only one I got to know was Yael. The other three were bare-knuckled hashish dealers who flirted brazenly with the American girls under their protection. I hated how the girls swooned in their presence. So juvenile. In fairness, most *were* juveniles. They handled their fake IDs with the same care I showed my foil-embossed business cards.

I was turning back to my notebook when our bus screeched to a stop. Zev, our Birthright tour guide, announced that we'd arrived in Acre, one of Israel's oldest coastal cities. We filed out into a parking lot.

Zev spoke English not quite fluently, each word scraping on its way up his throat. His Acre lecture began with a brief history of the city. Jews built it. Then the Crusaders took it and built a fortress. Then the Ottomans buried that fortress with sand, building their own city on top. Napoléon tried to take the city and failed. Then the British came and put the Jews in prison. But since Jews are clever, Zev explained, the prison couldn't hold them. In essence, Acre was the perfect microcosm (my word) because it epitomized (also mine) our people's long struggle, one in which we've relied upon our ingenuity (ibid.). Zev closed by encouraging us to buy souvenirs.

Yael and I broke off from the group to get lunch. Rifle hanging off her shoulder, she led me down a cobblestone street. It was oppressively hot, even with the sea nearby.

"Aren't you dying?" I asked. She was wearing full uniform.

"I'm fine. I'm used to it."

"What about the sleeves? Why not roll them up at least?"

"Seriously?" She gave a nod toward the sun. "You want me to burn?"

Yael barely hung out with me for the first few days of the trip, though lately she'd shown me more attention. The change happened after I notified Birthright via email, as a courtesy, that I was considering going home early. There was no particular issue really, just that I was finding its Zionist propaganda campaign tiresome. I explained that I had nothing against propaganda, that in fact I was an expert in the business of propaganda myself, but its messaging was wearing on me. If Birthright hoped to be persuasive, I wrote, it'd be wise to tone it down. I offered to relay my feedback to its marketing team directly, via conference call if possible.

The morning after I sent the email, Yael approached me. She said rather bluntly that her supervisor had forwarded it to her and that, while she personally didn't care if I stayed or left, she had a job to do. Her tone was flat when she said it, like she'd been assigned many jobs in her life, what was another?

At the end of the cobblestone street was a falafel cart. We took our lunch into the shade, an ancient-looking tree giving us cover.

"So your diary," she said. "It's for TV?"

I'd told her I wrote commercials for a living. It was simpler—and possibly a bit more glamorous—to label myself an ad man. No wonder people like Lawrence were confused; the branding industry had a branding problem.

I encouraged her to visit me in New York. Maybe accompany me on a shoot?

"Maybe," she said, "but what's a *shoot*?"

I tried to explain, but I knew little about shoots myself. I'd never been on set before, not even for Smackdale.

Yael leaned back under a tangle of branches, her hair nearly toppling free from its elastic tie. All around us lay fallen seedpods.

"Is Zev full of shit?"

She looked at me oddly.

"I mean, is that true what he said? The Ottomans buried the fortress with sand so they could build a city on top?"

"Zev says it's true. So, for him, it's true."

Others from Birthright began lining up at the falafel cart. I hoped they might turn, so they'd see the two of us together. As a couple.

"Why waste time with the sand? Why not demolish it?"

Yael shrugged, her weapon-bearing shoulder barely lifting. As a breeze slipped off the sea, branches creaked overhead.

"Hey, can I ask about your gun?" I wasn't sure what to ask. I just felt I had to acknowledge its presence. "Is it heavy? I'm not asking to hold it—"

"I'm not letting you." A drop of tzatziki landed on her shirt collar. With an easy swoop, she licked it clean.

"Do you own it? Or does it belong to the army?"

She gave herself a moment to size up her next bite. "The IDF gives these away. Pieces of junk. They don't work anymore."

I paused. "Wait, it doesn't *work*?"

Yael studied what remained of the falafel sandwich in her hand before bringing it back to her mouth.

"You think it works," she said, after swallowing. "So it works."

* * *

I didn't share the group's enthusiasm for Tel Aviv. A nice city, sure, but nothing special. Whenever our bus wheeled past its vegan cafés and raw juice bars, I saw only a poor imitation of New York. The others were impressed because they had no means of comparison; they hailed from wastelands of cosmopolitan culture—say, the backwoods of Maine or the salt flats of Utah. They were, quite simply, the least-Jewish Jews I had ever met.

Their ignorance about even the most rudimentary aspects of Judaism astonished me. Whenever Zev would lecture about something very basic, they'd strike an attentive pose and nod their heads with the zeal of the converted. I couldn't relate to it, how the religion held novelty in their eyes. For me, being Jewish had only ever felt old.

I'd never had much use for religion. It wasn't so much that I rejected the possibility of God but that I didn't believe God would care whether I believed, and if that was the case, why bother believing? That's not to say Judaism meant nothing to me. I liked certain aspects, especially its accessibility. I never needed to try to be Jewish; I just was. All my life I'd been trying out for things: competing for a coveted spot on the traveling soccer team or vying for a speaking role in the annual middle school musical. But when it came to being Jewish, I could rest assured that, if I simply showed up, I'd have a place on the squad. The Jewish people were always shorthanded. There was never enough of us, and never would be.

Birthright, however, made us feel awfully numerous. To my credit, I did try to socialize with the others. On our last night in Tel Aviv, Zev wanted to take us out clubbing. This, he declared, only half joking, was the time to be fruitful and multiply.

Yael and the other soldiers distributed wristbands after dinner. I headed straight for the club's main bar, which was surprisingly empty. Later I learned the others had already filled up; they'd pregamed at the hostel without me.

After downing a few shots, I braved the dance floor. It proved a less than successful effort. Like an excess electron, I drifted from one dance circle to the next, struggling to involve myself in the busy physics of their rhythms. In time, everyone would be grinding in pairs, adopting rescue dogs together, applying for mortgages. All of Birthright would be multiplying except me.

I decided to step outside the club to call Josie. I hadn't spoken to her once during the trip, so it seemed appropriate to touch base. It would pique her interest, surely, to hear about my new friend, Yael, and how the two of us felt a real connection, our coupledom imminent. There was also business to discuss. Had Travis recounted any unfortunate details from his interview? How was Diego coping in my absence? I was about to dial when I stopped myself. It was nice not touching base with her. It was nice having distance from the sharp edge in her voice.

I was about to head back inside when I spotted my favorite soldier. Yael was sitting on the fire escape at the rear of the building, her rifle in one hand and a blunt in the other.

I climbed the short stretch of ladder that led to her and took a seat. "Can I try?"

"You?" she said. "You don't smoke."

Meaning what, exactly?

"You don't smoke," she repeated, "because *I* bought this."

I was thrilled to put my RazorBeat income to use. I pulled some bills from my wallet, but she refused my clumsy offer. She took one final hit and snuffed out the blunt on the iron railing. When a fleck of hot ash caught her foot, she muttered a Hebrew curse I didn't understand.

"Zev was right, you know. About Acre." I gave a satisfied grin. "I looked it up."

"Oh?"

"They did bury it with sand. The Ottoman king wanted to erase all memory of the Crusaders. But Zev neglected to mention the ironic part. Want to hear?"

Yael's eyes flickered and waited.

"The sand *preserved* the Crusaders' legacy. It protected their artifacts from the elements." I was unsure if she was following.

She used the butt of her rifle to clear off the rest of the ash. It fell as a sprinkle on the pavement below. "This king, he's an idiot? He doesn't know what he's doing?"

I could smell Yael's hair, then the burnt marijuana, then the salt air of the Mediterranean. They came in little successive waves.

"His plan backfired. That's all I'm saying."

She gave it a moment's thought and shook her head. "If you bury something, you secretly want someone to find it."

"Like a game?"

"No," she said. "Not a game."

The club's music boomed even outside, the pronounced bass line pulsing hard through our bodies, even our bones.

I leaned in close to Yael and asked if I could kiss her. She waited a breath or two to see if I was serious, then, seeing I was, spiked a laugh in my face.

"You always do this," she said, her eyes turning back in the direction of the sea.

"Do what?" I replied. "What do I do?"

"Not *you*. Americans." She snickered. "You always ask for things."

Surely, Israelis were much more aggressive in such matters. I considered leaning in again, until she set me straight.

"You want to kiss? So kiss. You want to leave and go home? So leave and go home." She shifted back toward me, the moonlight sharp and cool on her face. Her eyes weren't flickering anymore. "I've never read an email like that. I've done ten of these trips, and I've heard every complaint, but never so much *whining*. Why did you come here at all?"

I wasn't sure how to respond. I repeated, more or less, what I said on my application. That I wanted to go on Birthright to grow closer to Judaism, to find a community where I belonged, something like that.

"Well," she snapped, "*I* don't belong to you. They don't pay me enough." It was possible to hear a few squealing voices over the music. "I think that's where you belong. With them. Not with me."

I offered an apology, though her tone didn't change.

"I'm just not interested in you," she said. "Or men, actually."

The breeze off the sea was picking up. It teased at the full heft of her hair, flaring a few strands free from the rest.

"It must be hard," she continued, bringing her rifle into her lap. "Writing commercials."

I assumed she was being sarcastic.

"No, really," she went on. "How do you do it?" She said it terrified her, the thought of making something up, something not from real life. Then she pulled herself to her feet. She and the other soldiers had to perform a routine bathroom check at night's end.

"You Americans," she said, dropping low to the ladder. "You're always crying or puking or both."

* * *

It was 104 degrees when we got to Jerusalem. I fought through it for the first day, then the second, but by the third, my body had had enough. I only wanted to curl up in bed beside the AC. When I texted Yael that I'd be skipping Shabbat brunch, she showed up at my room with a challah roll and an ultimatum. "We're walking to the Wall in an hour. If you can't join, I'll tell Zev."

"We're *walking?*"

Apparently, this was how it went on Shabbat. The Birthright bus would stay parked for the day.

I told her I couldn't, not in this heat. Then I gave her my mom's copy of the Kaddish and asked if she'd put it in the Wall for me. She slipped the prayer for the dead into her breast pocket and was gone.

Lying in bed with nothing to do, I reached for my notebook. I tried coming up with more Prostate taglines—my output on the trip thus far had underwhelmed—but I felt too tired to focus. I turned instead to the page where I'd first written the Smackdale tagline. I let my eyes rest there, almost as a balm.

Everyday Briefs for the Everyday Hero. It's hard to believe in hindsight, but I'd had doubts initially. Or not doubts, just hesitations. Doubling up on *Everyday*—wasn't it a bit repetitive? When I expressed this to Diego on the eve of my Smackdale presentation, he surprised me by grabbing my hand and ushering me to a back table in a hotel bar of his choosing. *Everyday life* is *repetitive,* he exclaimed, his eyes quickening with the amber gleam of his cocktail. *That's why we need heroes. That's the whole point.*

I sat up in bed, set my notebook aside, and reconsidered. It was hot out, sure, but not unbearably so. The others were toughing it out, weren't they? I rushed to the lobby and found the group had left, so I ordered a taxi on my phone. (Destination address? WALL.) A teenager named Sayed speedily arrived in a two-door Honda stripped of its hubcaps. I hadn't considered the possibility that the driver might be Muslim, but I was thrilled with this turn of events. Sayed wasn't propaganda. Sayed was real. Contorting myself to fit the dimensions of his back seat, I pledged to do my part to foster interfaith dialogue. With knees at my chest, I was ready to broker peace.

Sayed had a weak grasp of English and a lead foot; we maintained a halting conversation while careening through alleyways sized to accommodate mules. His noisy diesel engine was drowning out my efforts to discuss geopolitics, so I turned to the personal instead. I brought up Mishaal. I briefly described his story and explained that, when he was young, he lived with my family. Was Mishaal a common Muslim name? Did Sayed know any Mishaals? He sounded confused. Was that *my* name? Was I Mishaal? The app had ordered him to pick up Seth.

Sayed's Honda had barely any AC. It would work for a blessed second before stalling out, torturing us with cruel gasps of relief. I felt parched as parchment, a Dead Sea scroll. The suffocating heat had me wincing with every breath. But I resisted. *An everyday hero,* I told myself, *doth not wince.*

At a busy intersection, Sayed braked for a group of ultra-Orthodox Jews. I observed with little interest as dozens of them streamed into the crosswalk; but then, without any provocation, they veered from their expected course. They were moving toward us. They were *encircling* us. Sayed shouted a word I couldn't understand, and they matched him with incomprehensible shouts of their own. I considered adding my own shouts to the mix, but I was too scared to open my mouth, let alone produce sound. I just sat there, silent and scorched and seized. Then Sayed slammed his whole palm down for a long shriek of car horn, and the circle closed in.

Heavy rain, that's what it sounded like, their fists pummeling fast and hard on the Honda's hood and roof and doors. When they started on the car's more breakable parts, the windshield and side windows, I sensed something was about to shatter, and that's when I just—I passed out. And everything went silent, as if the rain stopped or never happened at all.

* * *

The nurse had just finished adjusting my IV when Yael knocked. She came bearing a few essentials from the hostel: clean underwear, a toothbrush, even my notebook.

"How's the patient?" she asked. "Do you need to stay overnight?"

"Probably not," I said. "They're just monitoring." It was a bad case of dehydration, nothing more.

Yael took a seat at the foot of my bed.

"Am I the first?" I asked.

"First what?"

"Birthrighter you've visited in the hospital."

"Someone always ends up here. Every time." She set her heavy rifle down at her side. "Usually, it's a girl."

The wooziness had begun lifting. When Yael spoke, I could mostly follow the meaning of her words as they formed.

"Anyway," she said, "I did it."

Did what, exactly?

"The Kaddish." She leaned back a little. "Remember?"

It had slipped my mind in the past hour's frenzy. I told her I was grateful.

I recounted for her my run-in with the ultra-Orthodox, how violent it was, how they punched hard at the car from all sides. "All because," I continued, "the driver was Muslim."

Yael laughed but only thinly, a ripple. "It wasn't about the driver. It was about you."

I looked at her in confusion.

"They hate hilonim, especially in Jerusalem. When they see Jews driving on Shabbat, they throw bottles at cars; sometimes they even drag people out into the street and kick them in the ribs." She rose briskly from the bed and smoothed the starched sheet of her impression. "Welcome to Israel," she said.

On her way out, she gestured to my phone. It was vibrating at my bedside.

Was it my parents? Had I called them from the ambulance? I was mulling over how best to assuage their concerns when I looked at the texts:

LAYOFFS
Basically everyone
omg
RazorBeat s FFFUCKED
Hello?????

5.

I saw evidence of the carnage everywhere. Empty name placards, desks wiped clean. One-fifth of the staff had been let go, the non-billable departments suffering the largest share of the casualties. The longest-tenured RazorBeat employee fired was Gregor, a septuagenarian hippie IT technician with a face like a roof shingle. When HR delivered the news to him, Josie said, he started humming to himself, quietly at first and then at a pitch that rattled the walls of the whole office. He was spotted hours later sitting cross-legged on a city sidewalk. He was still humming—his linen shirt unbuttoned to the navel, the sunlight pale on his bare chest.

The most senior person to go was Diego. I'll admit that, when I heard, I felt a little wistful. But my mood lightened when I considered his vast office: no egg, no rhombuses, no figurine, no nothing. The space was now up for grabs. I was set on grabbing it.

I never feared for my own job, not really. There was a moment or two when Josie hadn't yet answered my texts that my confidence was slightly shaken; I fought the impulse to rip the IV from my arm, dash to the parking lot in my hospital gown, and summon Sayed to whisk me to Ben Gurion. But I heard back soon enough, and all was as expected: my placard remained in place on my unwiped desk.

Layoffs had wrapped up the week prior, but everyone was still buzzing: an all-office meeting was set for 11:00 a.m. in Central Park to address the agency's future. As I took my seat in copywriters' row, an account manager saw me and flew over.

"You're here!" Camille set down her coffee mug a little too close to my notebook. "It's just, you haven't been around, so I figured you were X'ed."

That's what we called it when Xavier fired someone. Not axed, X'ed.

I explained I'd been away on vacation.

"Ugh, SO JEALOUS. Where?"

I took out my phone and began swiping through. "These," I said, "were taken in Acre, an ancient city on Israel's coast. It has a complicated history, so it really epitomizes—"

"Who's that?" She lifted her mug for a sip.

"A friend of mine. An Israeli soldier."

"Like, a *real* one?" She sipped again and her eyelids fluttered. Then she crouched a little, her voice thinning to a whisper. "Seth, this whole thing is insane. I mean, Brooklyn from payroll? A total angel! She blew at her job, so it's not too surprising, but like—"

"Never met Brooklyn," I interrupted. Account managers would talk your ear off for hours. They were desperate to maximize human interaction before having to slink back into the cells of their staffing spreadsheets.

I offered her more details about Acre, but, to my surprise, she cut me off. She had a million unread emails, she said, as she grabbed her coffee and left.

I powered up my laptop and anticipated a flood myself. While everyone at the agency complained about the quantity of email we received, it didn't bother me. I liked a full inbox, in fact. It felt like having a full stomach or a full heart.

I hadn't checked my email for a good while, so I was anticipating a record number of messages. But for some reason, I couldn't log in. Not unusual—our passwords often expired without warning. All I had to do was contact IT. But with Gregor gone, who would I call?

As I reached for my phone, I noticed a red light winking, the sign of a new voicemail.

"Hi, Seth. Drop by my office? Thanks."

The deep timbre told me it was Xavier. At six and a half feet tall, X was a towering presence. And yet, despite his eye-catching height, he'd moved invisibly up the ranks. It was unclear what was propelling his rise; his most notable achievement was upgrading the RazorBeatz swill from Yellow Tail Chardonnay to a more artisanal selection.

When I arrived, his door was open.

"Have a seat," X said, and motioned to a swivel chair. Since his office was tiny and his wingspan considerable, he took care when gesturing so as not to knock objects off his desk. He kept his arms tight to his body, a passenger bracing for impact.

I felt the thin cushion under me exhale. "Just got your voicemail."

"From last week?" He bent to fetch a stack of printouts. "Speaking of which, where have you been?"

Israel, I told him.

"I've always wanted to go. It's on my list, right after Venice."

"Better go soon. It won't be around much longer."

He paused. "Venice . . . or Israel?"

I didn't have time for this. I had a terrific new Prostate tagline to present, one I composed during my hospital stay. If only Moon would set up a meeting.

"Don't worry." X fanned the papers across his desk. "It's good news."

A big relief, frankly, not that I expected any different. My thoughts turned to Diego's office. I wondered how it might look to have the Smackdale tagline engraved over the doorframe, a benediction under which all must pass who enter. Or perhaps that would send the wrong message. It was important not to stake one's career on past glories. *Innovation*, that was the hallmark of any true visionary.

"Seth, I'm happy to offer you your current position."

"Sorry?"

"Everything just like it was. Same desk. Same title. Same salary. Well, no *salary*. And no benefits either. But our freelance rate is competitive." X knit his face into a tight smile. "It's possible your take-home pay will net out the same, give or take."

The doorframe in my mind vanished. I stared blankly at his papers and sensed them staring back at me. I hadn't participated in a staring contest in decades, not since I was very young, though I still remembered how my eyes would burn and water and burn and water in the heat of competition, how they begged to shut themselves in defeat, and how I begged them not to.

X broke the silence. "It's a good deal."

"It's *bullshit* is what it is."

Freelancers—FreeBeaters, in our parlance—commanded no respect and lived on the cusp of poverty. To their faces, we'd express envy. *How terrific*, we'd exclaim, *to enjoy such flexibility!* In truth, we pitied them: lowly orphans of the agency world, pawing after table scraps. We urged them to partake liberally from our snacks drawer for fear they might otherwise turn rabid in our midst.

"Listen to me, Seth." X drew a long breath. I could almost feel him reeling air out of my lungs and into his. "Other folks in your shoes? They'd gladly trade places."

I took note of his mixed metaphors and wanted to explode. What qualified a man of such verbal ineptitude to decide my future? If anything, *I* should've been firing *him*. How fitting, to X X!

I demanded to speak to the agency's most senior partners, the ones who'd often sought out my talents, the ones who—I reminded him—held all decision-making power.

"They've decided," he said, gesturing again at the papers.

He leaned forward and laid his massive arms on his desk. "I should really bite my tongue, but you know who's to blame for this?" His mouth hung open. "Diego."

My body language stiffened. So I was caught. That was what happened. Diego had known about Josie and me for weeks, for months. Maybe he'd even installed a camera, that sick bastard. Jealousy had led him to rat me out. He was in love, wanted me all for himself.

"What, exactly, did Diego say?"

"When?"

"When you fired him."

X leaned even closer, his elbows screeching on the dark veneer of his desk. "*He* left *us*. And he's taking Lexus with him." He straightened and shook his head at the thought. "That's half our billings right there."

It seems absurd in hindsight, but I never once stopped to consider why the agency was letting so many people go. I just figured RazorBeat was kicking out the bad, keeping the good. Like survival of the fittest or something. Like nature doing its job.

X gathered the papers neatly and handed them to me. "Sign these."

I skimmed the top of the stack. "Then what?"

"Back to work, whenever you're ready. Everything like it was."

I began feeling short of breath.

"One last thing," he said. "Whenever I exit someone from the agency, I'm responsible for escorting them out of the building."

I blinked at him sharply.

"For security purposes. It's in the employee handbook. You definitely received—"

"I'm being . . . exited?" *Buildings*, I told myself, *are exited. Not people.*

He shrugged and said the policy was the policy. It was, he explained, what it was.

I tried to calm down, one deep breath at a time. I knew the walls of his tiny office weren't actually encroaching, yet I also knew they weren't backing up either; that no matter how I might beg them to relent a bit and give me more air, they'd never oblige, never budge. I'd had my job interview in this same office, and hadn't the size seemed tolerable back then? Indeed, it was a masterful performance, more polished than Travis's, certainly. I stumbled only once, just for a fleeting moment, when Diego asked the most basic question of all: Why did I want to write taglines for a living? And I told him, to my surprise, the truth. Because they're sticky. They can't be forgotten. Even taglines that nobody likes, they're still impossible to forget. And I loved the thought of that, of being unforgettable. I would be old and senile someday, and my words would still be lodged permanently in people's heads, stuck there forever. Attachment. That's what it was all about.

Attachment? Diego had replied. He admitted that, frankly, he'd never thought of it like that. I wasn't sure how to read his response, the way he kept muttering *attachment* over and over to himself, as if weighing the word on his tongue. Then, out of nowhere, he burst out laughing. He popped up out of his chair and embraced me then and there, installing me that same week at my very own desk, the very same desk that, X would soon explain, I had to clean out thoroughly and without delay.

I stared at X and studied his long, narrow face. Above the high terrain of his shoulders, it looked helplessly wedged there, like it had no way down.

"Did Diego leave me anything?"

He seemed confused by my question. "What do you mean?"

"Before he left," I said. "Before he emptied out his office. Did he set anything aside? For me?"

X said nothing. His eyes answered dimly in their sockets.

"Are you sure?" I pushed. "Like, *absolutely* sure?"

There must've been something about my voice, how it trembled a bit before breaking so distinctly into pieces, impossible shards of one emotion or another, that made him want to double-check.

* * *

Before X could exit me, I had to place my personal effects in a big cardboard box. Thankfully there wasn't much to pack: my Swarovski crystal, my hardcover *Roget's* from college, and a toy replica of a Lexus that Josie received on a client visit that I might have salvaged from her waste bin. As I picked up the box, it produced a sad thump: the Lexus had skidded off the thesaurus and rear-ended the award for a minor collision.

I marched with X to the elevators, past the all-office meeting. I hoped Central Park's frosted glass panels would shield me from view, but someone had propped open the door. I raised the box to conceal my face, all to no avail: Josie, Camille, and a handful of others saw me making the ultimate walk of shame. Camille's response—hand brought to mouth, smothering a gasp—rang false. Josie, on the other hand, looked genuinely distressed. She gestured to her phone, signaling I should text her ASAP. Her eyebrows shot up to reinforce the point.

My mood shifted instantly. I took pleasure—joy even!—seeing Josie's face flush with worry. Then again, it was to be expected. I was her closest work friend, both during and after hours. It was hard to imagine her surviving the agency without me. For that matter, how would the *agency* survive without me? Perhaps the whole place would crumble. Perhaps Memorial's columns would disintegrate into twin piles of dust.

As I stepped into the elevator with X, I felt newly unburdened, even triumphant. Really, there was no shame in being let go. I'd relegate RazorBeat to the past and find a new job that paid double. Out of obligation, I'd stay in touch with Josie. She might feel awkward at first (some amount of survivor's guilt would be natural), but I'd take pains to put her at ease. I'd look her straight in the eye at our next Thai Palace lunch and swear, *I'm doing great!* flashing a grin with the arrival of every dipping sauce. Then, at pivotal moments in the conversation, I'd undermine my own assurances, hinting at hairline cracks in the facade. I wanted her pity to seep into me, to flood me to my very depths.

X pushed the door open for me. As we stood together in the bustle of the midtown sidewalk, he encouraged me to mull over the freelance offer, but my mind was made up. *Fare thee well.* He turned and stepped back into the building, a tower entering a tower. Then it was just me, alone, on the street.

Or not completely alone: I was still carrying that box. I thought about dumping it at my feet and going home, but then I'd have nothing to hold in my hands, and I hated the notion of that, of returning home literally empty-handed. Then I thought about taking the box back with me to my tiny apartment, but this too was unappealing, because where would I store such a thing, given my limited space? The closet was full, so I'd have to find room in my living area, and there I'd see it every passing day. Even if I threw out the box, I'd still have the memory of the box in my apartment, and that memory would take up space of its own. I arrived at the only logical conclusion: there was nowhere in the world that the cardboard box belonged but RazorBeat. I deemed it my duty to return it.

I explained to Phil at security that I'd forgotten my ID badge upstairs, as happened not infrequently. He shook his head. He'd seen me exited with his own eyes.

"Call Diego's extension," I said. "He'll let me up."

"Diego? Isn't he gone?"

"Right." I was scrambling. "So call *my* extension."

"But you're down here."

"Exactly. You'll get my voicemail. And, as I state explicitly in the voicemail, you should try my cell if you can't reach me. Then I'll

answer and let myself up." Phil's face blurred with deep befuddle-
ment. I tried simplifying the steps. "Or," I proposed convincingly,
"how about cutting out the middle man and just calling my cell
directly?"

The elevator wasted no time ushering me back to altitude. I
breathed uneasily as we ticked higher, higher. Then I, The Future of
RazorBeat, stepped out at the bell.

My timing was horrific: the all-office meeting broke just as I
showed up, as if my footfall had precipitated some critical fracture.
Josie, even more distressed than before, saw me and rushed over.

"What's going on? You didn't text." She held up her blank phone
as proof.

X was striding past when he spotted me and did a double take.
"You've reconsidered," he said. "Well, I wish you'd said something.
Maintenance needs more time to finish wiping down your desk." He
turned to Josie and then back toward me. "Protocol."

"Xavier," I said, "can you give us a minute?"

He agreed to take leave, though he was cautious in withdrawing.
He wanted Josie to know he'd be just down the hall if she needed
him. Phil, I suspected, would be reprimanded.

She waited until he was out of earshot, then sharpened the air
with a pointed question. "Are you fired," she pressed, "or not?"

It was at this moment that I wished I could make the box disappear. Because no matter what I could've said, no matter how I
might've tried to frame the situation, the box gave shape to the
undeniable fact of what had happened. Overhead, the globe lights
were burning with intensity. They were laying harsh heat on us
from above.

"It'll be the same," I said. "Everything like it was."

She digested my words and spat them back out. "What does that
even mean?"

"Fired, yeah. But they're letting me stay on." I shifted the box from one hip to the other. "FreeBeater."

I went on to assure her she shouldn't worry about me.

"And me?" she snapped. "What about me?"

I finally understood the root of her concern. Dropping to a whisper, I explained that, while I initially feared the two of us had been caught, I no longer held that suspicion. I was X'ed for some other reason, but I couldn't yet say what it was. This was all coming, I continued, as a pretty big shock.

Josie had maintained a humorless glare this whole time, but here she let out a tiny laugh. It was like Yael's, though it cut more cleanly off her lips. "Come on, seriously?" she said. "You *cannot* be surprised."

It was her emphasis on that word, that *cannot*, that continued to echo for months after. I wanted to respond, to defend myself, but she was already on her next thought: "So you're gonna stay and FreeBeat it? After X X'ed you?"

It was all so painfully clear now—Gregor had left with dignity. He'd boldly stripped down and exposed himself to the elements. By contrast, here I was: fully clothed and clutching a cardboard box of my belongings in an office where I no longer belonged. This would be their lasting image of me. The former Future, forever.

Camille saw us and toddled over, a few other account manager ducklings in tow. "Seth! Hey, everyone, look who it is! How you doing?" In a lower key: "Didn't they X you?"

"Well," I began, setting the box on the floor, "*technically* X'ed, but . . ."

It was hard to sum up my situation with any clarity, much less confidence. I'd decide on a word, then back off it in the middle, leaving the first letters to fizzle into thin air. After a few more fumbling starts, Josie butted in on my behalf: "He's back from the dead, Camille."

Camille's eyes popped wide in astonishment. The other ducklings huddled closer. Josie had their full attention.

"It's true, Camille. He *died*. And now," she said, wedging hard silences between her words, "He. Is. Risen." She reached down into my cardboard box and took back her Lexus. The whole car fit in the palm of her hand.

Part Two

1.

It was almost winter, way too cold to be eating outdoors, but I liked taking my lunch in the elements. I'd sit in the park with a sandwich or salad and a large cappuccino I made myself. I took pride in the foam, how it held against my lips.

I'd worked at Sötma for only a month or so. Much to my surprise—and possibly my employer's—I proved a capable barista. I accepted the job at the Swedish chocolate bar and café out of something akin to fiscal necessity. It paid an almost respectable hourly wage, though nothing close to the RazorBeat freelancer rate.

I did FreeBeat for a stint, but I won't enumerate the daily indignities I suffered, the sideways glances and quiet sneers whenever I passed a partition of frosted glass. Those I could handle. The worst was when RazorBeat's exec team, in a shortsighted play for profitability, terminated all overbudget accounts. Not froze, *terminated*. All nonprofit clients were dropped as well. Prostate went from listed as "dormant" on status reports to deleted altogether.

I emailed Lawrence directly and told him to call ASAP. I assured him that, RazorBeat policy aside, we could keep working together. I just needed him to call so I could Reveal my tagline over the phone. (In person was always preferable, but I could make do.) He blocked my email first, then my phone number. He even took the rather cowardly step of filing a harassment complaint with RazorBeat corporate. My freelance contract was not extended at month's end.

I figured I'd land at a different agency. And, indeed, I got numerous interviews on the strength of my Smackdale work alone. Everyone remembered it fondly, had a chuckle. But what, they asked, had I done recently? The question betrayed their ignorance. *A brand*, I replied, *is impervious to the passage of time. It's a fixture. It endures.* Their chuckling would start up again later in the interview. *We loved Smackdale*, they'd reiterate.

I resisted asking my parents for financial support. Not that I was above asking for help; I just preferred not to tell them about my minor professional setback. (News of my hospitalization had given my mom heart palpitations, and that was only a case of dehydration; if I told her I'd been terminated, it might actually terminate her.) Besides, I'd return to copywriting soon enough. Sötma was just a breather from the agency bustle, a hard-earned sabbatical of sorts, one replete with quaint flourishes: icicle lights blinking at the threshold, steam tickling the air above the espresso machine, chocolate truffles sitting upright in white-tissue skirts.

I might've taken more delight in these flourishes were it not for Odette. The long-tenured store manager had no patience for romanticism; she assigned tasks in the spare diction of a hard realist. Sweeping, mopping, toilet plunging—this was the language in which she was fluent.

Odette never admitted it, but she hired me for one reason: I was Jewish. When she read "Seth" on my application (which I can only assume was the most well-written she had ever received, so breathtakingly eloquent that it rendered the matter of relevant job experience moot), she asked me if I knew who Seth was.

I was confused. He was me.

"In the Old Testament," she clarified.

As it turns out, Cain and Abel had a third brother. The one Cain didn't slaughter.

Odette was a born-again Christian who professed an appreciation for the Jewish people. She never elaborated, but it was implied: she'd ride out the rapture from a safe perch in the heavens, while I'd be left stewing in hell's hottest cauldron, my tendons bubbling sweetly off the bone. The least she could do was employ me while I awaited an eternity of fire.

I'd never met a born-again before, didn't even think any existed in New York. (Didn't they all reside in the middle of the country, sprouting and resprouting from the same wheat field?) In any case, I tried not to waste time on Odette's belief system. What plagued me was her managerial style.

"Remember," she'd snap, crouched on the bathroom tile. "Waterfall. Not snail."

"Got it, thanks."

"Waterfall?"

"Waterfall."

There are two ways to slot a toilet paper roll in its holder, but only one *correct* way: the tearable end must "flow" over the top. The reverse arrangement, which truthfully looks no more or less snail-like, was a no-no. If I committed one such minor transgression— a "snail" for short—she'd employ the schoolmarm's time-honored method of framing accusations as questions.

"Seth, did you forget your hat?" (Health department requirement.)

"Seth, are you on your phone?" (No texting during shifts.)

"Seth, did you sneeze into the air?" (Always blow into the shirt-sleeve, even if thin deposits of mucus collect at the elbow.)

I'd hoped working in food service might prove a more attractive undertaking. Or rather, that it might make *me* appear more attractive. I remembered, for instance, how the Birthright crowd fawned over this one Mizrachi bartender. With each cocktail order, he hustled ingredients into his sizable shaker, revved up his triceps for a roisterous spell of consummation, then released his potion like a postcoital exhale over a tired scoop of ice. It was an intoxicating display. I sought to conduct myself with a comparable swagger.

But this was the effete world of artisanal chocolates and imported coffee, a far cry from muscle-toned mixology. Simply put, there was nothing cool or sexy about the job. I often prayed no customers would enter and see me, at least nobody I knew. I could barely bring myself to show up some mornings. It all would've been untenable had it not been for Ramya.

A part-time art student, Ramya started at Sötma two weeks after I did. I took notice from the moment she walked into the store; I was manning the espresso bar when the door opened and there she stood: tall and thin, a crack of sunlight. It was the tentativeness of her entrance that most transfixed me, how unsure she looked stepping over the threshold, as if merely entering might mean initiating a disturbance. Then she fished her one-page job application out of her tote and, before handing it over, repeatedly pressed the paper flat between palm and thigh to work out, or at least conceal, any creases. An anxious gesture, though I later sensed this was simply her way, an impassioned impulse to set things right, again and again. If Josie moved through the world with an edge, Ramya sought to smooth everything over. She was beautiful, of course, but it was *how* she was beautiful—the way she extended herself with such sensitivity toward whatever surrounded.

As I got to know her better, I marveled at her approach to things. I was the kind of person who'd zip from one emotional state to another, but Ramya transitioned gradually, almost easing herself; I was reminded of a body of water and how it sleepily drifts toward the temperature of its season. Sometimes, talking with her, I felt I'd found my ideal therapist; I could say anything, share anything, and trust she'd receive it with an even composure that nearly bordered on indifference.

That's not to say she lacked fire. She was young—twenty-one, to be exact—and rebelling against her own symmetry with an art student's zeal for experimentation. Her hair had been subjected to some sharp and uneven chops. Punched through her right ear were three rings like a notebook's binding. A Chinese character clung to her wrist in permanent ink. Once, catching me staring, she asked if I'd ever before met an Indian girl with a *real* tattoo. When I confirmed I hadn't, she scored a satisfied nod.

I should state plainly I did not pursue her. Or, if I did, not in an active sense (at least not at first). Perhaps the most fitting articulation is simply that *I was drawn to her*, which, as a passive-voice construction, obviates the need to engage in the messy business of parsing semantics, such as who attracted whom, and merely affirms the basic and incontrovertible fact that, yes, attraction did take place. I should also add: it was mutual.

I knew things between us wouldn't last. It wasn't personal; she just didn't factor into my long-term plans. I had every intention of quitting Sötma and reclaiming my past glory at RazorBeat, unless a bigger or better agency came knocking. If Ramya truly cared about me, she'd be happy to see me go. I'd bid her farewell and, like a loyal patriot called to duty, return to the front.

For the time being, I enjoyed her company. She was my perfect complement at work, as we compensated for each other's ineptitude. Because she was sloppy with the espresso machine, I taught her my foolproof technique for frothing milk: how I'd hold the steam wand parallel to the pitcher wall, coaxing foam from exaggerated pulls. Next came latte art. While making the pour, I'd rock my wrist from side to side and then sharply withdraw, giving the leaf its stem, the heart its pinch. With the thrill of Ramya's eyes on me, I could almost forget the snot caked on my sleeve.

She excelled at the register, where I was a disaster. One day, a woman in a red peacoat ordered at dizzying speed: *Dark chocolate mocha with almond milk, double whip, extra hot. A large.*

I kept my head low, puzzling over the antiquated POS interface. It was, in Odette's view, *highly intuitive, designed for illiterates.* Just one snag: to input a drink order, you first needed to select small, medium, or large. Until the customer stated the desired size, it presented a test of memory: How many details could you recall with no container to place them in?

"Sorry," I said, hunching into a whisper. "What? A large *what*?"

Ramya overheard my confusion and swooped in to salvage the transaction. As she played the necessary keys, I stepped aside and performed a chore with the pretense of urgency. Dragging a wet rag across a mirror, I saw my backward face. It started blurry before it dried and went clear.

* * *

"What's the name again?"

"Lawrence," I repeated. "Ask for *Lawrence.*"

"And why can't you just use your phone?" Ramya asked.

I found myself growing impatient; Odette needed us back upstairs, and Sötma's basement was no place for extended conversation. It was kept frigid to prevent chocolate from melting, milk from souring.

Odette often admonished us for spending too much time down there together. Ramya in particular liked retreating to the basement, sometimes without me. She'd disappear for half an hour, then drag herself sluggishly back upstairs, her eyes with the stillness of thrown dice just come to rest.

"And what do I say when he answers?"

"You hand me the phone."

"You're being weird," she said, though not abrasively. Her lips were turning a shade of bruise in the cold.

"Wait, I'll get you my jacket." Our lockers were in the basement, near the stairs.

"No need," she said. "I feel fine."

I replied that she was obviously not fine, that she was clearly freezing. She was wearing only our standard oxford under her apron, along with our mandatory chocolatier's hat. An atrocious fit, but she wore it well.

"Please don't tell me what I'm feeling." She tucked her phone back into her pocket.

I tried apologizing, but she wasn't having it.

"When I feel something," she added, "I'll let you know."

Given the basement's bitter conditions, tensions could escalate quickly, almost as a necessary means of generating warmth. Again, I tried apologizing.

"It's fine. It works both ways, I guess." Her cell phone was back out now. Her knuckles grew sharp and pronounced from her grip.

"What do you mean?" I said. "What works both ways?"

I waited for her to explain, but she held silent. Then, after a moment or two, her face changed, as some passing thought or recalled memory brought out a self-conscious laugh. When I'd asked a few days back why she liked spending time with me, she noted, after a pause of uncomfortable duration, that she laughed a lot in my presence. It seemed a tepid endorsement. It would've been different had she asserted that I *made* her laugh. At least that would've established causality.

She stepped back and folded herself neatly at the waist, taking a seat on the stacked cardboard boxes of skim. "Why exactly do you want to talk to this person?"

"Because I need to tell him something."

She looked at me the way a psychic might study a crystal for hints of opacity. "Tell him what?"

I sat down beside her, though I feared a milk implosion. "He's a very important client. That's all." I told her it was too complicated to explain.

I expected her to probe, but she didn't. Perhaps she didn't need to because she already understood. Perhaps she did indeed have psychic powers.

In the silence that followed, a new intimacy took shape. It arrived out of nowhere, or at least its origin was hard to trace. I was grateful for its arrival. Then she smiled strangely. "You want to know what I'm feeling right now?"

I waited. The intimacy was already fading.

"Nothing," she said, training her wide eyes on me. "I'm totally numb."

"Because of the cold?"

She crossed one leg over the other, then leaned back, almost away from herself. "You could hit me, and I wouldn't even feel it."

I recoiled. I said I'd never do that to her. Never.

Her eyes went even wider. "Maybe. Maybe not." She gave a pained laugh, as if the humor of the moment had impinged on a nerve. "I barely know you."

The truth was that now *I* was freezing, but I didn't feel comfortable getting my jacket, not after this whole exchange. Ramya turned from me and dipped her stare into her phone. She dialed as directed, but it wasn't to be: the call went to Lawrence's voicemail. I wasn't discouraged, though. I'd try him again tomorrow.

* * *

My return to RazorBeat wasn't guaranteed, but I liked my odds. From my sporadic text exchanges with Josie, it seemed the agency remained in dire straits financially, which I considered great news. If I could reel in even one decent-sized client, X would hire me back with open arms. I had the perfect new client in mind. Truly, *perfect.* I couldn't believe I'd never thought of it before.

I didn't tell Ramya about my intention to go back to RazorBeat. I would've, had she been forthcoming about her own career goals beyond Sötma. When I once asked what she intended to do after art school, she scoffed and said there was nothing to do with an art school diploma; in this way, it resembled a piece of art—aesthetic, not utilitarian. She had ambitions, of course, but I sensed she'd buried them deep.

As the weeks passed, she opened up more. Mostly intellectual musings, though sometimes she'd divulge things of a personal nature. She'd confide in me about the latest drama involving her roommates: who'd eaten whose vegan granola bars without asking, and who'd retaliated with passive aggression that manifested as a stack of unwashed dishes in the sink. Not riveting stuff, though I found myself enchanted. It was an invitation into her home life. It was a way in.

One day, feeling bold, I asked a question that had been nagging me. What was she doing down in the Sötma basement by herself for those long stretches?

"It's nothing," she said, then gestured for me to follow.

On the top shelf of Ramya's locker was a cigar box. She pulled it down and slid off the velvet-lined cover to reveal a mix of medicine bottles, some pills lying loose and scattered.

I'd never done drugs in this way. Or, really, done them at all. Sure, I'd smoked weed a few times in my life, but nothing beyond that. The reason was Ian Beiselman. A short, stocky kid with dizzyingly terrible breath, Beezy was my lab partner in high school chemistry. When we were assigned to each other, I considered staging a walkout; Beezy would blather nonstop at uncomfortably close range about an array of distasteful topics, most commonly his sexual fantasies involving any one of a number of sophomore girls who had never exchanged even one word with him, let alone entertained ideas of romance. But here's the thing about Beezy: he was an exceptionally precise hand at chemistry. If you managed to ignore his sound and smell, you couldn't help but admire the tremendous care with which he handled his pipettes and the technical skill with which he dispensed three drops of bromothymol blue (no more, no less) into a titration solution. That winter, when Beezy was found unconscious from an overdose in his stepdad's garage, his death was termed an accident. But I wasn't convinced.

It became an unhealthy obsession. I'd tell anyone who would listen—parents, teachers, the school cafeteria lady—that Beezy absolutely, unequivocally had not killed himself by accident. And if they asked how I could be so sure (most never did, preferring to drop the subject), I'd describe for them Beezy's meticulous chemistry handiwork in exquisite detail, much as Beezy might've described an imaginary blow job from class treasurer Alexis Horowitz. He just wasn't the type to be sloppy. If he'd overdosed, it was intentional.

This all came to a head when I got a call from Beezy's mother. I was lying in my room after school one day when the phone rang, and a less than boisterous voice greeted me on the line. Mrs. Beiselman kindly asked if I'd refrain from spreading rumors about her son committing suicide. And I do mean kindly—there was a surprising warmth in her request, no malice whatsoever. She went on to say she was sorry for my loss, that she knew Ian and I were close friends (we weren't), and that she was grateful her son had had the gift of my friendship, even if only for a short time. Something about what she said or how she said it, I couldn't help myself. I started bawling. And Mrs. Beiselman, she heard my sobs and then she started sobbing too. And then this wild thing happened. She started saying maybe I was right, maybe Beezy (she called him Ian, of course) *did* mean to do it. And I rushed in to assure her that wasn't true, that it was an accident, no doubt about it. Though I'd already made my thoughts clear on the matter. So that was that.

Before we hung up, I asked if there was anything I could do to help. Truly anything. And for the first time during the call—the only time, really—her voice grew sharp and firm. She made me promise never to do drugs. So I did. I promised.

I was debating whether to bring any of this up when Ramya took my hand. She said, simply, that I shouldn't feel pressured to do anything. She despised pressure, she said, of all forms. I told her I agreed, that I utterly and absolutely *abhorred* pressure, then opened my palm wide to her, because, really, what choice did I have? Anyway, Beezy was the past. And if it hadn't been drugs, it probably would've been something else.

From that day forward, whenever our shifts overlapped, Ramya and I made a brief trip to the basement, huddling together in a less-frigid spot beside the boiler. She'd dole out one pill to me and one to herself. Typically the same kind, but not always. Sometimes I took an upper and she took a downer, or vice versa. But we preferred coordinating, like dressing up our minds in little matching outfits.

After a few weeks, Ramya stopped taking the pills, claiming that she got more satisfaction from watching me take them. I figured she was lying, but she really meant it. She'd light up when choosing what to prescribe me on a given day. In the hours afterward, she'd check in on me. Her voice took on the lilting quality of a doting caregiver's.

It wasn't my intention to develop a drug habit. And, really, I didn't think about what we did (or, I suppose, *I* did) in habitual terms. If anything, it was an antidote to the oppressively repetitive nature of barista work. As soon as I left Sötma behind, I figured I'd leave the pills behind too.

The drug use had varied effects on my job performance. Depending on the pill, I'd either labor over a single drink order or plow through dozens of orders with frightful efficiency. Sometimes I hadn't flushed one pill out of my system before swallowing the next. But that didn't bother me. I appreciated the continuity; I was being passed from one set of hands to another.

An unexpected consequence of the pills was that I felt moved to write. Not taglines, just ramblings. With my RazorBeat notebook handy, I'd sit in the park near Sötma during lunch break and splatter sentences onto the page . . .

If you ever see a ventriloquist act, please ignore the dummy's mouth. The more interesting stuff takes place on the other end, namely the dummy's ass, inside which the ventriloquist's arm is lodged.

The dummy's predicament is distressing on two fronts: 1) his body is being violated, and 2) he can't cry out for help. By giving the dummy the ability to speak and then usurping it, the ventriloquist effectively silences his victim. The audience recognizes the rape that's taking place, but they laugh anyway because they don't consider it morally wrong. After all, the dummy is inanimate! And yet the ventriloquist animates him.

At some point during the performance, the dummy will lash out and refer to his own ventriloquist as a dummy. Aside from the obvious wordplay, this joke underscores the tense power dynamics. Though the ventriloquist can give his dummy a voice, he cannot control what he says. The irony, of course, is that the dummy has no control either. Performance renders them both powerless.

I'd jot stuff like this down, not think much of it. But otherwise, the drugs didn't have a huge impact. If anything, they smoothed out daily life, buffing out the dents. The only real issue was that occasionally they made me ill. One day—truly the worst possible day for it to happen, as it turned out—things got ugly.

"I'm fine," I told Ramya, though I was anything but. The pills tended to either slow me down or rush me along, but this time I felt stuck in a lurching rhythm, two opposing poles pulling at me in spurts.

"It'll pass," Ramya said, as she gripped my hand, anchoring me.

But no anchor could help. I was in terrible shape, and I had an urge to puke. I gestured for her to avert her eyes, to walk away *now*, but she stood in place. Her composure floored me: she took off her uniform hat, inverted it, and instructed me to use it as a bucket. Just in time, thankfully. In the seconds after, she patted my back while I stammered through an apology.

A bellowing customer interrupted everything: "'ELLLLLLLLLLO. Anybody home?"

We typically scheduled our basement trips for when Odette was back from break, but we'd been getting sloppy.

Unsure of what to do with Ramya's mess of a hat, I dumped it in the trash near the loading zone, accidentally spilling a little on the floor. I did feel a bit better, but my coordination still wasn't right.

"Go upstairs," I said. "I'll take care of this."

Ramya rolled her eyes in mock salute. Who was I to give her orders?

"'ELLLLLLLLLLLLLLLLLLLLLLLLLLLLLLLLLLLLLLO?"

At this second call, Ramya bound up the staircase, her long legs flittering out of sight. Meanwhile, I riffled through the basement closet in search of cleaning supplies. I stopped when the chemical smells nearly caused me to hurl again.

I took a moment to map out my next moves. I'd tackle the stairs and, ignoring the customer, duck into the bathroom at the far end of the store. It was essential that I clean myself up first and foremost.

And Odette wouldn't be returning for a bit, just enough time to get things back in order.

The climb upstairs proved challenging. It wasn't so much that my legs were wobbly, but that the staircase itself—nay, the world— seemed to wobble. After a halting conquest, I was surprised to encounter a familiar face. I wasn't sure at first, since the world kept wobbling back and forth, and all I wanted was to take the world between my two hands and look it straight in the eye like a petulant child and demand in no uncertain terms that it stop, *stop right now!* But there he was. Moon. His blond bulb of a head screwed loose into his shoulders.

I dipped behind the counter to avoid detection, but it was too late.

"Seth? It's Seth, right?" He took off his sunglasses and rubbed the polarized lenses on his rugby scarf, as if shining up an old memory.

Had I felt up to the task, I'd have seized this lucky opportunity to engage him in a frank discussion about the state of RazorBeat and the prospect of my return. But I could barely discuss anything, barely formulate a sentence without it dissolving on my tongue. I was in need of my own ventriloquist.

I concentrated as best as I could. "What can I get you?"

"*What can I get you?* You BELIEVE this guy?!"

Moon was addressing Ramya, but her focus was elsewhere—or, more specifically, her focus was on me. Her fingers kept worrying the silver rings that ran up her ear.

"How are things?"

I had to bring the conversation to a swift and painless death. "Fine."

"Same here. I can't complain. Getting married, actually! How about this: SHE asked ME. We're in the woods last weekend, hiking Bear Mountain. Nothing special, just a boring-ass trail. Definitely no bears. You could hear the highway the whole time, to be honest. Then she gets down on one knee—NOT LIKE THAT, Seth, you perv . . . I'm really sorry about him." He clasped both hands in fake apology to Ramya. "Anyway, she popped it, right on the mountain." He slapped my shoulder as if testing a piece of protective gear, nearly causing me to keel backward into a shelf of ceramic mugs. "Fuck *tradition*, right?!"

I was sure my breath reeked, so I tried to keep my mouth shut and nod expressively instead. It was shameful enough to be seen working at Sötma. I didn't need him reporting back about a stench.

Moon went on, coloring in the details of his engagement, until his tone abruptly changed. He returned his shades to the high bridge of his nose.

"So tell me . . . how's this working out?"

"Sorry?"

"Can I level with you?" Moon swooped closer and pressed his huge palms to the display case, surely leaving a pair of greasy prints for me to Windex later. "You got a good thing going here, Seth."

"A good—"

"Salt-of-the-earth shit. What, like fifteen an hour? A real honest living."

The sober part of me wanted to scream. I had no desire to live honestly. I deserved better than that.

"Bet you don't miss RazorBeat, am I right?"

"Well, actually, the thing is—"

"See!" Moon slapped the case, prompting the white chocolate partridges inside to quiver. They'd arrived weeks ago and not one had sold. "*Freedom*, right? No more bullshit clients. No more fucking clowns to answer to."

There was, of course, one clown I answered to, and at that moment she shuffled in through the front door. Ramya dashed out from behind the register to distract Odette, keeping her at bay with inane questions regarding the holiday decorations.

"And you left on your terms," he went on. "That's huge!" To reinforce the hugeness, Moon reached for me again, grabbing where he guessed he might find bicep. Eyeing me over the top edge of his sunglasses, his pupils did a quick dance of dilation. "Now I need your help."

"My . . . help?" The daze of the pills cleared for a moment.

"Gift for the future mother-in-law." Moon cupped both of his hands a foot in front of his stomach, implying either she had a large appetite or, possibly, though less likely, she was expecting. Chocolate. He wanted my advice on chocolate.

Ramya shot me a glance; she couldn't hold back the boss much longer.

"Ah, who cares." Moon pointed to the partridges and set his wallet down on the counter. "Give me a dozen."

I went to reach for the tissue paper and gift box when I remembered I still hadn't washed my hands. I had visions of an ornery health inspector shutting us down, tracing the contamination source back to me.

"Ramya," I cried out, as I waved her over.

Odette lingered at the entrance, uncoupling two strings of icicle lights that thankfully had gotten twisted. At my request, Ramya plucked the twelve partridges out of their skirts as I set about working the register. But I couldn't locate the appropriate button. Where was the damn partridge?

"Man, it's good catching up." Moon tilted his head down slightly, letting any loose memories roll to the front of his brain. "Hey, remember Tulsa? Those dumb Prostate bastards . . ."

I was bad at the register even when sober, but now I especially couldn't manage. Employing the process of elimination, I began running my eyes over the fifty-odd buttons. I'd look at each and mentally cross it off: *Not a bird, not a bird* . . .

"Doing anything next Friday?"

"Friday?" I said, glancing up at him. (*Not a bird.*)

"Dinner with the boys," he said. "You should come!"

I'd now surveyed all my options twice, backward and forward. Not one partridge to be found. I was stuck. Ramya would know which button to hit, but I was too ashamed to ask. Not in front of Moon.

"Hey," I said in a whisper. "They're on me."

Ramya, without missing a beat, handed Moon his prize. She'd even managed to dress up the gift box with twin curls of silk ribbon.

"You sure?"

I winked, hoping to inspire discretion. And he did keep his mouth shut, though that didn't stop his hand from giving the glass display case one last thunder-slap of gratitude.

As he turned to leave, I remembered the seasonal button. *Of course.* That's where the partridges were categorized. They were listed as a holiday item, stashed behind a cartoon image of a Christmas tree.

"Next Friday? You in?"

I nodded blankly as I checked the price for a box: seventy-two dollars. Odette would probably take the money right out of my paycheck. Then, before I knew it, Moon was out the door, freezing air rushing in to take his place.

Odette padded over to where Ramya and I were standing. The wrinkles along her forehead appeared deep, almost engraved. I was sure she already knew about the vomit, about the pills, about everything.

She glared at me for a moment, then turned instead to Ramya. She stuck her index finger mere inches from her face, though Ramya didn't flinch. "Dear," she said sharply, "where is your hat?"

2.

The vomit incident was the wake-up call I needed. What was I doing with my life? Why was I languishing in a dead-end job, blindly ingesting prescription drugs dispensed by some tattooed art student? Spending time with Ramya was fine, but I couldn't lose sight of my future.

The next morning, I made three calls. First, I dialed Moon's work number and left a message. Yes, I'd gladly join for *dinner with the boys*. It seemed like a great chance to reconnect with some of the RazorBeat partners. I could forgive and forget, no problem.

Next, I called my mom and asked if she could meet next week for lunch. She was thrilled, since I'd been putting her off for months, disclosing scant details about my trip to Israel other than that I'd baked in the sun. I stressed I specifically wanted to talk business with her. She sounded amenable, if uncertain.

The last call I made from Ramya's phone. (I'd memorized her locker combination from watching her open it so many times.) Because she was busy upstairs botching yet another macchiato order, I knew I'd get a few minutes in the basement alone, which was all I needed.

"Hello?" he finally answered.

I'd rehearsed in my head a million times how I'd approach the call. The most important thing was that he not hang up. Every word had to hold him tight, hug him close.

"Do you believe," I began, "that your work means something?"

"Sorry, who is this?"

"Do you believe," I said, careful not to be heard upstairs, "that it matters? That the Prostate Cancer Research Group matters?"

"*Wait.*" He took a moment to make the identification. "I swear on my—leave me alone! Enough already!"

I afforded him a moment to air frustrations. Then I promised I'd never bother him again, so long as he answered my one question. Lawrence went dark for a beat. I could hear him clearing his throat with a dry effort. "Yes, it matters! Obviously it matters."

"Sir, I couldn't agree more." I paused. The dust-caked fans in the refrigeration unit were throwing their usual buzz. "What your organization does is deeply inspiring. And this is personal to me, Larry. Can I call you Larry? Because let me tell you something: my father had prostate cancer." I took a breath, let everything sink in. "I still remember the day when Mom and I received the news. We were devastated. We thought"—and here I swallowed hard—"it might be the end of the road. But you know what? He made a total recovery. Happier and healthier than ever. So yeah. It matters."

"I'm glad to hear that, but—"

"I never said anything about this in Tulsa because it's hard for me to discuss. I'm sorry, I get emotional about it. It's not professional of me. I'm sorry for being unprofessional. Do you accept my apology? But here's the thing, Larry. My dad's story? It's not unique. You help hundreds of guys like him every day. There are men all across America, all across the world, whose lives depend on your work. You and Gage and"—I couldn't recall any other grunts I'd met in passing—"*all* of you. You're heroes."

"What, exactly, are you selling me?"

My basement break was nearing an end. It was time to Reveal or go home.

"Larry, come on. I'm not selling anything. I'm calling because I'd like to make a gift. Can I do that? Can I make a gift?"

"A . . . donation?"

"I want to contribute, completely free of charge, my final tagline recommendation."

"Look, I'm not interested in—"

"You were right the first time! But this one is different. It taps into the true spirit of the Prostate Cancer Research Group. I swear, donors will love it."

Larry said nothing, which meant I had him.

"Ready?" I took a long breath for the sake of pacing. "*Men Saving Men.*"

I let him soak up the profundity of the moment. The silence gave me an opportunity to adjust into a more comfortable stance; I relaxed my shoulders, rolling them forward first and then back, and leaned closer to the boiler's enduring warmth.

"I appreciate your time, but never call me again."

I was incredulous. Just incredulous.

"This will be our last conversation. Thank you."

"*Men Saving Men.* It's perfect!"

"It's not perfect. It's actually kind of offensive."

"Yeah? How so?"

"Many women work here too."

"So we edit it! *Saving Men.*"

"Listen," he snapped. "It's wrong. It's all wrong. And besides, our legal team would never approve it."

"I'll convince them! Let me talk to—"

"We don't save men. We develop treatments. It's not the same."

"You do save them! You absolutely do!" I stopped, started: "Think of my dad!"

"We save *some* men. Not all." He paused. "All is impossible."

I proceeded to curse him out. I said his organization *was* saving men, and he was just too much of a wimp to declare it to the world. If he were a real man, I went on, twisting the knife, he wouldn't be so timid.

"Maybe," he replied, not quite chuckling. "But some things you can't say."

I lowered Ramya's phone from my ear. Before returning it to her locker, I put the corner part in my mouth and bit down, gently at first, then harder, *harder*, attempting to shatter the screen, not the whole thing, just the corner, but wow, phones are harder to shatter than they look. They're getting stronger all the time.

* * *

"*Dinner with the boys.* What should I wear?"

"He seemed like an asshole," Ramya said. "So dress like an asshole, and you'll fit in." As she bent to untie her paint-speckled boots, her hair held its part.

"Yeah." I plopped down on her futon. Then I explained that being an asshole was, unfortunately, Moon's charm.

"Charming to who?" she asked. "You?"

Ramya reached across her plywood coffee table for the Jack Daniel's and poured herself some. She also filled my glass but, in doing so, spilled a little on the carpet by mistake. It was the kind of miss typical of a drunk, but that was just her—prone to minor slips, as if she hadn't quite mastered the subtle mechanism of her own limbs.

Ramya's Bushwick apartment had imposing walls of exposed cinder block, tempered only by bamboo dividers draped with tapestries. She shared the space with a dozen fellow art students, and there was no shortage of activity. At any given moment, you might hear someone pissing, someone snoring, someone fucking, someone Netflix binging. And since everything took place unseen behind bamboo, the sounds all jumbled together. It was hard to decipher, for example, when the fucking was real or on Netflix. Whenever I caught glimpses of the roommates, I tried matching them to the portraits Ramya had given, but they looked interchangeable: the same loose-fitting neutrals, the same severe haircuts. They never acknowledged my presence, which I took as a sign of their jealousy. They wanted Ramya for themselves.

Though my apartment was a more comfortable place to unwind after shifts, I never invited her there. I was too embarrassed about its luxury—not palatial by any means, but a fine studio in a fine building. Appropriate for an on-the-rise copywriter, but far outside of a barista's pay grade. And that's what I was now: a barista. In truth, I couldn't afford it. I was a month behind on rent.

Ramya's bedroom was bare except for one centerpiece: her Apple monitor. It was, she said, the only thing in her life she'd ever splurged on. Even for an aspiring designer, it was impressive—higher resolution and larger than Josie's.

I wanted to discuss Moon in greater depth, but Ramya had no interest. She tossed me a controller instead.

"Play?"

"The infinity one?"

"*Procedurally generated*," she corrected.

Ramya was a die-hard gamer. She once spent an entire shift explaining her thoughts on the gaming world. The latest innovation, she said, was the use of deterministic algorithms that relied on random number generation. Rather than a fixed board, the playing field was an infinite world perpetually building upon itself, too expansive for even the game's creators to comprehend.

"You'll kill me in seconds," I protested.

She rolled up her wool sweater's bulky sleeves, the slender lines of her arms on full display. The level was already loading. "You'll be fine."

After selecting my battleship and weaponry of choice, I found myself launched into space. It was a split screen, so I could also keep tabs on Ramya. She appeared similarly adrift, though billions of light-years away, in a sea of watermelon-pink lava.

Ramya's description didn't prepare me for the game's visual impact. As I got pulled into the orbit of a hazy planet, it lurched into focus. Mountains swayed like anemones in a tide pool. Sluggish robots inchwormed across a shore of ruby sand. Surveying the landscape, I was struck by the fact that this world existed only for us, at this single moment in time. No other players had ever or, if I understood correctly, would ever encounter this exact environment again.

"I can't believe," I said, "the game creates its own universe."

"Yeah. Well, kind of."

"Kind of?"

"It's not entirely autonomous." Ramya unleashed buckshot at a gecko with wings. "Programmers deserve the credit. They created the algorithm that creates it."

I was thinking up a reply when she urged me to focus on playing. My battleship had gotten entangled in the sticky roots of a lotus.

"But don't you think"—I freed myself from the attacking flower, then rewarded myself with another sip of Jack—"this is a turning point? Computers aren't just solving things. They're building worlds. It's like artificial intelligence is already beyond us."

"AI," she said, slaying an even more imposing gecko, "is just cognitive processing. The really impressive stuff is ASI."

I nodded, though not convincingly enough.

"*Artificial superintelligence.* Smarter than the smartest human— and more intuitive."

Ramya's ship was being bombarded with wasplike artillery, though she accelerated out of range. It was striking how coordinated her movements were in this virtual realm, her real-world clumsiness left behind.

After she described ASI in more detail, I offered a bold procla-
mation: humanity was obsolete. I turned to her nervously to see if
I'd made an impact.

"We're not superintelligent, but don't assume we're useless. We'll
always be better at certain tasks."

"But computers evolve faster than we do, don't they? They'll
pass us."

"Not in everything. They'll keep progressing, obviously, but there
will always be gaps." She let loose a hot flurry of ninja stars she'd
kept stowed away the whole time. "If you think about it, that's our
only purpose. Filling those gaps."

I stared at her and forgot the rest. "So that's all humanity's
good for?"

In her eyes, I could see the electric colors of the game reflected and
the strict vertical line setting our two worlds apart.

"Come here," she said, from galaxies away.

*　*　*

Sex with Ramya was wild and intense and highly transportable in
the sense that I could carry memories of it with me throughout the
week, sometimes even into the next one. Whenever the momentum
between us threatened to wane, we'd have an overlapping shift at
Sötma that sustained us. Like how a light touch, if well timed, can
keep a porcelain plate spinning on a stick for an eternity.

Ramya insisted on blindfolding me during sex—any dark piece
of clothing or towel would do. I initially thrilled at this practice
and the freedoms it afforded. I'd let my imagination wander and
picture myself with Josie back in Diego's office, or Yael on the fire
escape, or a hybrid of the two in a more surreal setting—say, a sea
of watermelon-pink lava. But I tired of visualizing them. Ramya.
Ramya was who I wanted to see! My powers of imagination failed

when it came to her. I didn't know how to fantasize about the person I held close. My mind was always squinting at someone further off. What we lacked in sight we compensated for in touch. Ramya liked sex rough, though not in an imprecise manner. She'd guide my hand to a particular spot on her lower thigh and show me where and how to pinch, digging my fingers deep into the admitting flesh above her knee, forcing me into an awkward encounter with bone. I kept waiting for her to signal that I should ease up, but nothing. Not even a faint yelp. If there was some hard-and-fast boundary, some line not to cross, evidently I was nowhere near it.

We began flirting more brazenly at work, though Odette hardly noticed, too preoccupied with some thorny issue involving the upstairs tenant. Otherwise our routine stayed the same: I continued with my daily tasks on a steady diet of pills.

The day I met my mom for lunch, however, I had to be sober. I told Odette I was feeling sick, then rushed home to change out of my uniform into something agency-ish. I arrived half an hour late, though my mom didn't seem too perturbed.

"Spiffy," she remarked. "Big meeting today?"

Had I overdone it with the blazer? "You know how it goes," I said, while our orders went through to the Thai Palace kitchen.

First things first, she asked to hear my full assessment of Birthright, now that I had what she called "perspective" on the experience. I started by listing landmarks, what I'd seen and in what order. Then my tone shifted, and, for one reason or another, I let loose. I blasted the trip in highly critical terms, more critical somehow because I'd paid nothing and yet still felt myself cheated in some way, possibly even deserving of a refund. Birthright, I said, was a failed marketing campaign. A pathetic attempt to promote a positive image of Israel, an image that bore no resemblance to reality. It was a violent nation, and I'd witnessed that violence firsthand!

"They attacked my cab, just like this." I took my two fists to our wooden lunch table to approximate the sound.

"They? Who's *they*?"

"The ultra-Orthodox. Who else?"

"Here's the good news, Seth," she said, pushing broccoli florets to the edge of her plate. "You never have to go back." A bittersweet expression landed on her face, like someone dropped it there and walked off. "So I take it you didn't reach out to Mishaal?"

"Let's talk about something else," I said. "How are you?"

"Can't complain, I guess. Though my hip's acting up again. Supposed to see about an injection, but you know me, I'd prefer to do nothing. I take painkillers. But with my stomach, it's pick your poison."

I nodded crisply. "How's work?"

"The TV station? Oh, you know. About the same."

"How's the business side?" I tried leaning forward, but my tightly buttoned blazer denied me this inclination. "How are sales?"

"Not great, honestly." She slowed while segregating the last of the broccoli. "Not great at all."

"Maybe I can help."

"Oh?" Her eyes brightened. "How?"

This was my shot to set my plan in motion. I'd start by explaining the economic benefits of rebranding. Then I'd urge her to entrust this important endeavor to me. True, she was just a salesperson, but she held sway. How long had she worked there? Since I was born? And no, a tiny TV network in Maryland wouldn't have much budget, but RazorBeat would still be glad to add it to the roster. I'd serve it up on a silver platter under one condition: full partnership, same as Moon. As for Ramya, maybe I didn't have to leave her behind, not entirely. I'd bring her on as a design intern—unpaid, most likely, though I'd look after her financially. On a partner's salary, I could spring for a bigger apartment, big enough for her to move in, if she desired. All the space we'd ever need. Our own infinite world.

I was sizing up the limitless dimensions of my future when my mother stopped me short: "You're kind to worry, but don't. Besides," she said, "I'm retiring anyway."

I took the news like a direct hit. I could barely breathe from the full force of the blow.

"Retiring when?" I asked. "Next year?"

"Ha! They wish. I've already given notice. You should've seen the reaction on their faces! Wait, what's wrong? Honey?"

I tried not to look alarmed. Maybe I could still close the deal? Though it would be impossible now. My own flesh and blood was my only in.

She proceeded to tell me about her plans for retirement, how much she was looking forward to this "next chapter." I hated that phrase, how it cast her dull life in the glimmer of narrative. I wasn't actually mad at her, of course. Just furious at myself. I should've acted sooner, should've reeled in this client when I had the chance. I let my own mother slip out of my grasp.

After lunch, she insisted on walking me to the agency. I considered telling her the truth then and there, but found no value in it. She deserved a happy retirement, didn't she? Then, out of nowhere, she told me she was proud.

"Proud? For what?"

"Can't a mother just take pride in her son?" She often used the third person in this way, slotting distance between us and the roles we found ourselves in. "How about," she said, "you show me your office?" She gestured up at the skyscraper that stood before us.

My office?

"Desk, cubicle, whatever." She ran a quick hand through her dark shock of hair, taming it back. "I've never seen it!"

I stared blankly, unsure what to say next. I had no use for language in that moment. I could've dumped all my words in a puddle on the street and walked off.

"Well," she said mercifully, "perhaps another time." She gave me a big hug, then drifted to the curb and raised her arm. Soon enough a cab saw her away.

I stood outside the building for a few minutes in a daze. I stood and stood, hoping that the building might take me back inside, that the doors might open swiftly and breathe me in, inhaling me up through the elevator shaft and installing me at my old desk. I was weightless. I was as light as could be.

I remained dazed when I spotted Josie stepping out of the building. I'd texted her to come down and meet me, but she hadn't replied. I wasn't sure if she'd show.

As she paced toward me, I tried to muster up something resembling a hello. She stepped with more buoyancy than I remembered, then halted a few feet short to look me up and down. She didn't even ask what I was doing in the neighborhood or what had brought me back. It was as if my presence were a total nonevent.

"Why so fancy?"

I explained that I'd had lunch with my mom.

She flipped up my lapels. "Must've been a nice lunch."

She was in a rush but could do a quick coffee; we walked to the first place that wasn't Starbucks. I hadn't yet told her I was working as a barista—just a temporary gig, after all—but I figured she'd heard through the grapevine. It was probably a topic of much discussion at the agency: former wunderkind copywriter turned coffee maker. As it turned out, she hadn't heard the news. "But the job sounds like a good fit for you," she said. *A good fit*, those were her words. *Yes*, I thought, *and surely Albert Einstein would've made a fine auto mechanic.*

In line, she was her typical self, all wry smiles and winning barbs. Since I was now a "connoisseur" of the café world, she asked if I might be so kind as to explain what distinguished a cortado from a cappuccino. I felt the shame of my new occupation lift for an instant and seized the opportunity to impart knowledge; I began detailing what I'd learned at Sötma, the subtle distinctions between one drink and another, the small but critical adjustments in technique. I was finally finding my rhythm when she interjected, "Wow, riveting! And what's a—how do you say it in Italian—*latte*?" Her laugh burned a hole right through me.

When we sat down, I fought the impulse to tell her all about Ramya. I'd found someone younger, prettier, and wouldn't that sting a little? It wasn't so much that I wanted to hurt Josie but that I wanted to believe I *could* hurt her, that I was still capable of inflicting a wound.

She was in a talkative mood. I focused less on her words than how they streamed out of her, her shoulders rising and falling accordingly.

"I ran into Moon," I said, finally. "He invited me to dinner. Boys only, I think."

"You gonna go?"

I pretended I was undecided. Would she go if she were me?

"I'm the wrong person to ask. Do I look like a boy? Anyway, I barely see him." She tore open a sugar packet, then sunk its contents into her iced coffee.

"Probably for the best," I replied. I sensed she might be about to lead the conversation elsewhere, so I hurriedly added, "He's such a mess."

"He really is," she said. "Did you hear what he did at a client dinner last week? Literally snorted one of these"—she held up a second packet—"in front of everyone! Not even the refined kind. Sugar In The Raw."

I paused. "Can you get high off that?"

"Who knows. He got a nosebleed, then blacked out in the bathroom."

I sipped the macchiato I now felt foolish for ordering. "Someone dare him?"

She wasn't sure. She assumed he'd just dared himself.

"A mess," I repeated.

"Wanna know something, Seth?" Rather than swirl in the sugar, she let it settle at the bottom, where she could easily retrieve it by straw. She took a quick drag, and her cheeks puckered. "I can't think of a single guy at RazorBeat who hasn't sexually harassed me."

I quit wallowing for a second, blinked into sharper focus. This was a serious charge, and I needed to meet it with the requisite seriousness. But I also felt myself stiffening into a defensive posture. Was Josie painting me with that brush? What we'd done in Diego's office was inappropriate, sure, but consensual. Wasn't it? And why was she only bringing this up now? What did she expect me to do with this information?

"That's terrible," I said.

She sighed listlessly, a fluttering exhale. Her cheeks looked wan. They'd shed all their freckles for winter.

I told her I was sorry. Not for anything *I* had done, mind you—just a vague apology offered on behalf of men in general.

She laughed and crumpled the empty sugar packet into a pebble, then flicked it to the tile floor. "You are what you are, Seth."

I nodded, sipped my drink, and tried to absorb whatever I was. After a moment, I sought to fill another silence. "What about Diego?"

"What about him?"

"I bet he never . . . well, you know, I mean . . ."

"Are you *joking*?" Her eyes blazed out from their sockets. She set her elbows against the table's unsteadiness. "He was the worst of all of you."

"But he's gay. I can't imagine—"

"Gay?!" She nearly spat out in my face. "Who told you that?"

Had anyone told me? Wasn't it just obvious? I'd lost count of how many times he'd layered on insinuations, stared at me with palpable longing. I'd always figured—

"Total womanizer," she said. "Total."

I concealed myself behind another sip. The cup felt ridiculously small in my hands, like an insect I'd trapped and hoped to keep as a pet.

"He slept with the Lexus client, you know. Then got her to pull the account. Broke up her family in the process.

"He was real sleazy with me," she continued. She dragged her iced coffee around in repetitive circles on the table, leaving loops of condensation in its wake.

The looping stopped, and she settled her eyes on me. For a moment, her gaze cracked wide open. "I never said anything to you?" she began. "Never?"

* * *

I went to Ramya's apartment afterward, and this time all her roommates were out. Some exhibition. Theoretically, the place should have felt more intimate. Just the two of us—no background noises, no furtive looks through the countless gaps between one bedroom and another. But because of the space's odd acoustics, we found ourselves interrupted by our echoes bombarding us at uncomfortable angles. Each word we uttered intruded awkwardly upon the next.

As we were sitting on her futon, Ramya took a big swig of Jack. Then she wiped her mouth with her wrist, leaving a light kiss of moisture there. I reached for her wrist to kiss that same spot. It was a game, I thought; I'd kiss there, then she'd kiss there. It would be as if the two of us were leaving kisses for each other. But she didn't want her wrist used in this way. It withdrew into a sleeve.

She gestured toward the controller. "Play?"

I shrugged. I asked if she had any pills for me, but she said unfortunately she'd left the cigar box at work. That, I knew, was a lie. I'd opened her locker earlier in the day and found it missing.

I agreed to play for a few minutes, then lost interest. It was sad to think an infinite universe could grow tiresome, but I got bored of the same motifs: each planet was one of the same ten colors; each attacking creature resembled some animal, plant, or robot I'd seen before. Was this all infinity was?

"So why aren't you at this exhibition?"

"Too abstract." She was immersed, tapping away rapid-fire as usual.

"What's wrong with abstraction?"

"I like conceptual art better."

Wasn't all abstract art inherently conceptual? What is abstraction if not a concept?

Ramya wasn't listening. With a stab wound, a bar of life was sapped. Meanwhile, my player lay abandoned on the rocky banks of a molasses-like lake.

"You've never shown me your art," I said.

"Just dumb stuff for class. Assignments." She was mowing down everything in the path with a persistent barrage of bullets. I, on the other hand, was getting pecked alive by a lobster-clawed gorilla. Each time a part of my battleship got pried off, my controller gave out a plaintive vibration of pain.

"Who cares?" I said. "Show me anyway." I stood up and unplugged the console. My controller froze, a suffering patient brought to a merciful end. She stayed silent and set hers down on the cold strip of futon between us.

With the monitor still on, she clicked into her hard drive and dragged a folder onto the desktop. "Happy?" she said, Jack in hand. This swig was different from the first; she held the bottle at her lips for a shorter duration, so the motion was more sudden and the angle more severe.

When she stormed off into the bathroom, I had time to peruse. Her portfolio featured many iconic corporate logos she'd redesigned. Pepsi with a gradient blending the red and blue. Google with a hatched drop shadow for added dimension. American Airlines with the As juxtaposed like two outstretched wings.

"I love these," I said, when she returned. I'd planned to lavish praise no matter what the folder contained—it could've been blank, and I would've complimented the austerity—but I was surprised by my truthful conviction.

"Marketing Comms. It's a stupid prereq." She began playing a game on her phone. In her palm, colorful bricks were exploding as fresh ones fell into place. It made me think of Acre, the new burying the old.

"Hey," I said, clicking through the files. "You redid Sötma!"

With its nearly illegible cursive, the current logo was outdated. Ramya had given it a face-lift, using a sleek sans serif while brightening up the color scheme. She also rendered the umlaut as two yellow stars, an artful nod to the shop's European roots. This was not the work of a prospective intern but a prodigy.

"You should show this to Odette."

Another row collapsed, making room for more bricks.

"Or what if *I* show her?"

She kept her head down. "Be my guest."

I wanted to tear the phone from her hands. So she would face me. So I could explain that I'd worked with many designers—some good, most mediocre—and that Ramya had real talent. I wanted to nurture that talent and protect her from the world and its vast fleet of vile men. Maybe it was too late for Josie, but not for her. And maybe, just maybe, I wanted her to pinch *me* for a change. I wanted pain to radiate deep and down and through. I wanted a literal train to run me over, so she might have to bend low and listen for the faint thud of my pulse. I wanted her lips pressed to mine—each kiss like a desperate tug on a rope, hauling something heavy and inert out of the dark. I loved her, and I wanted to say *I love you*, but the more active form of *I am loving you, I am loving you*. But I didn't say that.

"You know, I used to work in this industry."

She kept her eyes on her phone. Bricks were exploding faster and faster. "Oh," she said. "What industry is that?"

3.

I stayed up all night, pacing my parquet floor, overworking my coffee maker until it wept weaker and weaker cups. It felt great getting back into the swing of things, and now I was a one-man shop. No colleagues to deal with. No fucking clowns, as Moon would say. The presentation was in my hands alone.

The next day, I greeted Odette more warmly than usual. She eyed me with suspicion. "Did you leave the basement lights on last night?"

I shook my head, shifting my laptop bag off my shoulder.

"So it was her," she grumbled. "Figures."

"Hey, Odette, can I talk to you?"

"What about?" She was counting bills at the register, as she often did between shifts. She'd inspect the watermark of each note larger than a twenty.

"Business, actually." I would've gladly bypassed her and met with the store owner, but I'd never been introduced.

"If you're angling for a raise"—she lifted another bill to the light—"I'm sorry to disappoint. The holidays haven't been what we hoped."

"You're right. They haven't."

Her face crackled. "Excuse me?"

I told her I had a surefire way to boost sales. I had to tread carefully, though; I didn't want to draw all the attention to myself. It mattered that, in the final tally, Ramya receive credit too, since the logo was hers, after all. If I did manage to bring in Sötma as a client, I'd see that RazorBeat awarded her a modest commission.

Odette gave the open register a hip bump, clicking it shut.

"I've been thinking," I began. "What *is* Sötma?"

"A store." Then she added, sharply, "Your current employer."

"But what are we? What's our brand?"

I opened my laptop while maintaining eye contact, like a predator careful not to spook his prey. I set it to presentation mode, held it up for her to see.

"Chocolate," she answered. "Also coffee."

"Exactly! And that's a little confusing, isn't it?" I tried channeling Moon's charisma, the way he'd enchanted our Prostate clients before it all went south. "Most customers know us for our chocolate. But that's not our bestselling item! Two-thirds of our sales are from the espresso bar." I studied Odette's eyes and adjusted my screen, upping the contrast. "We have what's called a 'brand perception gap.' Our reputation in the marketplace doesn't align with purchase behavior."

Odette looked puzzled. "So . . . we stop selling chocolate?"

"No. We rebrand. We're known as a chocolate shop that sells coffee. We should really be a *coffee* shop that sells *chocolate*."

Odette was fully engaged now, her gaze slicing through the haze of my laptop's screen. "But why are they buying our coffee? All these customers."

I hadn't expected to field questions during the strategic setup. At worst, I'd anticipated a glazed-over look or a broom handle thrown in my face.

"Well . . ."

"Because of the mocha! It's our signature drink."

She wasn't wrong. I'd made more mochas than lattes and cappuccinos combined.

"Chocolate," she said sunnily, "is what *sells* our coffee."

It appeared Odette had a bit more business acumen than predicted. Not a problem. In fact, it made my job easier. I made an executive decision to skip the remaining strategy slides and dive into The Reveal.

"Meet," I proclaimed, "your new tagline and logo." I held the laptop proudly at my chest, beaming.

She scratched her neck with the inside of her wrist. "Is this . . . for our website?"

The Sötma homepage was a blog from yesteryear, its single entry a typo-filled paean to cacao's therapeutic properties.

"For everything," I replied. "Web, signage, advertising. Your tagline and logo belong everywhere, because they're the foundation of the brand." I read my proposed tagline out loud, just in case she was struggling with the size of the type. She seemed more interested in the new logo. "Looks nice, right?"

She kept peering, taking it in, tracing the lines and where they led. I waited a minute before explaining that Ramya designed it.

"Oh." She blinked away from the screen and met my eyes instead. "Figures."

I tried hard to defend the quality of the work—*our* work—but it soon became apparent that my plan was hopeless. I looked around the store and counted appearances of the existing logo: it was printed on all our mugs, etched into all our display cases. The idea that a tiny café with a minuscule budget would undertake a rebrand of this scope was laughable. What did I think Sötma was, Lexus? As for the tagline, well, it's not even worth repeating. It wasn't my best work, if I'm being honest.

"What time is it?" she asked finally. My shift was about to start.

I stuffed my laptop back into my bag, then drooped toward the spiral staircase to fetch my apron and hat.

"Seth!" Odette's voice swept clean over every surface in the store. "Tell your sweetheart to remember the lights."

* * *

"There he is! The fucker!"

Moon greeted me by way of a high five. As he leaned over his place setting, the tip of his tie nearly skimmed his chowder.

"Here," he said, smacking the section of table to his left. "Saved you a seat."

And with that, everyone in the party moved over one. A big-hearted gesture, yet I doubted it was particular to me. Moon had probably done the same thing with each late-arriving guest, shuffling people down to open up that nearest slot. By definition, each new friend was his closest friend.

I was the only person not wearing a collared shirt. A miscalculation on my part—most RazorBeat partners dressed informally, so I'd wanted to fit in. But there were no partners present, no one even affiliated with RazorBeat. *The boys* were, well, boys. Moon's friends were nothing like the agency executives I'd been expecting; they behaved more like rowdy recruits at a college campus job fair. When they boomed with childhood stories of Moon (or "Rob," as they called him), they lacked, to borrow my mother's term, perspective; weren't they still, more or less, children? Though it was obvious they'd grown up around Moon, so clearly they weren't that young. They just acted even more infantile than he did.

I considered getting up and leaving, but then the main course arrived: lightly charred cuts of well-raised cattle, paired with stately bottles of red. With the full herd of waiters hovering beside our table, one of Moon's buddies seized the opportunity for an expanded audience. "To Rob!" He raised his glass, shushing the table with his free hand. "May you and Meg have a happy life. May you love each other always. May you cum together—and may she always swallow!"

With that, he took a huge mouthful of a tannic Cabernet hailed for its notes of green bell pepper and punchy finish and spouted it in the style of a whale across the table at Moon with remarkable aim. Droplets all over him, a few splattering onto our plates—we were speechless witnesses to a close-range massacre. The bachelor's white dress shirt was drenched, so I could read the dark-blond calligraphy of chest hair underneath. A normal adult would have been raging mad, but Moon lived for moments like these. Laughter overtook him, grabbing hard at his throat. Only when the maître d' came to issue a warning did he pipe down.

I downed my glass, poured a second. No, I wouldn't leave. I'd stuff my face for the full duration of dinner, then duck out before the check. Why bother ingratiating myself to him? In fact, why associate with him and his heathen friends at all? And how absurd, inviting me to his bachelor party. I was an acquaintance at best! He couldn't even remember my name at Sötma. We'd shared only a single meal before this: McDonald's in Tulsa. He had enough pals; he didn't need me. Besides, I didn't know "Rob." All I knew was Moon.

As my tablemates traded tales of the groom-to-be, I focused on maximizing my intake. Bite, sip, bite, bite, sip. I wished I'd brought pills to mix in.

"Hey!" Moon turned to me. "Are you ready for Heaven On Earth?" He pointed his steak knife toward the ceiling.

I asked what he meant, and Moon indicated he couldn't hear. He leaned in closer, his face only an inch or two from mine. When he blinked, I felt the breeze.

Then the maître d' came back, and Moon yelled, "EVERYBODY IN," at which point the boys compliantly brandished their credit cards. I was hoping to escape notice in the flurry of activity until Moon stared me down, along with one other reluctant soul at the far end of the table. I hadn't observed him until now, but he looked just as out of place as I did. He kept his eyes low while running both hands up through his blond hair, tending to its front-and-center spike so it wouldn't topple.

Moon asked the maître d' to pick a card at random, a little game of roulette. What had seemed an assured financial blow could now spell total bankruptcy. But no, I wouldn't let that happen. If picked, I'd outright refuse to pay. Better yet, I'd *shame* them. I'd explain that my livelihood was, for the moment, a paltry one. Peddling chocolate and coffee. In that order.

The maître d' played his part with composure. He covered his eyes, fumbled around performatively for his selection, then read out loud the unlucky winner. "McCloone," he pronounced haltingly.

The table roared in a hot upswell of joy. Oh, sweet justice! Even I couldn't help shrieking from the sudden release of tension. Perhaps this was what friendship with Moon was all about: hugging your bud with one arm, plunging the knife in with the other. Maybe he'd scripted this charade, just to see us sweat. Maybe he'd had our backs all along.

"WAIT!" Moon shouted, after the wave subsided. "First name?"

"Wesley," the maître d' answered.

A second quake rocked us, more raucous than the first. How fitting that our hero should escape unscathed! How totally Moon-like! In the unbridled excitement, I downed another full glass. But who was Wesley McCloone? I looked around the table and there was that lone spike of hair. Moon's brother was taking the bullet for all of us.

After dinner, it was time for Heaven. As we filed onto the escalator at the rear of the steak house, the jokes poured out. Someone quipped that getting into Heaven wasn't that hard, after all—you just needed to hold on to the handrail. Before long, we were at the entrance. Beyond the pearly gates, poles awaited.

I'd always wanted to visit a strip club. I considered going by myself on multiple occasions, though I sensed it was better to go with a big group. Better to diffuse the ethical burden, to spread it around.

My desire to see strippers was less about seeing them, more about seeing *myself* seeing them. Would I transform into one of those hormonally turbocharged gawkers who picks lecherously at his incisors with a club-sandwich toothpick? Or would I play the part of the nail-biting softie who inquires in a high-minded tone after the dancers' educational aspirations? Visiting a strip club was like visiting Israel, I figured. Both were morally questionable places. Both would expose who I was or might become.

As we crossed the threshold from steak house to strip club (though technically the entire place was designated a steak house, so that credit card charges would not arouse suspicion), we were greeted by a hostess with skintight sleeves of opalescent feathers. She led us to seats that were far from the main stage, but nonetheless afforded a view of the whole floor. Moon and I sat together on what resembled a red leather therapist's couch.

At Heaven On Earth, the waitstaff wore angelic outfits while the exotic dancers—in a daring bit of blasphemy—strutted in devil-themed attire. When someone from our group called for more drinks, a waitress bent to take our order, holding her plastic halo in place. By comparison, my Sötma hat wasn't so bad.

Soon after our drinks arrived, the strippers showed up, like they'd been waiting for us to take the poison. Moon pulled out a hefty stack from his wallet. "Lap dances for the dozen of us!"

But I counted only eleven. Wesley—after expending little effort to conceal his sulking—had slipped out of his big brother's grasp and gone home. But he didn't simply sneak out; he made sure to hug the others goodbye before leaving. It almost seemed they were more his friends than Moon's, as if their attendance were something of a favor.

The stripper closest to me shimmered in devil horns and tail, a scarlet thong bikini, and cinnamon perfume. I could feel a light burn of spice on my inhale.

"What's your name?" I said, reaching for politeness. I had to remind myself not to extend for a handshake, since I knew touching in these places was forbidden. I tucked my hands behind me, like a freshman dignitary addressing the Queen.

She answered with a blank expression, which I took to mean she didn't speak English. Our interaction was remarkable for its inaccessibility: we couldn't communicate, couldn't make contact. I found it oddly comforting, this distance between us. Perhaps this was the true appeal of strip clubs: to remove yourself from the reach of the world; to float far out of range, tantalizingly far, almost too far to pull yourself back. It was like Ramya's video game: that freeing sensation of being adrift from everything, even reality itself, in the name of illusion.

Then the music got louder and the strippers began to dance. Moon's—the least subdued of them all—undulated at his lower half as he sunk blissfully into himself, a birthday balloon with air let out. It was grotesque, if transfixing, how he registered his pleasure: the horrible slackening at the eyes, as if his face might wash off like makeup. But I had to remind myself: *he* wasn't the spectacle. It was rude to focus on anyone but my stripper. The last thing I wanted was to damage her confidence.

It didn't take long to fall under her spell. As she swerved ever closer, I found myself eye level with her navel. Then, seemingly to test her hold on my attention, she spun around, her pointed tail brushing my thigh. A possible violation of the rules? Touch was okay, perhaps, so long as I wasn't the one touching.

As I leaned farther back, I saw Moon had taken out his phone and was recording his lap dance as it took place. Surely, *this* was a violation. I delighted at the thought of him facing disciplinary action. A crack team of security guards would descend and rip the device from his hand, deleting the footage and bloodying the bachelor's nose for good measure. But no one showed. What's more, the stripper appeared to enjoy being filmed. She kept sweeping her red hair off her shoulders and signing the air with a lively penmanship of hip.

With my stripper facing away, I reached for my phone so I could record this unseemly display: him, holding the phone low at his waist, as if sizing her up from the directorial vantage of his member. But what if *I* was caught on tape? Someone filming *me* filming *him*—how would that look? Still, I wanted a record of his depravity, something to console myself with. But what consolation would it give me? The hard fact remained: Moon had prevailed where I failed. This uniquely shameful creature was RazorBeat royalty.

Or maybe there was nothing uniquely shameful about him. Maybe his shamefulness was illustrative of RazorBeat as a whole. For all its faults, Sötma was a healthier workplace. Ramya had it better than Josie, even if she didn't know it.

Ramya. She'd been out of my mind for most of the night, but I suddenly felt a desperate urge to see her. I was determined to head out as soon as my stripper was done with her routine. It was around this time that Moon tapped my shoulder.

"Ten thousand views and counting."

"Huh?"

Moon aimed his phone at me. "Say hi to the people at home!"

"Wait, are you—no!" I reached out to block his lens.

"Hey, relax. The live stream just finished." He tucked his phone back into his front pocket. "And no one wants to see your ugly face anyway."

"You were . . . streaming?"

"I prefer the word 'sharing.'"

"And Meghan, she's okay with all this?" Granted it was his bachelor party, but wouldn't she disapprove?

"Who cares." He paused. "I broke it off."

"You what?"

"Yup, yesterday." Moon slotted his cocktail straw like a golf pencil at his ear. "Lost half the deposit on the reception hall. But life goes on, right?"

The music turned deafening. All the strippers who'd been dancing in our section were now kicking off an ensemble piece onstage. Mine was off to a slow start, attending to a footwear malfunction. I was pulling for her to catch up.

"What happened?"

"She's batshit! Just like her mother. Look," he continued, unholstering his straw and then plunging it back into the depths of his drink. "Things were going great. Then we decide to get married and now everybody's involved. Distant cousins, the damn priest, even the goddamn state. I mean, have you ever dealt with city hall?"

The chorus line had devolved into an impromptu limbo tournament with little orchestration. The performance appeared detached from the gaze of the paying audience, but maybe that was the whole point. It was important to give the impression these women were enjoying themselves for their own sake, like the customers weren't even there. It was important to the customers that the customers not exist.

"Look, when it's just me and Meghan, we're happy. So please explain why the *fuck*"—he stared at me not unthreateningly—"we need all these . . . witnesses." He rolled his sleeves up as far as they'd go.

"So you're single now? Really?" Here I was, attending a bachelor party for someone still clinging to bachelorhood. It was absurd and yet somehow unsurprising. Moon was incapable of surprise; all he could do was shock.

"Well, hard to say." He took a long sip.

"What does that mean?"

A curtain fell, dividing upstage from downstage. The women theatrically dropped to the floor, like they were one living and breathing entity cleaved in two.

"I found a new girl. From RazorBeat, actually." He swirled his drink with considerable pace, whipping his ice cubes up around the rim of his glass. Then he took back his straw and plunged it cold to the bottom. "You remember Josie?"

4.

"Josie?" I choked out.

"You remember. Cute face, cute freckles. But not *young* cute. A little bit, shall we say, seasoned." His smirk stretched like a drawn bowstring.

All the strippers had gone backstage now. In the subsequent hush, the mostly male audience twitched like a smattering of crabs at low tide. There was a briny sheen to the air, a saltiness on the tongue.

I knew it was in my best interest to hold back. I knew I would've been wise to smile and nod, simply let the subject pass without comment. "How could you do that?" I snapped. "How could you sleep with her?"

"Come on, man! She's not *that* old. And like I said, she—"

"No. No. I mean . . . I just . . ." A deep breath drew into and out of my lungs. It returned to me a sense of composure. "We were kind of together. She and I."

"Oh, shit." Moon's eyebrows arched high. "*Together* together?"

I explained, as maturely as I could, that we'd opted for discretion in our relations. As a result, we hadn't formally defined things between us. But yes, we'd been together, in all the ways that mattered. Never mind, of course, about her actual boyfriend (though this hardly seemed a detail worth mentioning).

Moon looked chastened. He shrank beside me. "And this was a recent thing?"

I confirmed that, indeed, it was. "Started after Smackdale."

"Smack what?"

A pinch of irritation seized my throat. "Adult diaper brand. 2013 winner in multiple categories, including—"

"Wait!" Moon's eyes bulged as he leaned forward. He'd sprung back to his proper size. "That's ancient history. That's, like, forever ago in fuck-years." He threw his hand to his heart, as if swearing some oath. "Seriously, you can't ding me here. She's a hundred percent free meat."

"Free . . . meat?"

"Fair game. That's what I mean." He drew back to his side of the couch. His hand had migrated away from his chest, loosening its grip with a dose of relief. "Man, she's got some appetite, right?"

I refused to engage. I simply refused.

"When she wants it, she *really* wants it, you know what I'm saying? It's like basic sustenance to her. It's like nourishment." Moon chewed at a hangnail. "Honestly—and don't get me wrong, I'm not complaining—it's a lot of pressure sometimes! You know, what if I don't perform? Even just one time? I'm not saying this ever happens, so it's purely a theoretical now, but . . ." His gaze thinned out. His face contorted under the weight of deep concern. "The poor girl might starve to death, right before my eyes. I mean, literal *starvation*. Do I need that on my conscience?

"Hey!" Moon said, clapping out a new possibility. "Maybe we could trade notes?"

My limbs stiffened at their joints. "Notes?"

"Come on, don't be bashful! I'll kick us off. Or should you go first, since you got there first?"

I kept waiting for him to give up the bit, but it wasn't a bit. And he wasn't giving up.

"I mean, you've been down that road. You know the twists, the turns." He swallowed hard and sucked at his teeth. He too seemed to be suffering a form of hunger, if less acute. "What do you say, my good man? Shall we?"

I needed to be careful. I wanted to lunge at him and smash his billboard-wide forehead—a terrible idea, slugging somebody at his own bachelor party with all his friends present. But this wasn't, I reminded myself, a bachelor party at all. And everyone else had snuck away after their dances, either heading home or slinking off into one of the Heavenly Pleasure rooms. It was just me and Moon now, no one else.

I decided to cut straight to the heart of things. I would tiptoe around RazorBeat no longer. "Can't believe you still work there," I said, finishing off the first drink within reach.

"Yeah, me neither." He chuckled. His shirt's wine stain had mostly dried, leaving a large infection-pink splotch at his middle.

"You should leave," I said. "Go to another agency." Now I gripped my empty glass hard against the table. "Though I'm not sure who would want you."

The bachelor's eyes twinkled in mild disbelief.

"You're not a writer. You're not a designer. You're just a glorified middleman." I aimed to keep picking him clean with my claws. "You don't create anything."

Moon nodded along with my words. Then he leaned closer until his hot breath practically wet my ear. "Maybe you're right. But here's the reality. Our clients? They don't create anything either!" He threw his hands in the air with such zeal, they threatened to fly off his wrists. "Take our old friend Lexus. They don't make shit! Everything is outsourced. Company A makes engines. Company B makes batteries. Company C makes tires. What does Lexus do? Simple addition. A + B + C. Then they slap their name on at the end and jack up the price.

"But *creation*," he added, "that costs extra." He proceeded to brag about the new car he'd recently bought and how he'd custom ordered it. Far better, he said, than anything rolling off a Lexus assembly line.

He flagged an angel for another round, then turned back toward me. He must've sensed some hint of distress. "Listen," he said. "We'll never have to worry. You and me?" He smacked my thigh. "We'll always land on our feet."

It was impossible to defeat Moon: he'd align himself in such a way that it shielded him from attack. A shrewd tactic, though I wondered if he really believed we *were* aligned. An appalling notion. I didn't want to be on his side. I wanted to get as far from him as possible. It was suddenly loathsome to me how desperate I'd been to return to RazorBeat, how I'd been willing to sell out everyone in my life in the process.

"You know," I said, accepting yet another drink, the one I suspected would send me reeling and spinning and possibly heaving late into the night, "I was X'ed. Xavier *fired* me."

Moon took a long sip. I wasn't sure what I was expecting—encouragement, an explanation, perhaps even an apology—but he just sipped in uncharacteristic silence. Soon enough a new stripper approached him with an offer. He listened and politely declined, insisting his heart belonged to someone else. I figured he was referring to Josie, until it became clear he was asking about the redhead. Had she clocked out for the night? He'd hoped to say a proper goodbye.

I decided I'd had enough. I abruptly got up to leave, though the alcohol in my system made it difficult to stand without keeling over. I stuck out my arms to regain my balance, nearly striking a woman who was scurrying past. Neither angel nor devil, she wore a hairnet and clutched a metal tray of dirty dishes. In Heaven's hierarchy, she was hard to place.

"Wait," Moon said, as I began walking away. I stopped, turned, and faced him, just to see if there was an olive branch.

He held up the bill in its bedazzled holder, waving it in my direction. "Split it?"

*   *   *

When I arrived at Ramya's, the cabdriver yelled at me to wake up. It took me a few moments to gather my things; I had to make sure my phone, wallet, and keys were all on my person. What an odd phrase, *my person*. It sounded like someone I'd never met.

My phone died in transit, so I hadn't texted. I wasn't too worried, though. Ramya stayed up late, and her front door was usually unlocked. I stared up at her third-floor window and observed a steady flutter of shadows.

My knocks on the building's entrance elicited no answer, but they were enough to swing open the poorly bolted door. I clutched at the rust-pimpled banister and managed to drag my person up impossible flights, one by one. When I arrived at her mess of a residence, Ramya was wide-awake, along with her roommates; they were all standing around in the kitchen with cigarettes held at their waists and half-empty beer bottles crowding the countertop. Ramya greeted me with a slight movement of her eyes.

Their discussion proceeded around me. I was a boulder that had rolled into their burbling stream—physically present, but not too great an obstacle to disrupt the flow. They were debating the artistic merits of a classmate's work, after their department chair disparaged it for being derivative.

"So what?" one said.

"Everything's derivative of *something*," another said.

"How about a beer?" I asked.

Ramya flashed me the same blank look the stripper had given me. Like a swatting away of my question, like my language wasn't hers.

I opened the fridge and helped myself to an IPA that was handsomely branded, its logo shaped like a rusted pitchfork. It looked like it could've been brewed in a toolshed by your long-lost uncle living in the heartland. An indie label designed for broad appeal: everybody, at one point or another, has lost an uncle.

As the roommates continued their rambling, I could make out snippets of conversation. Someone asked for a more precise definition of "derivative," so someone else answered that call. Finally, they all agreed: it was stealing.

"If you're starving, stealing is justified," one said.

"So the real question is, are we starving?" said another.

Even up close, the roommates were indistinguishable. Varying ages, heights, races, genders, but their faces were tuned to the same frequency of disaffection. They were all desperate to stand out from the crowd, so nobody did. They reminded me of cockroaches, how one might appear and scurry away, then another, then another, and you could never tell the original from the new ones, never assess the true extent of the infestation.

They each took turns piping up in the course of discussion, but not Ramya. During our time spent alone, she wasn't always vocal, but she found ways to make herself heard. Why was she holding back now?

I decided to give her a pinch, just to wake her up a bit. It was, after all, the gesture she insisted on introducing into our love life, the one that punctuated our intimate moments. And indeed, I liked thinking of it as a form of punctuation. It was a means of giving pace, of adding breath, of applying syntax to—

"OWWWWWWWWWWWWWWW!"

The cockroaches stiffened into a single glare. My hand, I observed with horror, was still attached to Ramya's leg, in plain view of everyone. I was unsure whether to pull it back, which would all but confirm my guilt, or leave it for the jury to see. I hadn't meant to do harm, of course. I'd probably just pinched a little too hard, or else I'd missed the usual mark. An error not of judgment but execution—too much force, too far from target.

Ramya looked at me, her face frozen as a footprint. Then she let her gaze slip down to the kitchen floor. Was she embarrassed of her outburst? For attracting attention needlessly? No. She was just ashamed to be with me. She'd tracked me into her life like dog shit on a boot sole, and now mess was everywhere. My hand loosened from the site of the pinch, as one of the roaches made a hasty approach.

"Ramya, I'm sorry, I'm so sorry, I'm—"

I'd never been punched in the face before. I was fortunate to receive the blow directly to my eye, which allowed me to capture the full experience with near-cinematic accuracy: a closed fist, like a moon rock, growing larger until it eclipsed all surrounding light. Then: *contact*. I sensed no pain at first, only a sharp impulse to muster a counterattack, but I felt myself drop to the tile floor. Three dimensions bumped down to two. Ramya's roommates stood as flat as headstones in a semicircle around my limp person. My limbs spilled out in all directions, a cracked jar of Seth.

I scanned the crowd for Ramya, but she was already gone.

5.

Subject: New York City?

Dear Seth,

How are you feeling? Hope you're healthy again. When can I see your TV ads? :)
My girlfriend just finished her army service. We're taking a vacation from Tel Aviv in 6 weeks. Be our tour guide?

xo Yael

I put my phone away as I sat in the park across from Sötma. Still no word from Ramya since last night. No text, email, voicemail. Nothing. I expected at least a brief message of concern, given that one of her roommates—Lord knows which one—had clocked me, right in her kitchen. In fairness, I might've had it coming. I hadn't been on my best behavior.

I checked my phone one more time: still nothing besides Yael's note. Why were she and her girlfriend coming *here*, and why should *I* be their guide? I'd encouraged her to visit, sure, but it was one of those cursory invites, the kind Americans extend all the time to one another, always with the understanding that it would be unspeakably rude to accept. And even though I might've invited Yael, I hadn't said anything about significant others. No, I had no intention of showing them around the city. Not to mention I had no money to do so. I'd been struggling financially for weeks, but Moon's bachelor party left me broke. Heaven had soaked me dry.

The more I reflected on the prior evening, the more I despised him. He'd called off his wedding because of, what, an aversion to interlopers? How deranged! If he loved his fiancée so much, why not elope? He was too immature for marriage, clearly. He was barely adult enough for adult entertainment.

And then there was Josie. I had to physically restrain myself from calling her and unleashing a tirade. Had she no self-respect? What was she thinking, sleeping with somebody like him?! As much as I tried not to, I couldn't stop picturing the act itself: Josie and Moon—her underneath, him on top. Despite my best efforts to peel the two apart, or at least fix them in an alternative arrangement, I kept imagining them in this exact position: his enormous thrusting body obscuring hers completely. I could see nothing but his nakedness and his alone, the shape and size and even sound of him grossly consuming the whole, rather than merely half, of the image.

I was disappointed in Josie's judgment, of course, though her motives weren't unclear in the least. It was a business decision, plain and simple. Moon was a high rung on the corporate ladder.

Ramya was above all that, thankfully. She wasn't with me for reasons of influence or status; we embraced each other as equals in a food-service economy. And was it such a lousy way to spend one's days, getting high in the presence of a loved one, pushing café items until sundown? Sometimes, when Odette went on break, I imagined *we* were the chocolate store's owners: a couple of flirty upstarts, fumbling toward a far-off goal of profitability. Though, in my mind, Ramya was really the head of the operation; I was her humble servant helping her realize her dreams.

As I walked back to Sötma, I tried to visualize her. Not her outer beauty, which was too easy. Her intellect. Her mind. But if I'm being honest, I kept failing. Everything I knew about seeing I'd learned from my eyes—how narrowly they focused on what was immediate, what was right there.

* * *

I hurried downstairs to check my phone whenever Odette's back was turned. Some more testy voicemails from my landlord, but nothing from Ramya. Our next overlapping shift was Tuesday, so I hoped to hash things out by then.

Her silence was starting to offend me. Maybe I hadn't carried myself in the best manner, entering her apartment unannounced, snagging a beer from the communal fridge. But I was the one who'd been assaulted! It was my eye that had swollen shut.

When Odette stepped out to meet Sötma's owner for lunch, I took the opportunity to write a letter to Ramya. Not an angry one, but not an apology either. I explained that I wasn't a mind reader. If our relationship was going to work, communication was critical; we both had to vocalize our feelings. (I considered attaching my essay on ventriloquism as supplemental reading.) And while we hadn't ever formalized our relationship, I wanted her to know I felt comfortable using the word "girlfriend" to refer to her. I was vocalizing. I was showing her the way.

When I broke into her locker later that day to deposit my letter, I was met by a surprise. New pill bottles, dozens of them.

Ramya had obviously restocked at some point in the past week, though this far exceeded her usual supply. Most of the bottles looked full, brand labels hastily peeled off. I opened a few to inspect the pills more carefully and saw multiple colors and shapes I'd never seen paired before. Pink triangles. Baby-blue circles. I was struck by how tiny they appeared, how little they weighed when I released a sample into my open palm and examined them in the basement's cool light. *Babies*, I thought. They reminded me of babies. I felt an impulse to keep them, tend to them, and see what in time they might become.

After a moment or two, I swallowed the handful. Then I tore my letter to shreds and ran upstairs to the customers I had to serve.

*   *   *

A total blur, those next few days. I felt anxious in anticipation of seeing Ramya that Tuesday, so I took more of her pills to calm my nerves. Her stash was big enough that I figured she wouldn't notice. *A drop in the ocean* was a phrase that brought me peace of mind. I repeated it often, swam laps in its rhythms.

I was talking to myself quite a bit, actually. As customers rolled in, I took their orders while inaudibly muttering, the pills sometimes making my jaw spasm. I fell back into the old habit of composing taglines in my head, though now I'd dare to whisper them under my breath. An elderly woman in a leopard-print shawl: *Forever on the Prowl. A* traffic cop clutching his belt buckle with both hands: *Upholding the Law with Force.* The pills, it seemed, gave me back my voice.

When Tuesday morning arrived, I woke up sober and antsy. I craved reading material for my commute, anything to distract me. I scanned my bookcase and grabbed an old copy of Derrida's *Archive Fever*, which had been assigned years ago by a particularly pretentious professor. I remembered nothing about it except it was written toward the end of the philosopher's life. Later works appealed to me; they often contained more profound insights, penned under the presumption of looming death.

I tried to give Derrida my full attention, but the packed crowd of the subway car only compounded the density on the page. Why had I picked such an impenetrable slog? I gave up well before the final stop.

Odette was working the register when I arrived. She pointed to my black eye and remarked, "Looks a smidge better."

"Where's Ramya?" I asked.

Odette was again lifting bills to the light. She said nothing, simply drew her forefinger across her low-jutting neck—a gesture suggesting beheading or, more colloquially, a firing. I felt an immediate sting return to the spot where I'd been punched.

"Wait, you *fired* her?"

She paused a beat and met my stare. "Want to be next?"

When it came to conflict, Odette was the total opposite of Moon. Whereas he engaged in a warfare of deft deflection, she met her enemies head-on.

"What happened?"

"Went AWOL. Skipped her Sunday shift too."

"Have you talked to her?"

She shook her head no and kept counting cash. She locked eyes with a crisp Thomas Jefferson, straining to see through him.

"So technically you haven't fired her. Not yet."

Maybe it was only semantics, but until a boss actually notifies an employee, then—

"*Fin-ished*," she reiterated, cracking the word like a whip. "She just wasn't cut out for this job. Showing up late. Spilling grinds. Leaving the lights on." Her face scrunched in increasing solemnity. "One snail after the next.

"Then that whole nonsense with the logo," she went on.

I couldn't hear this. The presentation fiasco was mine alone. And even if Ramya hadn't been the ideal employee, didn't Odette believe in second chances? Wasn't that the entire basis of her belief system?

"Not to worry," she said, running her money-tainted hands under sink water. "I've already got a replacement lined up." She patted them dry on her starched apron and shook off any remaining droplets into the air. "Starts next week. Travis or something?" She paused. "Strange-looking kid. Says he knows you. You used to work with his girlfriend?"

I glared at her with my one and a half eyes.

6.

A light snow was falling—so light, so fragile, it was hard to imagine it had survived the long journey down from the immeasurable height of the clouds. But "survived" isn't really the right term, I guess. Snow doesn't live through anything. It just falls.

I'd stepped outside to call Josie after closing up. I kept calling and calling until finally she picked up.

"I'm at the office," she began.

"Still?" Though really, it wasn't that late. We'd stayed together on countless occasions much deeper into the night.

"Yeah," she said. "Working on a pitch."

I could tell from her voice she was telling the truth. Pitches were more exhausting than normal projects. As an agency, we worked harder for the clients we didn't have than the ones we did.

I told her we needed to talk.

"Do we? Why do we *need* to talk?" Her tone implied I had a puerile understanding of necessity.

"Just grab one drink with me. Please?"

"Not a chance, sadly."

"Fine," I replied. "When's good for you?"

"Never? Look, Seth . . . I'm so swamped."

I felt no sympathy. *She* was the one sitting comfortably in an ergonomic desk chair; *I* was the one who'd just finished disinfecting Sötma's bathroom floor in the wake of a pertinacious clog.

"Never mind," she said. "Let's just talk now."

Now? I wasn't prepared to talk now. I wished we could've switched over to RazorChat, a medium in which I felt more assured. On the phone, her voice was markedly sharper than mine. It sliced deep through the tough skin of each silence.

"Okay, so about Travis. Your Travis."

"He's not my anything."

I slapped myself in the chest to dislodge some snow. Flakes had been accumulating in my parka's seams. "He's going to work at Sötma? Out of all the possible jobs in New York, all the possible career paths, he's got to—"

"Hold on one second." The line went quiet, and I could hear her imparting stern instructions to another RazorBeat designer. Had she been promoted to creative director? Already? "Yeah, so what? I was the one who encouraged him."

I felt the cold in my bones. "Why would you do that?"

"He had no other options! His label fucked him, and he's not exactly getting flooded with freelance offers. Can you believe HR never even called him back? Not even after I referred him?" She sounded a seething note. "It's just so . . . unprofessional."

I'd never confessed to her, never owned up to torpedoing his candidacy. I wondered how much he'd told her, or if he'd been too angry, too ashamed. I imagined our training sessions on the espresso machine might prove a wee bit tense.

"Anyway," she went on, "fifteen bucks an hour isn't awful. And if nothing else, it'll keep him busy."

Her tone irked me. "Is that what you think I'm doing? Keeping busy?"

"Aren't we all?"

I told her to hold on a moment, since I had an incoming call. Ramya, hopefully, but it was only my landlord for the hundredth time. He'd stopped limiting himself to business hours.

"Seth? You still there?" Josie barked. "I'm about to hang up."

"*Wait.*"

"What exactly am I waiting for?"

Shivering, I began jogging in place to bring feeling back to my hands, my feet, all the parts of me farthest from my heart. I took comfort knowing that, no matter how low the temperature dropped, my heart would be last to go numb, one lit bulb in an otherwise shuttered house.

As the silence extended, I wondered if Moon was there with her. I remembered how she'd act after sex, dressing herself with sudden remoteness, arms quietly retreating back into sleeves.

"Here's what I want to know," I said finally. "It's his title, right? That's why you're sleeping with him, because he's a partner? Just tell me that's the reason. I can accept that. I really can."

She unleashed a long sigh. I sensed The Reveal was coming.

"Seth, you make everything about you. Everything . . ."

"Well, I think—"

"What I do is *my* business. And what do you care?" She firmed up her voice, tightening the hard bolts of it. "You haven't worked here in forever."

I could brush off that comment coming from Moon, but from Josie it stung more. I reminded her it had only been a few months.

"Really?" She laughed. "Feels a lot longer."

Snowflakes were sticking to my hair, so I shook off what I could. "Josie, I need to know. Do you like Moon? Seriously?"

I hadn't allowed myself to entertain this possibility. It seemed too far-fetched, an emotional bond between them—how does one fall for somebody who snorts turbinado sugar crystals in the presence of clients, who holds a bachelor party in the dim afterglow of a botched engagement?

"Meh," she said. "Less than you like him, I think."

"What the hell does that mean?!" I was about to lay into her, but then she coughed a few times into the phone, either as a ploy to elicit sympathy or because she was actually battling something. The uncertainty gave me pause.

"Listen, Seth. I need to go. I'm buried over here. Two pitches tomorrow, then another on Friday."

I hoped that RazorBeat whiffed on all of them. But what good was hope? No, I had to *personally* make sure her pitches were failures. I'd successfully sabotaged Travis's interview, so there was nothing stopping me from striking again. Though the circumstances were very different now. It would be pointless to try. Pathetic, even.

"Good luck," I said, my voice brittle. "I'll look after Travis, I guess."

"No." She took time between breaths. "Look after yourself."

*   *   *

I debated going. I kept debating en route. I debated even as I knocked on the door, which, with its lone surviving hinge, barely held. I cried hello and heard somebody shuffling down to meet me at the entrance. Sporting gray overalls and a dark walrus mustache that obscured his mouth, he looked me over once and declared with composure, "She's not here."

"Can I come up anyway?" I gestured toward the snowy weather. "Please?"

He examined his wrist. "You get five minutes."

As I walked up the length of the stairs and entered Ramya's apartment, Walrus kept watch over me. I made sure to turn my head from side to side, providing him a good view of my still-glistening bruise. I was proud of the mark, of what it said. My person had absorbed a blow and survived.

The apartment's configuration seemed more confusing than before. Had more bamboo dividers been erected? It took most of my allotted time just to find Ramya's bedroom, and I barely recognized it. Everything had been cleaned out. Mattress, dresser, mirror—gone.

The only thing of value left was her Apple monitor, resting on its shiny foot.

"Told you." Walrus reappeared. He was tug-of-warring a thick strip of jerky between hand and teeth. "She's. Not. Here."

"Where'd she go?"

"Why don't you call her and ask her yourself?"

I'd dialed Ramya dozens of times unsuccessfully in the past day alone. Maybe she and her roommates were getting a good laugh out of it, watching her phone buzz. And each time she'd tap the decline button, like touching a pinkie to cake frosting.

"She never answers," I said.

"So maybe"—another carnivorous bite and yank—"that's good-bye then."

I would've sat on her bed to collect my thoughts, but all that remained was the box spring and four skinny posts: skeletal, the picked-clean carcass of a mammoth. During one of our intimate nights together, I'd commented on the creakiness of her bed, though Ramya insisted it wasn't loud, or at least no louder than it should be; being blindfolded, she said, simply sharpened the other senses, and I was probably hearing better. That's what was good about the blindfold, she explained. But I disagree. The best thing about it was that, over time, it grew comfortable. It was a relief to suspend my eyesight during intercourse. I could lose track of our two bodies. I could fade one into the other.

While I stood there, Walrus sauntered back into the kitchen. I could hear him opening and closing cabinets.

This was my opportunity.

"Hey, DOUCHEBAG!" he shouted. "That's our door!"

The last hinge had snapped when I jetted out of the place, sprinting as fast as possible without falling. I had to be careful: it was tough to find my footing on the stairs with such an enormous monitor in my arms.

It was a nice monitor, worth a thousand at least. If I pawned it, I might make back what I'd lost at Heaven On Earth. But I couldn't. It had sentimental value. It held our twin infinities, Ramya's and mine. When I got to the subway station, it was almost midnight. *We'll be moving momentarily*, declared a prerecorded voice. Sitting across from me on the stalled train, with one hand on a stroller, was a teenage mom. Long on top, her hair was closely cropped by each ear, like mowed grass around a monument. Why was she out so late with an infant? But I had no right to judge. I had a piece of stolen hardware in my care.

A group of uniformed men was attending to the subway station walls. With long squeegees held like bayonets at their shoulders, they were applying new ads. They took care to align the edges, smoothing out any air pockets. It was therapeutic watching them. There was something calming about how the ads flattened perfectly into place.

Ten minutes passed, then twenty. Growing bored, I reached into my backpack for Derrida. My swollen eye stopped at one particular passage: "The memory without memory of a mark returns everywhere, about which we ought to debate with Freud, concerning his many rapid statements on this subject: it is clearly the question of the singular archive named 'circumcision.'"

An archive? Of what, exactly? And "memory without memory of a mark"—what did that mean?

I'd never given circumcision much thought, not until Birthright. It was our last night in Israel, and Zev wanted to tell us the story of his family. On his father's side, all sabras for generations. (He bragged about how deep into the desert soil his roots went.) But his mother's side was different. They grew up poor in Poland, and when the Nazis invaded, the SS conducted strip searches in their village. Some neighbors paid a surgeon to try reversing their circumcisions via skin graft, but Zev's great-grandfather adamantly refused. In hindsight, he made the right decision. No, he didn't survive, and in fact he was shot twice in both kneecaps and left to bleed out in his own kitchen, but at least, Zev continued, he died with dignity. The surgery always backfired anyway. It never fooled anyone.

The ad installers had come and gone. In their wake, the station was plastered with glossy images of a brand of lip balm I'd never heard of, with a tagline that made no sense. Then the subway doors closed, and we lurched onward, the baby waking to the late-night groan of metal against metal. To soothe his cries, the mother held out her pinkie. He swallowed it in his fist, like it was all his.

7.

The thing just sat there looking more and more stolen. I considered wrapping it in a sheet, so the monitor wouldn't glare at me quite so unflinchingly from across the modest width of my apartment.

Days had passed, and she still hadn't called back. I decided I'd hang on past the beep. I'd leave a voicemail pouring out my feelings for her and mentioning the monitor and how I'd kept it safe, rescuing it from her filthy cohabitants. It wasn't to be: her mailbox was full.

How would I go about locating her? She took her art classes at Parsons, I knew that, but which building? I thought about calling the cops, but I feared how that might look. Her bruised leg, my black eye? Not to mention the monitor in my possession. But maybe it was worth incriminating myself. What mattered was Ramya's well-being.

It didn't make sense, though. Abductees don't often have the luxury of moving their belongings into storage. So where was she then?

The next day at Sötma, I took another extended trip to the basement. I first cleared out all of Ramya's pill bottles, transferring the supply from her locker to mine. Then I snuck into Odette's "office," a glorified closet tucked next to the loading zone. I had one objective and one objective only: find Ramya's emergency contact card.

I'd just finished copying down the phone number of "Vivek Prasad, father" when I heard Odette coming down the stairs. I hurried to file the card away and close the office door, but then I realized I'd left her lamp on. I reached for the thin gold-beaded chain, but—

"Seth." She held a splayed set of measuring spoons.

"Hey, I was just—"

I shut my mouth and braced myself. I deserved to be fired and had deserved it for some time. I'd been spending most of my shifts getting high in the basement, then dragging myself like a wet paintbrush up and down the same stretch of stairs. And now she'd found me rifling through her desk. *X me*, I thought. *X me and be done with it.*

To my surprise, no reaction. She looked dazed, focused on something far off. I turned off the lamp in her office. Still nothing. Buoyed by my good fortune, I sauntered toward the stairs and asked if things were okay.

"Not really," she said. "There's been a death."

Ramya was my first thought, the only thought that mattered. I clutched hard at the knobby end of the spiraling banister. "Who?"

She collected herself, then angled her face toward mine. "The man upstairs."

It took me a moment to realize she meant this literally. But why so forlorn? Didn't she hate the upstairs tenant? Wasn't he a nuisance for her, always registering noise complaints?

"Anyway. Stuff happens," she cheered weakly, setting each spoon in the quiet concavity of its next-largest kin.

I considered offering condolences, but I lost my nerve. Then, to my surprise, she knelt beside me, her apron's trim gracing the unfinished basement floor. It seemed she was praying, and I felt oddly grateful to be witness to this moment, to be present, if only on the periphery, in her praying, but that wasn't it at all. She was reaching for the bottom drawer, putting the spare spoons back where they belonged.

* * *

My name was Sam Tipton and I was an associate dean at Parsons School of Design. I was calling to inquire about Ms. Ramya Prasad's whereabouts. She'd skipped classes, and the faculty was growing concerned. Though not *alarmed*, I would add. For some reason, this felt like an important distinction.

I'd done research to prepare. According to Google, the Prasad family resided in an upper-class stretch of coastal New England. When I zoomed in, I found myself facing a three-story colonial with green shutters and a stand-alone garage.

Most everything on the internet about the Prasads centered on Ramya's father, a pharmaceutical researcher who'd been published widely. One article included a photo of him looking pensively into a microscope. I'd seen that same pensiveness in Ramya.

I took a pill to steel myself, cleared my throat, and dialed. "Hello, I'm Sam Tipton, associate dean at—"

"DAD! It's for you."

I considered hanging up then and there. I immediately recognized Ramya's voice. Had she recognized mine? I hadn't even considered that she might be home and—

"Hello?"

I was choking down a second pill. "I'm Sam, and I work at Parsons—I'm a dean, actually—and I've got questions regarding your daughter's whereabouts."

"Her *whereabouts*?" he echoed, slicing thinly into the syllables.

Fuck. Her whereabouts were obvious—she'd just picked up the phone.

"Listen," he continued feistily, "I'll tell you people one last time: I'm *not* paying."

"Of course, of course," I stalled.

"If you're asking me," he whispered, possibly so that Ramya couldn't hear, "you should refund the fall tuition too. A total waste." Then, after an exhale, Dr. Prasad changed his tune. "It's not your fault," he continued. "It's really not your fault."

His compassion shook me more than his rage. I felt an impulse to correct him, to accept some share of the blame, but I sensed it might cause offense to do so, that he wanted the fault to reside with him alone. I pictured Ramya occupying that huge house with him and wondered if it was the kind where floorboards are always creaking underfoot, where even the lightest step echoes into every room. When he asked if I was still on the line, I left him with my silence.

In the hours that followed, I settled on a working theory for Ramya's disappearance: her father disapproved of her arts education and demanded she move back home. I could relate to such familial tensions: when I decided to major in English, my engineer father nearly disowned me. His relief was palpable after I found employment as a copywriter. Perhaps not all writers were doomed.

Knowing Ramya was alive and well put me at ease, but I still missed her. I started upping my pill intake. (I counted out the remainder of her supply—329 in total—so I could keep track and eventually compensate her for what I owed.) But even with the extra pills, the days dragged. I'd get lost in pulling espresso shots and forget Ramya wasn't on register. I'd turn around to meet a long line of scowls.

It got so bad that I started looking forward to Travis's arrival. I needed the extra set of hands, no matter whose.

* * *

Walking into work the next day, I gave Odette a sunny greeting.

"Well," I said, "where is he?"

No reaction.

"The rookie?" I leaned in. "The fresh meat?"

She was stacking cups on top of the espresso machine to warm.

"You said Travis was starting today."

She continued her stacking. "Not anymore."

"Seriously?"

She gave a shrug.

"Well, that's just perfect," I said. "And I'm left doing twice the work."

She mumbled something salty under her breath.

"Excuse me?"

Odette was motoring at an unusually low volume. Then she repeated what she'd said, tilting her chin toward the light so I could watch her pass each phoneme out through her thin lips: "There's not gonna be any work."

No work? But business was booming! The cold weather was bringing droves of people into the store. We were selling mochas at a blistering pace. Rather, *I* was selling them. Solo. Which was why I needed—

"Lease ends at the end of March. And then"—Odette performed the same beheading gesture she'd used for Ramya. "The whole building," she said. "Leveled."

It was an oddly pristine word, too tidy a term for something so destructive.

"Big-shot developer swooped in. After, you know, our land-lord . . ." She trailed off.

The man upstairs, I thought. *Not just a tenant. The landlord.*

She continued stacking cups with her tiny hands. They were such a blur, I could barely tell one apart from the other.

"Seth." She looked at me like we were meeting for the first time. "Can you please make a bank run? We're all out of quarters."

I couldn't believe what I was hearing. Quarters? *That* was her priority? What we needed was a Save Sötma! campaign. A full-blown marketing blitz to rally customers behind our cause, complete with a tagline that conveyed our inestimable value to the community. But, without a lease, it was a lost cause. No way around it: leveled.

Odette set the last stack of cups and shuffled off toward the spiral staircase. I didn't know what else to do, so I followed orders. I walked to the bank and requested as many quarters as I could carry. It seemed fair to pocket half for myself.

8.

We settled on a kitschy French restaurant with its windows spray-painted white at the corners for snow. Yael, Dalit, and I were seated at a table meant for two, our conversation growing cold over salmon fillets. Thankfully, there was alcohol to liven things up.

I raised my glass when the wine arrived. "Congrats!"

"For what?" Yael asked.

"The military. You got out." I reached toward Dalit, so we could clink.

"You never leave the IDF. They can always call you back."

"Then don't answer." I gave Dalit a smile.

"And how about you?" Yael pointed to my eye. "Did you join?" The stubborn bruise still hadn't faded completely.

I asked what the two had planned in the city.

"Many things." Yael reached for her hand. "We'll miss you."

"Tomorrow is the 9/11 memorial," Dalit said. "He can't join us?"

"Too busy," Yael replied. "TV commercials."

Dalit responded with interest about my line of work. In her enthusiasm, she found greater fluency; I countered with a barrage of hard-to-translate idioms. Anyway, I said I had no desire to see the memorial. Nothing special, that's what I'd heard.

Dalit took a long sip of wine. "An Israeli designed it."

"Are you sure? *Our* memorial?"

She nodded.

"Doesn't sound right to me," I said, topping myself off.

"Not right?" Dalit turned to Yael in confusion. "What could be wrong?"

The electric candle on our table kept flickering. It was engineered this way, to provide the impression that even the lightest breeze might snuff it out.

Yael's girlfriend excused herself for the bathroom, one of those tiny ones with the toilet crouched behind the door. In her absence, Yael unloaded. She said I was spending the whole dinner being rude, that I was even ruder now than she remembered.

I apologized. I told her I was going through a bit of a rough time. "Financially," I specified.

She didn't understand. Didn't TV pay well?

"And if you're so poor," she added, "shouldn't you be spending less money?" She pointed to the three wine bottles I'd ordered. They stood tall at the center of our table.

Perhaps, Yael continued, she might be able to help me. Their hostel was being fumigated next week, so they'd need somewhere to stay. For a couple hundred dollars, would I put them up? It might, she added, serve both of us.

When Dalit returned to the table, she inched her chair a little closer to me, away from Yael's stern expression. "What did I miss?" she asked. Then she reached for the only unfinished wine bottle and took it by the neck.

*　*　*

"Can I speak with Ramya?"

"I'm sorry, who is this?"

After many days of deliberation, I decided to call her father again. This time I'd be myself. But when he asked the simplest of questions, I froze. *Who was I?* A friend? A boyfriend? Ex-friend or ex-boyfriend? An ex who'd been X'ed?

I described myself as her former coworker from Sötma.

"Oh," he muttered, a passing ripple of recognition. "The coffee shop."

Well, technically a chocolate *and* coffee shop, but that was one battle I'd already fought and lost. Regardless, the shop wouldn't be in existence much longer. Soon Odette would reach into the register and withdraw her last wrinkled bill.

"Can I speak to her? Can I?"

He rejected me outright. Besides, he said, she wasn't even home.

"Fine." I picked up a pen. "When will she be back?"

"Not for a while. Months, probably."

I could feel my grip tighten around the pen.

"Where is she?" I asked, turning desperate. "I have something to give her."

"Then mail it," he said. The man had no patience for a romantic barista. He rattled off an address in Allentown, Pennsylvania.

To confirm, I asked if he could repeat—

"No," he shot back. "And never call here again."

I entered the Allentown address quickly in my phone. I also jotted it in my notebook, just to have it someplace real.

* * *

I didn't tell Odette I was leaving. She wouldn't have permitted it anyhow. It was a hectic time as we prepped for the Easter rush: subbing out partridges with bunnies and lining the insides of wooden gift boxes with iridescent grass. And even while we hustled to prepare the store for the holiday, we set about initiating its dissolution. Odette had me box up "nonessential" items, so I was constantly pausing to consider the indispensability of whatever found its way into my hands.

I also wasn't sure when I'd leave or how. I couldn't afford to rent a car, not even with the extra money I received from Yael and Dalit. Borrowing a car also wasn't an option, since nobody I knew had one in the city. Except, of course—

"Hi there, Moon." I released my words after a stiff exhalation.

"You sack of shit. How are things?"

"Fine, fine." I gripped the phone tightly. I was ready to spout apologies, if necessary. What he did with Josie was his business. What he did for a living—literally, his business. But he plowed through pleasantries, asked what I wanted.

"Car," I managed. "Need to borrow your car."

En route to Moon's apartment, I tried to imagine what it might look like. Maybe like Diego's office? A minimalist gallery of polished lines and glass finishes? No, nothing so sophisticated. Moon wasn't the type to display an appreciation for high art or, frankly, any artistic sensibility. He likely couldn't even spell "aesthetic."

I couldn't help wondering, had *I* made partner, what my apartment might've looked like. It likely would've manifested a restrained approach to luxury: top-quality furnishings, not too showy. The truth, however, was that I had no idea. It was increasingly hard for me to envision a lifestyle for myself that involved RazorBeat. Josie wasn't wrong that it felt like ages ago. I hadn't been The Future in forever.

It took me some time to locate the old redbrick building, as it was wedged between two glimmering high-rises. I buzzed the button marked MCCLOONE, stepped into a dusty lobby, and a rickety elevator sank to retrieve me. After a protracted struggle with its sliding metal gate, I secured myself behind it and suffered an upward lurch. Then, before I knew it, I was *inside* his apartment. No hallway, not even a foyer: I was live bait in the dead center of Moon's enormous loft.

"Fuck, man!" Moon sprang up from an oversized puke-yellow beanbag. "Get in here," he said, suggesting a hug, but I couldn't approach him. My hands, trembling, couldn't solve the elevator's latch. My jailor kindly released me.

"Bourbon?" he offered.

"Probably shouldn't." I paused before adding, "I'm borrowing your car."

"Excellent point. A beer instead." As he sauntered toward the far-off kitchen, I took stock of the place: high ceilings with interlocking wooden supports; casement windows with old-fashioned cranks; exposed brick with mortar caking out of the edges, having never been scraped clean. It had clearly served as a factory at some point, though there were no traces of what had been manufactured here, simply the scale of production, the extraordinary volume of it. Possibility. That was the apartment's appeal. You could turn a huge space like this into anything, so long as it remained nothing. The apartment found its ideal tenant in Moon, as he'd added scant adornments. And what had been added was colorfully impractical: beanbag chair, pinball machine, lava lamp. It looked as if a middle schooler had decorated the place, and not just any middle schooler but one particularly lacking in maturity, the kind who, when made to repeat a grade, cannot summon even an ounce of shame.

"You cool with a can?"

Before I could reply, Moon threw a perfect spiral of lager at me. I mustered the necessary athleticism to make the catch, protecting my face against further injury. As I popped the tab, a loud shush came between us.

"So," I said, "aren't you going to introduce us?"

"Shit!" he exclaimed. "How rude of me."

Before heading to Moon's, I'd readied myself for the possibility that Josie or Meghan—or both—might be present. I was determined not to let any encounter with a third party faze me; the only thing that mattered was that I take possession of Moon's car, so I could go to Ramya as soon as possible. I hadn't prepared, however, to come face-to-face with a replica of a human skull sitting on his coffee table. It had been eyeing me since I'd staggered free from the elevator into the loft's expanse.

Moon reached down and palmed it like a grapefruit. He cocked his arm back, readying to chuck the skull in my direction, until I frantically waved him off.

"Come on, I'm no idiot!" he said. "Twenty grand for my Chinese friend here." He mixed up his grip so he was now addressing his friend directly.

"I'm sorry?"

"Xiang-Xiang. Born into a family of humble yam farmers in the Yunnan Province during the rainy season of 1897. But really, who the fuck knows."

He extended the top part of the dome for me to grab. Was there proper etiquette for holding a skull? I double-gripped my beer; my hands were full. "How did you—"

"Acquire her?"

"Acquire her," I echoed.

"You're not gonna believe this." He salivated in the suspense. "eBay! I outbid more than a hundred sick fucks like me. Seth, it's insane what people will pay. Dealers really have the market by the balls. Xiang-Xiang," he went on, "has an uncut calvarium, a pretty rare find." He zipped closer to me and, with the tip of his thumb, traced a half-moon around the skull's upper circumference. "So I had to pony up extra for my girl."

"But why—"

"Oh, and you'll love this! As a copywriter." Moon cleared his throat. "The description on eBay said: 'In fair condition. This item has been previously used.' That *killed* me."

I forced a smile and nodded, my head heavy and full. My own skull was weighing on me like a dark thought.

Moon rolled up the gray sleeves of his baseball tee while keeping a hold on Xiang-Xiang. "Look, Mao was a savvy dude. He faced two problems: lots of enemies, little cash. So he killed two birds with one stone: slaughtered some dissidents and sold off their remains. But that was a long time ago. China won't talk about it now, too ashamed. A real black eye for them." He jabbed at me with a smirk. "No offense."

Moon adjusted his stance, squaring his shoulders. "Now I know what you're thinking: skulls are a horrible investment. And you have a point. I mean, people are dropping dead all the time, so the supply keeps growing and growing, right? Why toss twenty grand at an unlimited commodity?"

I kept my mouth shut.

"But you got to remember, investing is all about diversification. And when inflation bites you in the ass, what do you want to be holding? Physical product. Real assets." He hoisted her in the air, light raking through her eyeholes. "This is as real as it gets."

As he wrapped up his little speech, I wondered how many times he'd given it before. Perhaps I was simply one of many guests over the years who'd been subjected to these musings, though something about how he looked while speaking, how his eyes kept darting and drawing wide, told me I was one of a select few. Maybe the only.

I was staring hard at the skull when Moon changed his grip. Its eyes—or lack thereof—were now glued to his broad chest.

"Drink up," he prodded, so I did. Then I made my way back toward the elevator, his car keys in hand.

Part Three

1.

I found myself at the headspring of many highways. I needed the one that led west from New York City in a straight shot—to feel ejected, expelled, spit out clean as a pit. Allentown was two hours away, one and a half if I floored it.

Moon's car was more than up to the task, though he took his sweet time before letting his lime-green Land Rover out of sight. "Now this," he explained, proud to showcase its gadgetry, "unlocks the roof rack. And this controls the passenger seat warmer . . ."

But there was no other person to warm. All I'd have with me was a packed duffel bag, along with Ramya's monitor.

I was eager to leave Moon behind, when he asked a reasonable question: "Where are you taking her?"

I was focused on adjusting his mirrors. "I'll be back soon."

"Not what I asked," he said, clapping me hard on the shoulder through the open window.

I told him, quite simply, I had to take care of an errand.

"Let me guess. Liquor run?"

I nodded, if only to avoid verbally incriminating myself. I'd just turned on the ignition, feeling the roar of the engine run through me, when he hit me again, a little harder.

"Hey! So what, I'm not invited?" He wore a broad scowl.

"Oh, I mean—"

"When's the party?"

"Thursday. Next Thursday." I found it easier to lie while seated tall and upright in the captain's chair.

He took out his phone to set a calendar reminder. "You mean *this* upcoming Thursday or the one after?"

I hesitated. "After."

"And remind me"—he winked—"where's that shithole you call home?"

I watched as Moon painstakingly entered each character into his phone, then read back to me where I lived. As I began pulling out into the street, he didn't wave goodbye. Instead, he waited for the vehicle to inch out, then gave it an ass-slap to the rear fender, as if to say, *Yes, good girl, keep going, keep going.*

* * *

I was only one exit away from Allentown when the traffic got bad. I decided to pull off for a quick dinner in Bethlehem.

The city looked better than I remembered, having driven through once with my parents when I was young. The steel industry's abandoned infrastructure along the river had been reclaimed as rows of luxury condos and retail outlets, along with a sizable casino. There was a billboard depicting a woman in a black strapless gown with her bare arms extended high in triumph before the roulette wheel. GIVE YOUR NIGHT A GOOD SPIN, it read. The words floated just above her, beyond her fingertips' reach.

I saw a KFC at the next intersection and pulled in. As a kid, I'd loved the fast-food chain, over my mother's objections. She called it *the Anti-Kosher.* Seated opposite me in the booth, she'd pretend to shield her eyes for the entirety of the meal.

Bethlehem's KFC was empty except for a noisy group of women seated near the door. They reminded me of a focus group I once observed. It was my first project, before even Smackdale: I was told to stand behind a two-way mirror and take notes while a room full of middle-aged moms opined about a test brand of laundry detergent. It struck me as a colossal waste of time; whenever one woman would express an opinion, another would raise her hand and regurgitate the same thing verbatim. I kept waiting for the moderator to nudge their answers apart, but he just kept applauding them for making their voices heard. My view of them changed, however, at the end of the session: after the moderator dispensed $150 checks as compensation, they stood up and waved a smiling goodbye at the two-way mirror. It seemed less a polite courtesy than a mocking gesture. The mirror hadn't fooled them at all, and in fact they'd fooled *us* in some sense. Stupidly, I waved back, forgetting they couldn't see me.

I was in the Rover eating my KFC when, halfway in, I felt like hurling. My mind kept drifting to the nauseating image of Moon holding that skull. *Acquired*, that was the term he used. I couldn't shake it.

Then my phone rang. For once, it wasn't my landlord.

"Where are you?" my mom asked. "You sound far away." No matter where I was, this was always her opener when we spoke by cell phone.

Near Allentown, I told her.

"Pennsylvania? What are you doing out there?"

"Work." I set the food aside. "A focus group, actually."

"Who's the client? Never mind, you probably aren't allowed to say . . ."

"No, it's fine." I held out for a long beat. "Land Rover." Lying to my mom worked best when I blended in truthful elements with the falsehoods. It yielded a durable alloy. "How's retirement treating you?"

"It's funny, I don't feel retired yet. Part of me thinks this is just an extended vacation, and soon I'll be back at work."

"Maybe you rushed into it."

"At my age, you don't rush into things. Just the opposite, in fact." She shouted something inaudible to my father. "Say hello to him? He's futzing with the cable box. It's doing that thing where we only get the Golf Network, which I don't mind, to be honest. It's kind of soothing. I just look at the trees and the grass and the white sand, the traps or whatever they're called. I'm not sure how they get them so white, maybe bleach? I really hope it's not bleach. Anyway—"

"Don't bother him." My dad was always fixing stuff, his hands reaching into the heat of some appliance. I suspected he damaged things around the house on purpose, just to put himself to use. "How are things otherwise?"

"Well, I have the hip replacement coming up, as you know."

Did I know? I had no recollection of her telling me, and it seemed like the sort of thing a son would—*should*—remember.

"Allentown," she continued, "has a nice-sized Jewish population. Used to, at least. The numbers have dropped a bit, but still—"

"I'm not staying long," I cut in. "It's a business trip, remember?"

"Right." She chuckled for no good reason. "When it's over, maybe you can explain to me the appeal."

Appeal? Of what?

"Driving something so huge. More trouble than it's worth, no?"

I let her ramble a little more before putting the Rover in reverse, then shifted gears with a final goodbye.

* * *

"You have arrived at your destination."

I looked up at the large Victorian building. Only a few lights were on in the windows, just enough to illuminate the long stretch of front yard where crocuses were forcing themselves up through a layer of frost. There was no signage on the property, though I recognized the place from pictures on the website. *BrookeHaven Rehabilitation Center: For Women of Courage.* I liked the archaic syntax of the tagline. It sounded like something born of myth.

It was late to be ringing the doorbell, but that didn't stop me. I beamed with the confidence of a couple of pills moving through my system.

A BrookeHaven caregiver greeted me with a cold glare. "Yes . . . ?"

"I'm here to see Ramya Prasad."

There was a not-so-subtle mole on the woman's left cheek. It was where you'd expect to find a dimple, though she wasn't smiling.

"Sorry, I should've gotten here earlier, it's just—"

"Is that yours?" She gestured to the souped-up Rover parked on the street.

"It's borrowed," I said. "From a friend."

She nodded crisply, some intuition confirmed. I feared my jaw might be heading into spasm, so I nonchalantly drew my arm up and propped my fist under my chin.

"And what's this?" She pointed at the white-sheeted companion by my feet.

"Property of Ramya," I said obliquely.

"Please excuse me a moment." She spun around and muttered something to someone out of my field of vision.

While the building's exterior appeared residential, the inside was your typical health-care facility. Clipboards attached to doors. Blue alarm lights affixed to the ceiling. Pinned to a bulletin board were maple leaves cut from construction paper on which residents' names were written in thick marker. I spied RAMYA in the lower right corner. Her leaf looked forlorn, bottom of the pile.

"When are visiting hours?" I asked. "I can come back another time."

Visiting hours? She shook her head.

"So when can I see her?"

"After detox. And that's *if* she agrees to see you. And"—she looked quizzically at the concealed monitor—"*if* you pass our inspection."

A chilly wind blew through, nearly taking the sheet with it.

"Listen." I leaned closer, attempting a fatherly tone. "How's she doing?"

"She's here. That's a start."

"Tell her hi? From me?"

"Not your messenger," she answered.

I asked that she please make an exception. I emphasized that, despite how things looked, I was harmless, really. Plus I'd driven a long distance.

"Then you better get going," she advised, "if it's a long trip home."

I was desperate to persuade her, but then another caregiver appeared by her side, and then another, and it became clear I was facing a blockade. I started making my way back to the Rover, shuffling through the yard with those little hits of white and purple and yellow, when she yelled for me to wait.

I spun back around, dizzy with hope.

"This goes with you," she said, "or it goes in the trash."

She didn't kick the monitor exactly, more a hard nudge courtesy of her shoe's black sole. The door slammed with her behind it.

* * *

214. That's how many pills I had left. Or actually 208, after I shoved a hearty handful down my throat and waited for them to take hold of my brain, or soak into my brain, or shake up my brain, or do whatever it was they did in there.

I considered putting the Rover in drive and heading home. But I couldn't do that. I'd promised my apartment to Yael and Dalit, for one thing. Also, it seemed pathetic to come all this way for nothing. No, I owed it to Ramya to stick around.

I searched on my phone for inexpensive motels. It didn't matter how run-down the place was; I needed to conserve what little money I had left. But everything was booked or outside my budget. When I spotted a hotel chain that had been a former client, I called to inquire about the possibility of a comped room. The concierge listened as I described in detail the monthslong work I'd done, a rather labor-intensive corporate rebrand that had been praised, if not effusively, by *Ad Age*. Could he get me something at the corporate rate at least? He placed me on hold. Minutes passed. More minutes. I hung up after an hour.

I was lucky, at least, that the car was spacious. Recalling Moon's demonstration, I managed to recline the back seat for a makeshift bed. It was comfortable enough, though the cold outside was brutal, more winter than spring. I took the sheet off the monitor to use as bedding and fabricated a quilt out of floor mats. Just like that, I settled in for the night.

I lay back and stared up through the huge moonroof. It was difficult to see stars in New York City, but not here. I could pick out a few constellations I'd learned in childhood: a dipper, a crab, a man's belt. All these random objects in the night sky, as if some massive shipping container had cracked open and spilled out its varied contents across the cosmos. I'd never stopped to consider the randomness of it all. I accepted it, and that was that.

2.

Subject: ???

Seth,
You forgot to leave us your key. We had heavy bags with us and couldn't enter! It's good now . . . Dalit talked to the doorman. Anyway, thank you for letting us stay here. It's a nice apartment. Where are photos of your artist girlfriend? I want to see you together ☺
The 9/11 memorial was fine. The museum is underground like Yad Vashem. But please explain . . . The gift shop sells clothes? Who buys 9/11 sweatpants? Who wears a tragedy for fun?

xo Yael

I set down my phone on the Rover's center console, sat up in the morning sunlight, and considered what clothes to change into before heading to BrookeHaven. It would be smart to dress up slightly, a way to start fresh with the nurses and invite more formality into our interactions. But when I opened my duffel, I found I'd packed no outfit that would suffice. For that matter, I'd packed hardly anything at all. A prodigious stash of pills and little else.

I ventured out on foot in search of provisions. The first place I passed was a coffee shop that served breakfast. It lacked Sötma's sophistication, though the espresso options were acceptable. When the barista took my drink order, I tried to keep things simple.

"I'll have a skim latte, since you already steamed the milk."

She shook her head a little, not understanding.

"In that pitcher." I reached over the counter to direct her eye. "You should have enough left over from the latte you just poured." I spun to point at the customer who'd gone ahead of me, but he'd taken his drink and left. "Just give me whatever's in there. Seriously, I don't mind! It's less work for you."

She turned away from me and grabbed a fresh pitcher. I forced a few reluctant coins through the tip jar's gash of a mouth.

Next was a pharmacy for some essentials. I scanned the shelves for the cheapest brands, determined to spend as little as possible. I was glad to see, for example, that men's briefs were sold in discounted five-packs, though five pairs seemed excessive. Or was it? How long was I planning to stay in Allentown? Ramya's rehab stint would be over fairly soon, I figured. A few days, a week at most. After all, addiction to pills isn't like being hooked on heavy drugs or something. I wasn't sure what she was taking (or I was taking), but the pills didn't strike me as all that serious. They didn't change you on a fundamental level, not in any lasting way. They passed through swiftly, swimming the length of your brain like a lake, little ripples felt along the shore. This was my experience of them at least.

I was debating how much underwear to purchase when I noticed, out of the corner of my eye, a familiar friend. I'd never actually encountered Smackdale in person. What an unexpected pleasure! When I reached for a pack from its expertly calibrated placement on the middle shelf—no bending or straining required, easiest for seniors—I realized I'd been foolish not to seek out this experience sooner. It was gratifying to hold the fruits of my labor, to feel the weight of my words in a tangible way. My friend, I was heartened to see, hadn't changed a bit. The branding was just as I'd intended.

Only one slightly disconcerting difference: my tagline was nowhere to be found. I dropped the pack to the floor and reached for a new one, figuring it was faulty, some one-off printing error. Again, nowhere to be found. I took out my phone and rushed to check the Smackdale website. Previously, my tagline spanned the top banner of the homepage, though now I could see it was gone. The replacement: *Go Freely Wherever Life Takes You.*

This? They killed the everyday hero for this?! Not only was the phrasing wordy; it was paradoxical. How can one go freely while being taken? Not to mention the double entendre: go, like venture onward, but also go, like go to the bathroom. It was crass. It was insulting.

I picked up all the packs I'd dropped to the floor and stuffed them into my jacket. Then I hurried out through the store's exit, bracing for an alarm to sound. Nothing. Just a soft slap of daylight.

I spent the next hour or so circling BrookeHaven in Moon's car. Each time I rolled slowly past, I tried to peer inside and catch a glimpse of Ramya, but to no avail. I wasn't discouraged. I felt certain she could sense my presence with my every loop, something in her quietly stirring. I could've parked and went inside, or at least given the doorbell a hopeful ring, but something compelled me to keep hugging the road and not let go.

After making countless trips around BrookeHaven—and all the neighboring buildings on the block—I'd memorized practically every visual detail one could hope to glean from the vantage point of a passing motorist. The same lamppost greeted me, followed by the same mailbox, then the same run of potholes. It was repetitive, but not numbingly so. Intimate, actually. Like treating a lover to a series of light caresses.

The "refuel now" indicator began blinking, just as I noticed something else blinking in my rearview. A cop car was signaling me to pull over. My first thought was Smackdale: I'd been caught on camera. I couldn't imagine the pharmacy would press charges, not for such a joke of a theft. That's how I figured it would look anyway. Like a joke.

I decided, as the officer emerged from his vehicle and lumbered toward the Rover, that I would try laughing the whole thing off as a prank. A very *stupid* prank, I'd be sure to stress, one never worth repeating, though maybe, just maybe, he could find the humor in it? Or, maybe, no—better to give him a confession. I'd look him in the eye and admit what I'd done, and when he inquired about motive, I'd turn my head and stare off into the distance and mumble a few words about incontinence, the hard shame of it. Then I'd extend my arms to meet his handcuffs, daring him to heap more shame on top of what I already had.

I lowered the window as the cop neared. Before I could confess anything, he asked for my license and registration. The first I produced easily; the second had me reaching deep into Moon's mess of a glove compartment.

He took both, grunted thanks, and lumbered back to his car, where he'd need "a few minutes to sort things out." A few minutes became ten, twenty. I grew more nervous. It wasn't only the Smackdale packs that were stolen. Practically everything in the car—the monitor, the pills, even the car itself—belonged to someone other than me.

The cop slammed his door shut behind him. "Clean record," he huffed, as he handed back what I'd given him. "Not sure how you're clean, but you are."

I was itching to drive off, but it was clear the cop wasn't through. He dipped lower to peer in through my open window, to make an assessment. "You living in this thing?"

I turned to see what he saw: the back seat folded flat, blanketed with mats, and a balled-up sweatshirt I'd used for a pillow.

"Must be a nice friend," he said, "to let you borrow such a nice car."

I smiled dimly, but he wasn't looking at me. "Gonna tell you this only once," he said, still eyeing the back seat, his forearm flat against the car window's frame. "Leave those good girls alone." He pointed to BrookeHaven, though he didn't have to. I knew the good girls he meant.

He went on with his stern warning, impressing upon me that I was now out of strikes, out of last chances, out of everything. The whole time he spoke, I kept nodding to show I was intending to heed his warning, even when he told me, in no uncertain terms, that I had to stay at least one mile away from BrookeHaven at all times. And honestly, though I didn't say so, that seemed like one more strike. I could expand my circumference and continue circling Ramya forever; I could make a life with her at the center and keep driving deeper and deeper into it.

*　*　*

I was fortunate to look more or less average, such that it would be difficult for the police to monitor my movements with any assurance that they had the right guy in their sights. But the Rover was a different story. The Rover stood out. I parked her green majesty one mile from BrookeHaven, in a shopping district with lots of restaurants. I was walking past a busy deli when I felt a tap on my shoulder.

"Excuse me . . . Jewish?" His beard reached all the way to his suit's middle button. "Are you Jewish?"

I was often stopped on the street by Hasidim in New York City, and it always unsettled me. How were they picking me out of the crowd? Maybe I didn't look average; maybe some part of me screamed Jewish, and I couldn't silence it if I tried.

"Let me guess." He squinted. "From out of town?"

"New York," I said.

He extended for a handshake, as if my answer had won me a car. "Rabbi Jacobwitz. No, *Nadav*," he self-corrected. "Not so formal." His fair face shook out a smile.

"Seth," I replied.

He offered me his prayer book and brandished black tentacles of leather. "Can we lay tefillin? Can we?" I'd seen people participate in this ritual in Israel, and it didn't appeal to me at all. The look of it was very . . . bondage. I said no, and to his credit, Nadav didn't push. He packed up his paraphernalia for another day.

"So." He opened his arms to the street where, behind him, a leashed pug was settling into a squat. "Allentown?"

"Here on business," I said. "Focus group."

He wasn't familiar with the term, so I defined it as simply as I could. "You pay people for their opinions."

"They must be important, these people."

I explained that they were totally ordinary, not important in the least. They were nobodies; that was the point.

He let my explanation hang in the air, evaluating it. A smile eventually found him. "Then why listen to them?"

I stared at him and he stared back, though not quite meeting my eyes; he was looking past me or around me, much as the cop had fixed his attention on the back seat. Then the young rabbi sharpened the angle of his gaze. Suddenly there was no escaping it, like he had me pinned.

"My fiancée," I blurted out. "She's sick. Recovering here in the hospital."

Was there a hospital in Allentown? I could only assume so. The rabbi offered something in Hebrew, then patted my back as if taking its temperature. He said he was grateful I'd opened up to him, that this openness was a mitzvah.

He dropped a hand to his beard, spun a small curl in and out of its end. "I run the Chabad down the street," he said. "Come for dinner tonight."

When I declined, he waved a hand loosely in the air, dismissing my objections like gnats. He repeated his invitation and refused to leave until I took down his address.

After, when I was alone, I took a seat on a nearby wooden bench. It was a pleasant place to sit, shaded by a stand of pines, and I wondered how many people had sat on that bench before me. It didn't matter, of course: they were somewhere else now. I sat there as the afternoon slipped away, the sun sinking with its own weight.

* * *

I could hear my mother's voice scolding me for not bringing a gift, not even flowers. But it was, I assured myself, in character: a fiancé in my position wouldn't remember flowers. His distraught mind would be elsewhere.

As I stood outside the Chabad House, I heard the rattling of Nadav working through a series of locks. Then he swung open the door, his long beard catching its cut of the porch light. Replacing his charcoal suit was a gray button-down flannel that billowed at his arms.

"Should I take off my shoes?"

"They're your feet," he said, and led me inside.

True to its name, Chabad House was an actual house, serving as the main residence for the rabbi and his family in addition to hosting prayer services. I'd been to a Chabad only once before, during my freshman year of college. It had initially seemed redundant with Hillel, until I understood their different functions: whereas Hillel was a sprawling glass structure with its doors always open to interfaith dialogue, Chabad welcomed only those within the faith. (The Chabad tagline: *Where Every Jew Is Family!*) But if Chabad-goers were more rigid in their dogma, they also had more fun. They believed in celebrating God heartily. In other words: libations.

Walking through Nadav's foyer proved treacherous: toys strewn all over the carpet, including many ponies with rainbow-colored manes and wheels for hooves. I could hear the stomping of bare feet in rooms off the main hall.

Nadav ducked away, only to return accompanied. "Seth, this is my wife, Hana."

I stepped forward, then froze—was I permitted to shake hands with an Orthodox woman? I seemed to recall all touch was forbidden, though I wasn't sure if I'd made this up, a boundary I'd invented. I offered a distant smile, not unlike the one I'd given the Heaven On Earth stripper.

Hana reciprocated with a quick hello. Then she spun back into the kitchen to core a head of lettuce, her hair covered except for a few stray curls bouncing to her step.

Nadav gave my stomach a playful backfist. "You hungry?"

Starving, in fact. But first I had to clean myself up.

Nadav led me down a long hall to a bathroom. If I'd asked to take a shower, he probably would've obliged (*Where Every Jew Is Family!*), though I didn't want to take advantage of his hospitality. Still, I needed one. I felt disgusting after sleeping in the Rover, then spending much of the day on foot.

I locked the door behind me and stared into the mirror. Perhaps, in a few days' time, I'd recount this whole experience for Ramya, the bizarre strangeness of ending up in the bowels of an Orthodox rabbi's home. Though it might not strike her as strange, or maybe strange only in the abstract. I'd never told her anything about the incident with the ultra-Orthodox in Jerusalem, never mentioned Birthright at all, never even shared that I was Jewish. It was suddenly difficult—as I dampened the rabbi's white hand towel and dragged it over my face, then up and under my shirt, en route to a light scrubbing of my armpits—not to resent Ramya for what seemed like evidence of a cruel disregard. And yet I knew it wasn't her fault. I rarely talked openly about being Jewish with anyone. I wasn't hiding it, of course, though sometimes it felt to me that concealing being Jewish *was* being Jewish; or, to put it another way, that I was less a Jew myself than someone quietly sheltering a Jew inside him. I wondered if the Orthodox ever felt like that too, that their Judaism was a secret they carried. Probably not—they wore their faith in plain sight.

I folded up the hand towel I'd soiled and hung it back on the rack. Then I stepped out to rejoin Nadav and his family, but not before reaching into my pocket for 202 and 201.

I returned to a table of steaming platters. Their aroma gave the air greater texture: garlic sharp, rosemary smooth. The rabbi, Hana, and their four kids spaced themselves evenly, leaving one seat open for me.

"Triplets. The girls," Nadav explained.

I hadn't noticed, but yes, of course: all three wore pigtails in the same style, just long enough to meet their shoulders.

"And this is Asher," he continued.

I reached over a pair of lit candlesticks to shake the boy's hand. He appeared a little older than his sisters, possibly around kindergarten age, and his skin looked pale, a good shade lighter than the rest of the family's.

"Asher's a baseball fan," Hana added, tonging string beans onto his plate.

"And a world-renowned novelist. Haven't you heard of him?" Nadav poured me a tall glass of water, which he tasked his daughters with delivering. It passed haltingly down the length of them.

"World-renowned, huh?" I feigned admiration, playing along. "Yes, the name rings a bell."

As Nadav uncorked prayers unfamiliar to me, I stared at Asher. I didn't want to be rude, but there was something about his face I found hard to turn away from: a haziness around his eyes, a slight blurring between them and their sockets.

I reached for the hot dishes as soon as the triplets had finished serving themselves. I'd noticed that the pills often made me hungrier than usual.

"Do you work?" Hana asked.

I set my cutlery down for a second. "Not as successful as the acclaimed Asher over here"—I'd stretched the joke a step too far— "but I'm also a writer."

I watched Hana closely as she digested my answer with little more than a nod. I considered elaborating, but what could I say? What could I claim as my own? Barely anything in the world still had my words attached to it.

I felt a soft thud on my foot. One of Asher's shoes had fallen off, though it became clear he'd dropped it for me to retrieve. He was playing a game.

The rabbi picked a string bean off his fork. "The world needs more writers."

"Nadav studied English literature before yeshiva," Hana interjected, using a knife to slip some dark meat from the bone.

"Oh?"

"It's all literature," he said, behind a conspiratorial grin. "The Mishnah, the Gemara . . . all of it."

The triplets were entertaining themselves with leg kicks under the table, until Hana settled them down with a glare. Asher had finished with his game; he grew silent but for a high-pitched wheeze.

"What do you like to read?" Nadav pressed.

I fit one too many cubes of red potato in my mouth, then forced them down. "Lit theory," I mumbled. "Derrida, for example. But no one reads him anymore."

"No one reads, period." His shirt pulled tight to his wiry frame as he leaned back.

I nodded and heaped more cubes onto my plate.

"So where should I start?" Nadav sat upright. "Which book?"

It struck me as a surprising inversion: Weren't rabbis, I said, usually the ones to dispense reading recommendations? He chuckled, but only obligingly, before settling into a pose of mild impatience.

"*Archive Fever*," I said, not divulging that I'd found it impenetrable, retaining little more than a sentence or two.

"*Fever*," he echoed, setting it in his memory.

It was at this moment when all motion at the table stopped, and everyone's attention locked on Asher. His wheeze had turned into a cough, then a series of coughs. They started loud and dry, then louder and wetter, growing increasingly concerning as each charged up from low in his throat. Hana stood up from her chair and, with an almost alarming lack of panic, walked over to him. She folded a napkin in thirds and held it to his lower lip, catching any spit-up. While doing this, she massaged his chest—clockwise first and then counter, as if speeding up time and just as soon rewinding it. When Asher's head jerked with the force of the coughs, his yarmulke almost slipped off. Hana made sure it held in place the whole time.

After the child's coughing fit finally passed, Nadav tried to pick up our conversation where we left off. He had countless questions for me; he kept repeating this, telling me how many questions he had, until I started to suspect that he didn't have many questions, that he had only a couple and this was a method of spacing them out. I didn't mind, since I was having trouble speaking anyway. The pills had taken hold of my jaw, only select words making their way past my clench. I spent dessert smiling and nodding.

Hana was clearing our plates from the table when she broke in with a question of her own. "What's her name?" she asked.

I stopped mid-swallow. "Her name?"

"Your fiancée," Nadav said, reaching for his wife's hand, though she didn't have a free hand to give him. "We'll say a mi sheberach."

That, I knew, was the prayer for the sick. On the rare Shabbat when I'd accompanied my parents to synagogue, I heard congregants call out the names of ailing loved ones so the rabbis would repeat them. The idea was that God was listening and, upon hearing the names repeated, would tend to those in need. Being named meant being healed.

I locked into a wobbling gaze with Asher. He smiled at me while fidgeting with the same napkin his mother used for his coughs.

"Yael," I said, "is her name."

Hana flashed a look of relief, perhaps because the name was identifiably Jewish, perhaps because I'd finally produced a name after an extended pause.

"Yael," she sung. "To ascend—"

"Hana," her husband sliced in sharply. "He knows what it means."

* * *

It was dark outside as I was preparing to leave Chabad. Nadav had offered me their spare bedroom, but I declined.

"He probably wants to get back to the hospital," Hana explained on my behalf, her voice warming in pitch.

So I said my goodbyes, waving first to the triplets, who were busy galloping ponies up the uneven terrain of the living room furniture. Then I turned to wave to Asher, only to find he was already rushing toward me. He caught my leg in a bear hug and refused to loosen his hold.

Escorting me to the front door, Nadav took thoughtful strides and then, at the moment of parting, initiated one of those handshakes. You know the kind: you slap someone's hand and, rather than letting go, drag it in forcefully, almost violently, toward your heart.

"You're not at all curious?" he asked.

I was confused.

"Cystic fibrosis," he whispered. "Asher."

His tone suggested I'd been waiting all dinner to learn Asher's diagnosis. I was still finding it tough to speak, so I tried to convey compassion with a downward tick of my eyebrows, a small tilt toward empathy.

He saw the gesture and smiled it away. "When you're a father, you'll understand."

I tried for more compassion, but the pills left too much slack in my face.

"It's not funny," he said sternly. The rabbi proceeded to lecture me about his experience of fatherhood, how it had changed everything for him. "Your world goes like *this*." He flipped his hand like a cut of meat beginning to burn on one side. Softening, he urged, "Come back tomorrow."

I said I wasn't sure. "Maybe for lunch?"

"Dinner. I'm in Bethlehem tomorrow until sundown."

"Oh? What's in Bethlehem?"

Nadav brushed my question aside, returning to the invitation at hand. "Asher adores you," he said. "Come for him."

I thanked the rabbi again, then soldiered in the direction of the Rover parked not far away. The streets were a grid, much like in Manhattan, except the distances between blocks were shorter than I was used to. I found it hard to form meandering trains of thought, each sentence clipped between one curb and the next.

I decided I'd go see Ramya at BrookeHaven. Perhaps it was the pills, but I just wasn't too worried about the cop's warning anymore. I knew the nurses wouldn't let me in, but maybe I could sniff out an unguarded back entrance, an open first-floor window. The phrase *Women of Courage* echoed in my mind, like a taunt.

Before heading there, I opted to grab a drink at the nearest bar. It looked ramshackle from the outside, its metal awning rusted and bent. Smoky air overtook me at the door as I entered, neon signs turning the top-shelf liquor blue.

"I'm just the barback," the mop-haired boy answered when I asked for a double shot of bourbon. "I'll go get Lindy."

I nodded and sat on a stool near the door. When Lindy emerged from behind the bar, she leaned in to take my order. Her face was narrow and bone-stiff, earrings swinging heavy as globes. "Hon?"

"Bourbon, please. A double."

"Don't think so," she said, dipping a bare arm into the well. "Start with one."

She looked the same age as Odette but moved more falteringly. I downed her pours in quick succession, passing her back the empty glass as spiteful proof. *See? See what I can do?* The more I drank, the more emboldened I felt. It occurred to me that I was drinking expressly for that emboldened feeling, a kind of *liquid courage*, and this phrase delighted me until I remembered I'd heard it before, many times actually; that it was a cliché, certainly nothing I could call mine.

I asked Lindy for a paper napkin and a pen. Then I hunched forward at the bar and, without much thought, began scribbling. I wanted to prove I could still write a decent tagline, and I used the same process I'd learned at RazorBeat, pouring out as many words as possible and letting the meaning multiply on its own. I wasn't even sure what I was writing a tagline for, but that didn't matter. I didn't need a product; I just needed words. If I poured out enough of them, the right ones would find each other.

I'd nearly filled the whole napkin with my dense scribbling when Lindy leaned in again. "What are you drawing, hon?"

I stayed focused on what I was writing, or what I hoped was writing itself.

"I see a face," she said, referring to the scribbles. Then she pointed out all the components: two eyes, a nose, and a mouth.

I still refused to look up at her and risk breaking my concentration. The words continued to pour out of me, less and less napkin to absorb them. I began writing words over other words, which was rendering both sets illegible, but it seemed the only way to hold them all in one place.

"Who's it supposed to be, hon?" she asked, rasping sweetly.

"It's *not* a drawing." I sounded like a brat, but I didn't care. "I'm writing something. Something with lots of meaning. Something you'll hear on TV one day and then remember forever."

"I still say it's a face." She squinted. "Is it you?"

I stumbled out of the bar after an hour. On account of the alcohol and the pills, I began experiencing an uncontrollable twitch, and when I tried to suppress the twitch by stilling it at the source, it migrated to some different part of my person, and in this way I started to feel less like a single entity than the sum of multiple twitchable parts, multiple places for the twitch to escape to, though ultimately the twitch was trapped because there was nowhere to flee that wasn't me. On second thought, maybe it wasn't the best night to see Ramya. I twitched my way back to the Rover and heaved myself in. It was then that my phone buzzed with a text.

my pops died, need my girl back

3.

I knew his dad wasn't really dead. This was classic Moon, right out of his playbook: say the most outrageous thing to elicit a quick response. And sure enough, as soon as I relayed my condolences in a rambling text full of participles and gerunds and everything awkwardly ing-ing at once, he changed topics, making quips about the latest crop of RazorBeat hires, how the ass in the office had gotten better since I'd left, how it was a shame I wasn't there to partake.

but seriously, he went on, when u dropping her off?

Our exchanges persisted like this over the course of a couple of days, and it began to seem that Moon was less concerned with the prompt return of his vehicle than simply staying in touch. When he asked if I was excited to party on Thursday, I offered a vague reply—enough to assure him I was his friend, not his carjacker.

When I wasn't corresponding with Moon, I spent much of my time camping out behind shrubs next to BrookeHaven. It was hard to keep myself from marching up to the front door, but increasingly I felt I needed to remain outside, that it was a test of devotion. I took to wearing Smackdales during these marathon sessions. They proved as absorbent as advertised.

I took pills to keep me company whenever loneliness set in. It wasn't simply the effects of the pills, but how the ritual of taking them reminded me of Ramya, the way she dispensed them into my attendant palm as we huddled together in Sötma's basement. I told myself I'd quit as soon as the two of us were reunited. I saw no issue with consuming them liberally in the meantime.

Ramya's room at BrookeHaven was on the top floor. I say this with only partial certainty, since I never got a clean look, but there were often movements at one particular third-floor window—a graceful sweep of the curtains, say—that seemed suggestive of Ramya or at least fit the contours of memory. It was frustrating not to see her, but a familiar frustration. I was back in her bed, blindfolded once more.

When I felt I'd lasted as long as I could, I'd slink away through a vacant lot and head to either Lindy's bar or Chabad. Both served liquor, at a cost. At one, I had to pay cash. At the other, I had to endure long conversations with Nadav. Together we'd sit on his porch in frayed wicker chairs and, over chilled vodka, discuss a range of subjects in the twilight after dinner. Not entirely unpleasant, though I was wary. I knew how rabbis worked, how they drew people in. And I did feel closer—to Judaism and to Nadav. Whenever he offered to top me off, I'd watch my glass fill with clear liquid. All that clarity was appealing. It kept me coming back.

"Finished," he said, reaching into his black leather satchel, its strap slung over the back of his wicker chair. He took out a copy of *Archive Fever.* When he flipped through, I saw he'd underlined sentences, paragraphs, almost entire pages.

I sipped my vodka and breathed out into the early-evening air. "A little dense, right?"

He laid the book flat on the small table between us. "Well, you can't understand Derrida without reading Yerushalmi. And you can't read him without Freud. And to make sense of him, you should start with the Talmud." He dipped the vodka bottle toward me, to ask if I wanted more.

I suspected this was the moment I'd been fearing, the rabbi dispatching me on a wild-goose chase for enlightenment. And yet I sensed there was truth in what he was saying. In college, I'd been attracted to deconstruction because it seemed like a shortcut. It was faster to take things apart than put them together.

I could hear the triplets roughhousing in the living room. I turned to look in through the porch window and there they were, straining, screeching, reaching for fistfuls of one another's hair. But Nadav paid them no mind. He took up the book again and leafed through it intently, in search of a particular section. I feared an oral exam was coming.

"What do you think this means?" he said, holding his drink high, as if giving some toast. "'If Judaism is terminable, Jewishness is interminable. It can survive Judaism.'"

I sat silently for a moment, hearing only the not-so-faint violence of his daughters. "That they're separate," I said. "One can exist without the other."

"And what's Jewishness, you think?"

I could've answered *Seinfeld* or Larry David or maybe bagels. Instead, I held my tongue. I could see through the window that Hana had entered the living room and was reprimanding the girls while holding Asher by the hand.

"Jewishness," Nadav continued, dragging his forefinger slowly around his glass's rim, "is just the perimeter. It's everything on the outside."

"And the center is God, right?"

Nadav didn't rush to correct me, which I took as approval. But no. He wasn't finished making his point. "Jewishness," he explained, "is a Jew with no faith."

I visualized a person with a gaping hole in the middle. Basically, a bagel.

He inched his chair closer, until we shared the same beam of porch light. His voice was whittled down to a fine tip. "You know what the Talmud says? About the hidden tzadikim? Every generation gets thirty-six righteous men. And these men, they're so good, so honorable, each is worthy of being the Mashiach. And the thirty-six, they're walking among us as we speak. Incognito. Hidden."

I offered a noncommittal nod, just to indicate I was listening. Above us, a few moths had gathered at the light and were fluttering in short spurts against it.

He set his drink down again, using Derrida for a coaster. "But Maimonides, he adds a special twist: the Mashiach will only reveal himself when all Jews"—he stretched out his hands into a scattered people, then returned them to each other with a swift interlocking gesture—"come together as one."

"And then?"

"And then?" he mocked. "Shamayim! As it is written."

The Chabad House was silent now, but for the sound of moths above us on the porch.

I asked if this was prophesied in the Talmud. He nodded with the full weight of his head, along with the yarmulke sitting atop it.

"When will it happen?"

"It happens," he said, a little coolly, "when we will it to happen."

Nadav poured himself more vodka and dropped back in his chair. There was usually a boyish sheen about him, but now it seemed dimmed. If not for his beard, he would've looked unremarkable, like anyone you meet on an ordinary day and immediately leave behind.

I told him I wanted to read the prophecy, since I presumed this would please him. I worried about overcommitting myself, though part of me did want to commit in this way, to be Jewish how Nadav was Jewish, to be versed in it. I'd always been hesitant to get too involved in Judaism; it seemed prudent to remain at a distance, to stand somewhere along the far periphery and just observe it, as one might a bonfire. Though now I wondered what I'd really gained from this distance and what I was giving up.

Nadav was smoothing his beard with heavy, listless strokes. "Why do people lack faith, Seth?"

I made up something about how faith is difficult, how it asks a lot of us. It seemed true enough.

"It's because," he said, "they don't understand it." He was staring down to the bottom of his glass. "They think faith is about the future, when actually it's about the present. Believing in what *is*. Not in a hundred years or a million years. Right now."

I waited for him to say more, but he didn't. The moths overhead had flown away. Either they'd heard enough or they'd found a brighter light somewhere else.

*   *   *

The next few times I visited Chabad, Nadav wasn't home. He was, according to Hana, taking care of business in nearby Bethlehem. "How biblical," I said.

Whenever he was out, which was seemingly quite often, Nadav let me use his study in the basement. I'd stay down there for long stretches, coming upstairs only to use the bathroom or grab something to eat. Mostly I nourished myself with alcohol and pills and reading material. The rabbi had photocopied me some Kabbalah passages in English, which were maddeningly circular in their logic. Like this one, from Moses Cordovero: "God is everything that exists, though everything that exists is not God. It is present in everything, and everything comes into being from it. Nothing is devoid of its divinity. Everything is within it; it is within everything and outside of everything."

Everywhere and nowhere! What a slippery God. It sounded awfully lonely, though. Like God was an exile. Or a Jew.

I wanted to write down my thoughts on the passages, but I'd left my notebook in New York. I suppose I could've written them on any piece of paper, but it felt necessary that the thoughts be written in that particular notebook, that to write them elsewhere would be tantamount to losing them. I'd spiral like this at Nadav's desk for hours: wanting to write down my thoughts, not wanting them to be lost.

"Seth? You down there?"

Hana almost never spoke to me directly.

"Don't mean to disturb you," she continued, "but can you do me a mitzvah?"

I could see her ankles on the top step. They had the whiteness of sugar cubes.

"Nadav promised to take Asher to a baseball game, but he's running late as usual. He won't be back in time." Her long black skirt flooded into full view.

"Tonight?"

"I'm sorry, I know it's last minute, and if you need to be with Yael—"

"Happy to do it."

"It's a long walk to the stadium," she explained, scurrying into the downstairs closet and yanking Asher's fleece off a hanger. "But fresh air is good for him. And I'll show you what to do if he starts up again, but he's been better lately, so who knows."

As she handed me his fleece, her eyes made a pass over the desk. There was a half-empty handle of vodka and two pills (163 and 162) in plain view. She didn't ask any questions, didn't even flinch. Then she plucked two tickets out of her purse and gave me the pair. Her fingertips made brief contact with my palm, enough to deliver an electrical charge, had there been one.

"Thanks." She added, "He loves baseball."

"Me too," I lied, fetching my glass for her to rinse.

* * *

For the first few blocks, I was on high alert to administer chest compressions if needed. He didn't cough once. He barely made a sound, in fact. Then, when we were halfway to the Triple-A stadium, not far from where I'd parked the Rover, he piped up. "Name your favorite IronPig. Go!"

My favorite IronPig? I couldn't name a single player in the majors, let alone some bush-league affiliate. "You first."

"Axel Woo. Wanna know why?" Asher stopped to gather himself. Then his knee popped up as high as his chin and hung there ridiculously, before his tiny arm punched through.

"So he's a pitcher?"

Asher nodded. He was worming a pinkie through his little mitt's webbing.

"Pitchers," I explained, "don't pitch every day."

"I know," he said. "They need rest."

We continued walking, and I had to remind myself to slow my pace, my strides twice as long as his. I paused for a moment to check my phone: a few landlord calls, a few Moon texts, nothing from anyone who mattered.

"Do you know if Woo's pitching today?" I asked.

Asher didn't answer. He slipped the mitt off his hand and set it on his head, a double-decker yarmulke.

"How about this?" I said, bending to meet his eyes. "Let's forget the baseball game. Let's do something else instead."

He looked at me curiously while digging in his pocket. He pulled out two baby carrots and snapped them with his teeth.

I expected vigorous objection from Asher, but he didn't question me, didn't hesitate, not even when I began leading him back the way we just came. As we walked, he took the opportunity to tell me all about Axel Woo's career, how he'd been drafted high and fallen short of expectations. I said something about pitchers being susceptible to injury, but he stopped me right there, said that wasn't his problem. The issue, he insisted, was nobody understood Woo. "They don't use him like they should," he said.

When we arrived at BrookeHaven, it was just after sundown, the sky mostly squeezed dry of its light. I rushed Asher to my usual spot behind the bushes, showed him how to bend back the low branches for a better view. He was enjoying this little outdoor adventure, though he soured when I asked to borrow his glove.

"Whyyyyyyy?" he said a bit too loudly.

"I'll give it back in a few minutes. Promise." I just needed it to turn a doorknob, force open a window, all without leaving fingerprints.

Asher balled up into a cry. I knelt next to him.

"Never mind," I grunted. "Keep it." I thought his mood would clear, but he just let out more despairing cries. He was probably going to beg for his mom or Axel Woo or anyone who wasn't me. "Listen, let's play a game. See that front door over there?"

He shook his head no.

"Well, you'll see it when you get closer. I want you to walk up to it and ring the doorbell. When they open the door, say the magic word. Say *Ramya*."

He nodded while nibbling a carrot the size and shape of an adult's thumb. I asked him to repeat the magic word, just to confirm he had it right.

"*Ramya*," he said, a wet smile sprouting under tears.

I wasn't sure why I hadn't thought of it sooner. The BrookeHaven staff would never let me inside, but they wouldn't slam the door on a kid. The appearance of a little Orthodox boy would disarm them; it would make for the perfect diversion, the perfect opportunity for me to slip in unseen through the back, or at least toss a pebble against the pane of that top-floor window, just to see Ramya press her face to the glass, seeking out the source of the disturbance. Though, of course, she'd know the source. She would sense it.

I watched as Asher crawled his way through the dark skirt of the shrubbery and stumbled out across the BrookeHaven front lawn. From his first few steps, it seemed the child was losing his nerve. He'd inch forward, then turn back toward me with a fearful glance. It was mostly performative, this fear. I had no choice but to play along. I coached him on in whispers, all the way up to the front door.

When Asher struck the doorbell with his kid-sized baseball mitt, its loud chime cut sharply through the hollow evening. It was louder than expected, not at all hushed in a way the neighborhood could simply ignore. And who's to say how the sound was carrying in the BrookeHaven building itself, how it was ringing in the ears of the women in treatment and the women treating them. The boy looked over at me one more time for my approval, and I gave him a big thumbs-up, though I saw now how wrong this was. Seriously, what was I thinking, putting a child in this position? What kind of person would do such a thing? I felt around hungrily in my pocket for some answers. 161, 160, 159.

I listened as Asher rang the bell a few more times, each ring cutting deeper than the last. Eventually I couldn't take it anymore. I sprinted out from behind the bushes and met him at the front door, where he was sitting and staring down at his lap, mitt back on his head. I could see he was crying again.

"I said the magic word, but nothing happened. Nobody came."

I peered into BrookeHaven's windows, and it seemed all the lights were off. From the look of it, the women of courage had found safe harbor elsewhere for the evening.

"Asher," I said, "please don't cry." I reached for his tiny shoulder and gave it a light squeeze. "It's my fault. It's all my fault, okay? Do you understand?"

It wasn't too late, I told him, to catch the last few innings. Wouldn't he like that? To see Axel Woo on the mound? Then I took a look at my watch. It was, in fact, too late.

Asher looked up at me and, with a sweep of his mitt, wiped at his tears. "Your magic," he said, his voice firmer, "doesn't work."

* * *

Thankfully, for such occasions, there is ice cream. The parlor was a short walk from BrookeHaven, much closer than the stadium. I didn't tell Asher where we were going, just that it was a surprise.

It was a warm spring night, and our moods brightened. As we strolled along a residential avenue, Asher likened tree buds to little green snails coming out of their shells. I nodded approvingly, one writer to another.

I thought I detected Asher's slight wheeze, but he assured me he felt fine. Still, I remained on edge, and not just because of him: I'd taken a few too many pills. I began to imagine that, rather than dissolving in my stomach, the pills had fluttered up into my head and, like a swarm of hungry moths, were eating holes through whatever they could find, through the very fabric of my thoughts. It was hard to keep thinking straight with so many holes. I hid my unease behind frequent smiles.

The ice cream parlor looked busy from the outside. "Come on," I cheered, happy for his company, happy not to be alone with my holes. "It's my treat."

He looked up from the well-oiled palm of his mitt. "Not kosher."

I held my index finger to my lips, the universal sign for secret keeping. For God's sake, the kid could have one scoop! Even if Hana wouldn't approve, I felt somehow I had Nadav's blessing, that he would've encouraged us to indulge at least a little in life's sweetness. But just as I was leading Asher in, I remembered that dairy was supposedly bad for respiratory conditions. Slipping him an unsanctioned dessert was one thing, jeopardizing his health was another. I tapped Asher on the shoulder, unsure how best to explain my sudden change of heart. Then, right as I prepared to crouch down beside him on the parlor's cold wooden floor, I saw Ramya not more than a few yards away from us. There she was, standing by the blackboard that listed the flavors of the day.

I was doubtful at first. A hallucination? If I reached for her, would she ripple out of existence? She was wearing a white polo shirt, in a group of young women all wearing the same thing, all chaperoned by a nurse in a lavender turtleneck. They appeared cultlike—though, as usual, Ramya had a way of setting herself apart from those around her. She looked older than when I'd last seen her, or maybe it was just that sharpness had replaced softness in a few places: the center part in her hair was accentuated; her brown eyes stared more crisply out from their sockets. In one hand, she held a child-sized waffle cone with a plain mint scoop, and I watched with great delight as she scraped her plastic spoon at the scoop's curve, gently, scraping barely anything at all, taking only what had to be taken, what was bound to melt regardless. All in all, she looked great. She looked real.

I took Asher by the hand and dragged him toward her. "Ramya!" I cried, and she turned. Like magic.

As I charged closer, the other white polo shirts stood by silently while lavender turtleneck stepped out in front. I expected a loud confrontation, but she kept her voice low. "You need help," she said. "You need *serious* help."

That had been a popular insult back in middle school, though it seemed turtleneck wasn't aiming to be insulting. She kept repeating the words calmly, no anger whatsoever. I would've preferred had she shouted them.

I wanted to say more, but I wasn't sure what to say, my words mostly falling through the holes. The best I could do, it seemed, was to keep calling out Ramya's name, so I did, louder and louder, until I was sure I had her full attention and everyone else's in the ice cream shop, every customer turning to glare, even the servers freezing with their forearms mid-scoop.

I could hear the other women of courage talking among them-selves, and not at all discreetly; they were pointing and laughing, commenting that I was high off my ass, that I smelled like shit, that I'd probably shat myself. Ramya wasn't participating in all that. She just gazed in my direction, her face scrunched in confusion, as she kept asking, "Who is he? Who is he?"

"It's Seth!" I yelled. "I'm Seth!" I realized later, much later, she meant the boy.

I gripped Asher's hand even tighter and begged the turtleneck lady to let me through. But she said she couldn't do that, that I had to leave right away. And, she added, if I continued with my stalking, she'd no longer hesitate to get the cops involved a second time. Though they too, she said solemnly, couldn't give me the help I needed.

"Please." I remembered the monitor. "I have something to give her!"

But turtleneck was no longer listening. Instead, she was crouched and addressing Asher, asking his name, his age, other dumb ques-tions like that.

One of the servers stepped out from behind the counter and demanded we leave her establishment. Asher and I had no choice but to do as she said, though I was struck by that word, "establishment," how fragile a person seems compared to something like that. We found ourselves standing on the sidewalk in the thick of the night's silence—or near-perfect silence, but for a wheeze.

I tried to put Ramya out of my mind and tend to Asher. As we started back toward Chabad House, *his* house, I said I was sorry we'd missed the game. From his standpoint, he seemed happy enough; he kept stretching his mitt high above his head and snapping it shut, pretending to secure some miracle catch. There was a game taking place in his imagination. I wondered if I was on his team, if I was even there.

I was about to ask him more questions about his favorite player when he looked up at me with a raw flash of concern. He began coughing. Seriously coughing.

I yanked Hana's handkerchief out of my pocket and pressed it to his lower lip as instructed. When the coughs continued, I cleared a spot on the curb for us to sit and proceeded to hoist him onto my lap. Then I unzipped his fleece and slipped my hand underneath his shirt, rubbing his chest with rhythmic urgency, just as Hana showed me. The more I rubbed, the more I sensed that the problem lived not at the surface but buried deep in his lungs. Still, I continued rubbing the same area, trusting—if nothing else—in proximity. He kept coughing. I kept rubbing. I began to fear that the pills were messing up my coordination, so I tried rubbing faster, then harder, then both. I pictured the boy turning blue, medics arriving late, police pinning it all on me, locking me away in some windowless basement cell, rusty iron bars, damp concrete floor, and all I could think was *This is home now, I have a home.*

I wish I could say that, despite my condition, I rallied. That when it really mattered, I stepped up and rose to the occasion and saved the day and every other cliché people use to glorify themselves. But that's not what happened. After more failed efforts to expel the blockage, some main switch in me shut off. I passed out. It was the pills or the stress of the moment or both. My head drooped lifelessly in my lap, where I held him.

When I came to, there was drool all over my chin, and Asher was sitting a polite distance away from me. How long had I been out cold for? A few minutes, an hour? In any case, he was still alive. He'd survived all on his own.

He was fixing his yarmulke, which had come off-center in the chaos. Under the beam of a streetlamp, he looked paler than ever, translucent. "That was Yael, right?"

I stared silently at him in the light.

"In the ice cream shop," he said. "Yael?"

I didn't know how to respond. If I explained Yael, I'd also have to explain Ramya. And honestly, what sense would it make to him? For that matter, what sense did it make to *me*? I no longer even understood why I was lying. I'd layered so many lies on top of one another that I could barely see underneath them all.

Asher was himself again, feeling around in his pocket for any remaining carrot. All things considered, he looked fine, even reborn.

I thought about hugging him. I thought about wrapping my arms around his diminutive frame, interlocking them at his back, and working him like a pump—his lungs going full, empty, full—and in this way, I'd operate him, I'd sustain him, I'd make it my job to keep him alive.

He found one last carrot and offered it to me. Then we walked off together, hand in hand, in the dark.

4.

I spent much of that night crying in a car I didn't own, in a parking spot that, as it turned out, wasn't a real spot.

It started shortly after I dropped off Asher at home. He hopped to his front door, poking his mitt through the mail slot. Hana lifted him up high, then just as quickly put him back down.

"So," she said, "who won?"

I'd planned to fess up. I'd planned to explain everything: that the night had taken some unexpected turns and that I had carelessly put the well-being of her child—her only son—at risk. But before I could, Asher piped up: "IronPigs lost."

I smiled awkwardly at him, then at Hana. She said that was a shame.

I gave Asher a good-night high five to his glove and hurried to leave, but Hana asked me to wait a minute. She returned with a gigantic basket full of green apples, jelly jars, and a box of matzoh, the top corner of which poked through the shrink-wrap.

"For you. And for Yael." Light from the foyer fell out around her, softening the edge of her every motion, every gesture.

"I can't accept this. I can't."

"I don't know how much of this she can eat." She slowly rotated the basket, inspecting its contents. "But either way."

After she passed me the basket, I continued insisting I couldn't accept it when I noticed a handwritten note, presumably Asher's, affixed with tape. It read *Mr. Seth & Mrs. Yael,* and he'd crayoned two little stick figures holding hands, their arms rendered in the style of intersecting rivers on a map. My stick figure appeared to be smiling, while Mrs. Yael, with her poor health, wore a frown.

"You really must," she said.

The bar wasn't a long walk. I took one stool for myself, one for the basket. Lindy gave me a ginger ale, which I used to wash down a few more pills.

"Special girl?" she said, eyeing my evening companion.

"All yours," I said, after a gulp. "Take it home. As a gift."

She brought the soda gun back to my glass and pulled the trigger in its wide mouth. "My husband'll get jealous." She then let out a cackle that suggested she had no husband, that the very prospect was a joke.

Lindy turned to add ice to another man's whiskey, and, as she turned, I sank deeper into loneliness. My person, it seemed to me, was all I had left. I resolved to do away with him. If I swallowed Ramya's stash, that would do it. I'd owe her for the entirety then, though perhaps she could forgive the debt.

I called out for more ginger ale, but Lindy was still busy with the other customer. I called again. Impatiently, I raised my glass high in the air, and it must've been that upward thrust that pried the glass from my grasp and sent it to the counter. It shattered, obviously.

The barback was fetched to show me the door. Eager, he shoved me out onto the sidewalk with purpose, knocking me to the ground. A minute later, he returned with the gift basket. He lowered it almost tenderly into my lap.

I clutched my prize and stumbled off toward the car. I was twitching and clenching and teeming with moth-holes but I managed, after a few missteps, to track down where I'd parked it. I was confused at first when I arrived at the Rover, since it looked different from when

I'd last seen it. The most noticeable difference was that the passenger window had been relieved of its frame and—with a shattering that surely exceeded in magnitude what I'd caused in the bar—lay in countless shark-tooth-sized slivers, some on the curb, some on the passenger seat where Ramya's monitor had been. I'd worried that someone might break in and steal it, and clearly, I'd been right to worry. If that wasn't enough, a parking ticket was tucked under the windshield wiper.

I brushed away enough of the broken glass so I could sit. Picking up one of the largest slivers, I slit the shrink-wrapped basket down the side. A few apples rolled out and fell in a plodding rhythm.

I'd just bitten into one when my phone rang. Moon. He'd been texting more, but he'd never actually called.

"Yeah?"

"'Ignore the dummy's mouth. The more interesting stuff takes place on the other end, namely the dummy's ass, inside which the ventriloquist's arm is lodged.'"

"Sorry?"

"Ass-raping dummies?" He made the sound of a train whooshing past, the one for when a person's far gone. "This is a whole new side of you!"

Even in my intoxicated state, I sensed the sharp reality of a threat. "Moon, are you . . . in my apartment?"

"Not in love with your interior decorating. A little blah, if I'm being honest."

I paused. "What the hell are you doing there?"

"Me? Oh, you know." He sprinkled in a laugh. "I came to party!"

I could hear another voice in the background. Was it Yael? No, she and Dalit had left days ago. "Moon, who's there with you?"

"Just Sergei."

"Who?"

"Sergei, you believe this asshole?! No respect!"

Was this Moon's henchman? Were they ransacking the place as retribution? Aside from my old desktop and TV, there wasn't much to steal. Ramya's monitor was the only truly valuable thing in my possession, and I'd managed to lose that on my own.

The pills had me twitching more intensely now, shrill little bells ringing up and down the length of my spine, but I tried to collect myself to deliver him a stern message. "You both have to leave my apartment building. Immediately."

"Well, that's impossible, since Sergei's working the night shift."

The doorman. Of course.

"He let you in?"

"Hey, man, YOU invited me!"

It sounded like the TV was on. I pictured Sergei reclining on my couch, his buffed black loafers up on my coffee table, while Moon raided my pantry for snacks, leaving pistachio shells and pretzel crumbs everywhere.

"Look, Moon, I'm sorry—"

"Tell me, what's so great about Allentown?"

I crouched low out of instinct, but the shattered window provided no cover. Had he been following me?

"Manhattan," he continued. "Now that's a respectable city. Tulsa, a bustling metropolis by comparison."

I always felt uncomfortable around Moon, but this was something else. "Moon, listen—"

"*Robert*," he asserted, almost shouting. "My name is Robert."

"Fine. Robert." I'd been waiting so long for a span of silence, I hesitated when it arrived. "I'll bring the car back, promise. Just give me a few days."

"Sergei, a few days? What do you think?" He paused. "He says sooner is better."

"Please," I said wearily. "I'll try."

"He'll try! What a hero. Hey, Serg, pass the remote. Nope, wrong one. That one's for the volume. I need the real thick one, yeah . . ."

"Robert," I pleaded. But there was nothing to say, except I was sorry. And really, I *was* sorry. Sorry I wasn't there with him. It sounded like fun: hanging out, watching TV, trashing some idiot's apartment. It hardly mattered that the idiot was me.

* * *

"Hey, I know it's late." I waited for Josie to speak. "How are you?"

"Designing my life away. As always."

"How's RazorBeat?"

"Crumbling without you. We'll just never recover."

I sat up in the back seat, careful not to plant my palm on broken glass. "Look, I'm calling about Moon. Don't worry, I'm bringing it back."

"Huh?"

"His car." I did indeed plan to bring it back, just not yet. I had one last stop I had to make first.

"Seth, do me a favor? Hang up and call him yourself."

"I did! Or he called me. Either way, we talked." For all I knew, he and Sergei were still in my apartment, polishing off the rest of my snacks while cracking themselves up with recitations from my notebook. Maybe they were ripping out pages right now, slipping the most embarrassing ones under my neighbors' doors, alerting them to the deviant in their midst. "Let me ask you something. Do most cars come with tracking devices?"

"No idea."

"When you were staffed on the Lexus account, was it a feature?"

"I'm a graphic designer, not a mechanic."

I could see now that it was a stupid question. We never familiarized ourselves with clients' products, preferring to maintain distance from the hard details of their existence. In branding, the product barely exists anyway. It's a blank canvas.

"Been out of the game too long, I guess."

"The game?" She shot out a laugh. "Who are you?"

"Well, it's just—"

"Don't be a drama queen. I'm sure you've still got it, whatever you think you had."

"Thank you," I said. "That actually means a lot."

"Hey, you okay?" She paused. "You sound kinda . . . different."

The parking ticket was still pinned against the windshield, its corner lashing like a little blue flame in the breeze. At any moment, it might flutter away.

"Josie?"

"Yeah?"

"Are you happy? At RazorBeat?"

She made a nondescript popping with her lips.

"Then why do you stay?"

She gave a sarcastic reply. Her voice sounded hollow, like the rich part had been scooped out, leaving the rind. "I don't know," she said finally. "Inertia, I guess?"

"But you're not stuck there. You'll keep moving up."

She could barely tell up from down, she said. She was too busy to think straight.

"So quit," I said. "Open your own agency."

"Seth Taranoff is giving *me* career advice? Really?"

I heard Josie's tone, even as I refused to hear it. The pills were beginning to fade from my system, but not before sending me one last surge. "You could be your own boss. Take on only the clients you want. Manage your projects however you—"

"See, this is exactly the bullshit men always put on women. There aren't enough female-run businesses, go start your own! Like, it's not enough just to be successful. You have to build a fucking empire."

"All I'm saying is . . ." But my voice petered out. I didn't know what I was saying, because it wasn't really me saying it. I'd absorbed the pills and they'd absorbed me.

"Hey," she said, "maybe it's good he's tracking you?"

"Why?"

"So you can't disappear."

I stared out through the broken window. I told her I doubted if Moon cared.

Josie grabbed a quick breath. "You hear about his dad?"

*   *   *

The skies had been building up to this performance for more than a week. When the rain fell, it bounced off the sidewalk a foot in the air, dumbstruck. In my New York apartment, I would've slept through the storm; but here, with rainwater shrieking in through the gaping hole where the window used to be, I couldn't ignore it. As I groggily struggled to fix the breach with the leftover shrink-wrap, I couldn't believe how undeniable the weather was. Evidence lay everywhere, puddling in bucket seats and cupholders.

My patching attempts were unsuccessful, so I gave in. I threw open all the doors, even unlatched the sunroof, and let torrents stream through the interior, washing away most of the glass shards. The Rover had grown increasingly messy since I'd taken up residency, so it was cathartic to watch the rain purge this makeshift home of mine. Food wrappers and other trash poured out of the car. Plastic-wrapped packs of Smackdales floated off with a faltering buoyancy. And Ramya's pills, which I'd stashed in loose piles throughout the vehicle, dissolved into dull pops of color. They too were gone. As for the monitor, maybe it was for the best that someone had stolen it. The rain would've ruined it anyway.

Seizing this rare opportunity to shower, I stripped and took to the pavement, careful not to step on glass. I hadn't been fully naked in a long while, and it was refreshing to find my person was more or less unchanged. I splashed my face, underarms, crotch. When an oncoming car's headlights shone brightly, I was tempted to dash back inside the car in retreat. But I held my ground.

The storm passed just as quickly as it arrived; the trees stood tall again, dripping silence from the ends of their branches. I was relieved to find a dry sweatshirt I'd left in a sealed compartment. When I pulled it on, I felt a lump in the pocket. So there was, it turned out, one handful of pills still intact.

It was nearly sunrise when I started the ignition. I turned the heat to full blast, though most of the warmth escaped through the busted window. As I touched my foot to the gas, I wondered if Moon was tracking his beloved four-wheeler from afar, watching over our every move. If so, I didn't mind. I was just grateful to be seen.

There were signs for the highway I needed, so I followed them. It was lucky I was traveling south, rather than east, as traffic was minimal; aside from a few early-morning delivery trucks, I had the road to myself. I kept accelerating, so Moon would see me accelerating: 90, even 95 mph. I was flirting with triple digits when the parking ticket up and flew away.

Part Four

1.

"Mom? Dad?"

My parents' house was situated at the bend of a long road, where it abutted identical houses on both sides. I grew up thinking this was normal, that all kids lived amid such vexing sameness, but Columbia, Maryland, went beyond. A 1960s planned community, the town was designed for peak conformity. Instead of multiple houses of worship, there was one conference center that religious groups rented on a rotating basis. It hosted services on Christmas, Yom Kippur, and Ramadan. Its walls were kept blank.

If our house stood out at all from the rest of Columbia, it was because of the garden my mother tended. An intrepid wisteria vine graced our clapboard facade, dangling its wealth of purple every season over the front door. But for years it wouldn't bloom. Frustrated, my mom did research and learned that a healthy wisteria plant is content to keep sending out shoots without flowering. The solution was to shock the vine into bloom by causing it distress. My dad was enlisted in this effort, stabbing its taproot with a handheld spade. He was brutal in a way few fathers are: obliging and precise.

I was relieved when my mom opened the door, though I was taken aback by her walker. I'd completely forgotten about her hip surgery.

"Honey!"

"Sorry for the surprise."

"Some surprises are good," she said, reaching to give me a hug, though her walker got in the way. It was too cumbersome to set aside, its hard-capped back legs stuttering on the bare floor.

I was grateful for an excuse not to embrace her. While I felt somewhat refreshed after my Allentown downpour of a shower, I still hoped my mom wouldn't get close enough to smell me. I thought of mammals who take one sniff of their wayward offspring and, failing to recognize their altered scent, cut them loose.

I asked how she was feeling.

"Me? I'm fine. You believe this nonsense?" She slapped the walker's frame, and it gave a clunking response. "But you'd like my physical therapist. He just left two minutes ago. Don. Or Doniyor, actually. From Uzbekistan. He trained as a doctor in the navy! Or their version of the navy, I'm not sure what they call—listen, come inside."

I wanted to hurry to my bedroom to get what I'd come for, but my mom led me into the kitchen to see Giles. Formerly a jumpy presence, Giles was a poodle terrier mix who had been slowed by cataracts. We'd never been close, but it surprised me how unmoved he seemed by my return. He, I knew, could smell me.

I sat at the table while my mom started on a batch of limeade. Since I was little, it was routine: whenever I'd arrive home, she'd fetch a pitcher and a can of concentrate from the freezer. I asked her to stop, sit down. I didn't want her laboring on her feet.

"*Stay active*," she said. "That's what Don says." She pulled the tab on the can, its syrupy innards birthed with a little coaxing.

"They gave you one, I see."

"Huh?"

"To test drive." From where she stood at the kitchen sink, she had an unobstructed view of the driveway, save for some errant wisteria creepers. "Did you pick that color? Yuck! It's turning my stomach."

Giles trailed my mom as she retrieved an ice tray. When she went back to the pitcher, he bumped his wet nose on her walker's back leg.

"Looks like a window's missing?"

I said nothing.

"Is that safe, you think? To ride around like that?" She added water and spun through the concoction with a long wooden spoon.

"Mom."

"If something flies in? A pebble, even?"

I took a tumbler from the cabinet and poured myself a glass. "It's just a stupid window."

She stretched her arms stiffly, raising herself a bit taller with the walker's support. Then she offered a smile, a small impediment to slow us from rushing into a full-on argument. "All I'm saying is, maybe they can get you a replacement? If you ask." She set the rest of the limeade in the fridge. "By the way, your boss called. A couple of days ago. But I told you that, right?"

I placed my drink directly on the hardwood table, where it might leave a ring.

"A woman. French name. Odette, I think?"

I told myself to stay calm, to keep my facial expression unchanged. Odette probably got their number off the emergency contact card.

I brought the limeade back to my lips and took a sip. "What did she say?"

My mom drew her hair up and behind her, then snapped on an alligator clip. "It's funny, you know. They give you these drugs, the first few days after surgery. They're really something! Your dad and I would have long conversations, and I'd only remember bits and pieces. If he said he was going out to buy a gallon of milk, I'd only remember the word 'gallon.' You think to yourself, why that specific word? Why not 'milk'—"

"Mom."

"She said you were missing at work, that you hadn't shown up for many days. So I just told her what you told me."

I looked at her with plain confusion.

"The focus group," she said. "In Allentown."

I nodded, waiting for some wave of relief to wash over me, but it never came. She began asking me questions about work. Was the agency pushing me too hard? Was I traveling too much? I asked to be excused.

I took a long hot shower to scrub off an eternity's worth of grime. Then, after getting dressed in my old bedroom, I found it on the desk exactly where I'd left it: my tzedakah box. As a child, I'd plunk in spare change, a few dollars, sometimes more. I'd planned to donate that money to charity—*Save the Whales! Save the Rain Forests! Save the Planet!*—but I never did. I hadn't saved up enough to save any of those, so why bother?

I picked up the box and was glad to find it heavy. Having long ago lost the key, I bashed the copper top with a stapler until it cracked open. I tallied more than expected: $178.34. I took particular care to uncrumple the bigger bills and smooth them into my wallet.

With my much-needed infusion of cash, I retreated to the basement. Furnished with just a twin mattress and a TV, it was the only unfinished room in the house, which made it my favorite place to escape. I'd used it for this purpose throughout childhood, except for when it belonged to Mishaal.

My mom acted like it was some big news story when Mishaal came to live with us, but no networks took an interest besides hers. It made for a short news segment: Bethesda-based human rights organization places Lebanese refugees in American homes. His English, we'd been told, was poor, but that was selling him short. Mishaal knew how to make the most of the few words he had.

When he enrolled in my school, he caused a stir with his searching eyes and long hair begging to be swept back into place. Quiet in class, he shined on the soccer field. He could thread any pass, pick any corner of the net. My classmates and I would try to tackle him, simply to punish him for his talent, and find he'd already slipped whatever trap we set for him. We became spectators in his presence, and our own athletic abilities regressed. We would drift out of position and study the grass at our feet.

His impact on the girls was especially pronounced. Some confessed their love for him openly; most expressed their affections by applying glitter stickers to the exterior of his locker. After ignoring me since kindergarten, they were now stopping me in the hallway. They wanted to know everything about what he was like at home, his living habits, his idiosyncrasies, all the parts of him they couldn't see. If I tried to change the subject and torque their attention ever so slightly away from him and toward me, they bit at my throat.

My mom delighted in having Mishaal around. A considerate houseguest, he once made for us muhallabiyeh, a Middle Eastern milk pudding swirled with pomegranate and pistachio salt. *Tastes like soap*, he said sheepishly. *It's delicious!* my mom said. *Soap wished it tasted like this.*

Eventually he had to go back. His uncles had contacted the embassy and explained that things were better at home, that they needed him to work. Mishaal didn't seem to mind, or if he did, he didn't say anything. During our last soccer game, he was red-carded for stomping the opposing goaltender's wrist under the back teeth of his cleat.

My mother's farewell was, as I expected, cringeworthy. Standing next to Mishaal at the airport's security checkpoint, she pulled him into her arms and—tears running down her cheeks—declared, *Take care, my son.* An over-the-top performance for the cameras (the network was filming as a personal favor to her, since the footage wouldn't air), though she did take it hard. Whenever neighbors mentioned him in casual conversation, she'd say it felt like losing a child. The hardest thing, she said, was not knowing whether he was okay.

I knew he was, since we kept in touch online. I thought about telling my mom, just to put her mind at ease, though I worried it wouldn't stop there, and she'd insist upon regular updates. I had no interest in playing messenger between her and her "son." I was her actual son. That was enough.

For a long while, I was the one who would initiate our chats, probing for details about his life back in Lebanon. Each nugget of information he offered me was priceless, something to bait the glimmering hopes of girls at school. But then, over time, the allure faded. I'd rush to gift them a new tidbit, something I was sure they'd salivate over, and they'd nod politely as they stepped past me in the cafeteria line. It was around then that I began ignoring his chats. I figured he wouldn't notice, since I'd always been more eager in our exchanges, but then he began reaching out with more frequency, asking about school, about my family, about me. On the rare occasions that I did reply, it was just to say I was sorry, can't talk right now, busy. But I had nothing going on. All I had was the basement, which was mine once again.

* * *

I was about to take Giles for his evening walk when my dad got home. He slipped off his coat and asked, "To what do we owe this pleasure?"

My dad relied on archaic sayings as his mode of father-son communication. He preferred to recycle dialogue rather than invent his own.

"Seth is here," my mom said, "to see how I'm doing."

Giles held out his neck as I collared him. My dad turned back to me. "Is that your SUV in the drive?"

"Temporarily."

"They loaned it to him for work," my mom explained.

"You see it's missing a window?"

I nodded.

"How'd it happen?"

"They gave it to him that way," she interjected. "I can't believe—"

"Someone smashed it," I said. "In Allentown."

"You didn't tell me that!" My mom flooded the foyer with fresh concerns. "Are you hurt? Did they hurt you?"

"I'd replace it myself, if I had the glass," my dad mused. He worked his hands in and out of the lamplight, miming a surgical procedure. "The thing is, damn power windows. With electric, it gets hairy. Used to be a lot simpler."

"Power windows aren't some new invention. They're older than Seth!"

My visits always devolved into squabbles. I'd come to accept that this was the only shape our love could take. We might try to mold it into something solid and whole, but it would always return to its natural state: a wash of weak bonds, loose as air.

"I'm taking Giles for a walk," I said, finally.

"I'm coming too."

"*You*"—my dad pointed at my mom—"should rest."

I dragged out the walk for well over an hour. I led the dog down many side streets with kittenish names: Youngheart Lane, Encounter Row, Forty Winks Way. It was absurd nomenclature, though I preferred it to Columbia's other ridiculous approach: borrowing from world geography. RazorBeat at least drew a connection between each conference room and its namesake; Kilimanjaro Drive was so flat, it could still a marble.

With dusk approaching, I heard crickets rubbing their wings together. I once learned that only males do this; the females spend their nights lying low in the grass, listening to what their suitors have to offer. Though some males choose to stay silent. They'd rather avoid detection from a predator, even if it costs them a potential mate. They put their own survival above everything else.

As Giles and I were about to head home, I decided to take one more detour. Mrs. Beiselman's house was only a half mile away, a small brick ranch located next to a laundromat. This wasn't the house where Beezy was found dead—his stepdad's place was three towns over—but I still couldn't help picturing it every time I walked or drove past: Ian Beiselman lying limp and lifeless in the garage. Once, when I passed, the garage door was open, and I took a peek inside. I'm not sure what I'd been expecting, though I was still surprised by what I saw. An endless amount of pink. Pink bicycles, pink tricycles, pink scooters, all adorned with pink streamers. I supposed for a moment that they'd all belonged to Beezy, until I remembered that my former chemistry lab partner had a baby sister. I'd never caught her name.

The lights were off at Mrs. Beiselman's house when Giles and I arrived. I considered walking up and ringing the doorbell anyway, before I stopped myself. What would be the point? What would I say to her? I decided in that moment on a different course of action. I resolved to rush straight home and come clean to my mom and dad: about RazorBeat, about Sötma, about sleeping for days in a car, and, yes, about the pills. I'd admit to needing help. Financially, certainly, since the tzedakah wouldn't get me far, but more than that. Maybe I'd even enter rehab, just like Ramya. There had to be a BrookeHaven for men: someplace as comfortable as home, sans the emotional baggage. And I'd strive to make friends with the other addicts. I really would. I'd sit respectfully in the circle and listen attentively to the harrowing tales of their experiences with hard drugs, stories spiked with dirty needles and pointed threats from turf-warring dealers and all kinds of unspeakable hardship. And when it was my turn to share, when they finally—if begrudgingly—asked about *my* past, I'd make an impression. I'd wow them with my brutal honesty, detailing my fall from grace: how I'd once been The Future before it all slipped away. How my words once reached far and wide and then, in a breath, were erased. Yes, I had it all planned out. I could see it.

Giles had had enough. He began tugging lightly on the leash, then yanking more aggressively as we approached the final stretch home. As he pulled me hard around that last bend, my heart sank like a boot heel in sludge. A brand-new car was in the driveway, parked directly behind the Rover. It was a Thunderbird convertible, cinnamon red. I knew what would happen next. I knew before I was even conscious of knowing, before I knew I knew.

When I opened the door, Giles leaped into the living room as fast as his aging limbs would take him. Typically he barked at strangers, but not this time. He was licking the black leather shoes of our surprise guest. Dressed more formally than I'd ever seen him, Moon was sitting, legs crossed at an easy angle, on our paisley couch. He was entertaining my parents with a glass of limeade in his hand.

"Honey," my mom scolded playfully, "you should've told us!"

By the look of it, the three were enjoying their conversation. Even Giles joined the fun, climbing up into Moon's lap. Soon he'd roll over and serve up the softest part of his belly so our guest would see exactly where to rub.

2.

Had it been anyone other than Moon, he would've requested a private word, frisked me for his car keys, and floored it back home. Instead, he engaged in a full evening of small talk, following my mother while she hobbled around the house and regaled him with the provenance story behind every tchotchke. There was the porcelain figurine of a shepherd that my great-great-aunt smuggled out before the Holocaust, though his staff had gotten lost en route. More recently, there was the fun-sized Torah scroll I received for my bar mitzvah.

"Fluent in Hebrew?" Moon turned to me. "Muy impressivo!"

I shook him off, but my mom overruled. "He reads beautifully."

Once docent and pupil left the room to continue their tour, I sidled up to my father, who'd just turned on the TV. He was doing that thing that killed me: watching a show with his thumb on the remote, preemptively turning the channel at the slightest hint of a commercial. For him, TV was a game to be outsmarted.

"Dad," I interrupted.

He turned, his thinning hair like a dry brushstroke on canvas.

"This guy Robert," I whispered. "He's not my friend."

He loosened his grip on the remote control. "He's . . . more to you? Is that it?"

This was one pitfall of having liberal parents: they were a little too eager to assume a progressive stance. I assured him he was absolutely *just* a colleague, nothing more, and how could he think otherwise? I sounded manic, but I couldn't stop. I needed Moon gone. I needed to detox my house of him, so I could begin detoxing myself.

"Well, he seems like a nice—"

"He *seems* like. That's what he is, a facade." I rolled up my sleeves and glared. "It's like that Thunderbird he drove here. You really think Ford makes it?" I inched toward him on the couch. "That's just the name they slap on."

"Who makes it? Chevy?"

"No, Dad, it's a Ford. *Ford* makes the Thunderbird. You're missing the point."

My father muted the TV.

"Your mom," he said, with a calibrated calm, "isn't out of the woods." He wrapped both his hands around the remote, like he was covering its ears. "They found a little something on the latest scan. Hopefully nothing."

"Something? What something?"

"We'll know soon. In the meantime, please—"

"But it was only a hip replacement." I said it like I'd undergone the procedure myself, like I'd had countless things in my body replaced.

"Sometimes other stuff can . . . pop up."

"Stuff?"

"Keep your voice down," he said, his words short and spear-tipped.

Mom and Moon returned from their tour of the house, Giles trailing. I tried looking for signs of serious infirmity in her appearance, some sort of tell.

"Good news," she announced. "I convinced Robert to stay the night."

I sprang to my feet in objection. The entire living room was perfectly still around me; it seemed like every piece of furniture had positioned itself for this very moment, had been bracing for it. Even

Moon stood motionless with his large arms at his sides. I'd never seen him so fixed in place.

"Mom, wait," I finally said. "Are you sure?"

"Nonsense!" she said. "He'll sleep downstairs in Mishaal's old room."

My dad, sensing a conclusion had been reached, resumed pecking away at the remote.

I stared at Moon and expected to find him gloating. This was his MO, wasn't it? Not just winning, but exacting revenge: mocking me and my boring, pathetic family in our boring, pathetic house, just like every other one on our boring, pathetic block. He was humiliating us, even now, and later in the evening too, when he reached over the top of her walker to hug my dying mother good night.

* * *

"Let me in. Moon. Moon!"

He took his sweet time unlocking the door at the bottom of the basement steps. He was wearing an old pair of my pajamas, the flannel pants snug around his middle.

"So?"

"So what?"

"Moon, what the hell are you doing here?" I looked past him into the makeshift bedroom. There was a clock affixed to the wall above the twin mattress; it read just after midnight, its digits glowing like worms in turned soil. "I mean, my *parents'* house? Seriously?"

"Nice digs." He wiped at some sleep in his eye. "Better than your apartment."

"Stop kidding around."

"I wouldn't have come," he said, "if you'd just answered my texts." A thick yawn stretched his mouth wide. "It's pretty rude, you know. Jacking someone's car, then going completely dark." He blinked and gathered himself. "Friends don't do that to each other. Friends don't fuck over friends."

I eyed him carefully for signs of sarcasm, but the earnestness was all over his face. He thought we were friends. He truly did. He even sounded invested, like our friendship was something valuable and rare, a bespoke Land Rover with a custom paint job. I'd always taken Moon's popularity for granted. He acted like he was popular, so I assumed he was.

Still, I wasn't feeling charitable. "I promised I'd bring it back in a day or two! You couldn't have waited?" I took the Rover's keys from my pocket and pressed them to his chest. "Look, you win. And I'm sorry about the window."

"Window?"

"There was a break-in. Somebody smashed through the passenger . . . Wait, was that YOU? Did you try to—"

"Seth, what are you talking about?" He ran his eyes into a squint. "Think logically."

"Me? Think logically?"

"Let's talk in the morning, buddy. Killer headache. Like a midget jackhammering on the back of my—"

"Just answer me this." I could hear my mother upstairs drawing a glass of water, the dreadful sound of her walker's two dragging feet. "Why not drive home right now? You have the keys."

"And leave you the rental?"

It was a fair point; I'd proven myself a flight risk. The Thunderbird would indeed make for an enticing flight, provided I had anywhere else to flee.

I studied the floor for a moment. "I want you gone. Please."

"Hey, listen—"

"This is my house, and you're not welcome here." The words came out harsh, harsher than I meant, but there was no way to round down their edges. I dug into my pocket and gripped my last handful of pills. With the proper force, I could've crushed them into a fine dust. I could've turned them over to the air and blown them all away.

I took a heavy breath and met Moon's eyes once more. "I'm sorry," I added. "About your dad."

"We weren't close. Wesley maybe, but not me."

"If I can ask, how did he die?"

Moon turned his attention to loosening his—*my*—pajama bottoms, plucking at the knotted drawstring with his thumbnail. He didn't say a whole lot. Just that his father loved drinking. That he loved it a little too much.

I nodded and adopted what I hoped was a receptive posture. Nadav had impressed me in that regard, how he listened with his entire body, leaning into the weight of what he was being told.

"Must've been hard on you," I said, "your father's battle with addiction."

"Battle? Who said anything about a *battle*?" Moon cocked back and stuck out his chin. "The guy got exactly what he wanted."

"Maybe. Or maybe he wanted to stop but couldn't." My tone was gentle, a light touch on a hard surface. "Maybe it was too difficult to change."

He stiffened against the basement door's threshold, sizing me up.

"You know what?" I continued. "It's like those people in Uganda you told me about. They lived their whole lives seeing themselves a certain way, and then suddenly the eyeglasses told them they were wrong. They couldn't handle it. They wanted to stay who they'd always been."

Moon gave up on adjusting the pajamas and brought both hands to his face. I thought for a moment he was crying, or maybe about to cry, but then he let them fall to his sides, and I could see there were no tears, no chance of them. He'd been kneading his forehead to work creases in and out of it.

"Want to know your problem, Seth?" He blinked at me with a keen intensity. "You think you understand everyone, and that makes you better than everyone. But you don't, and it doesn't."

"I'm only suggesting—"

"You're not a psychoanalyst. You're a psycho narcissist." He stepped closer to me, until I could feel his breath, the wet kick of it. His eyes, I could see, were pulsing. "You actually think you know my dad better than I do?"

I asked that he please keep his voice down, for the sake of my parents.

"They can't hear us down here. Besides, your mom can barely hear shit. Her right ear's been clogged since the day after the surgery. But you already knew that, right?" He shook his head in a slow and steady wag. Then he looked at me more intently. "Do you want to know why you were X'ed? You really want to know?"

I found myself staring at the clock. It seemed like it was time for something significant to happen, or perhaps multiple things, chiming all at once. I imagined myself at the center of all that noise, all that sound springing out from a mess of tiny gears.

"When we were choosing who to lay off, we didn't choose who to lay off."

"I don't understand."

"Can you let me goddamn finish?" He brought a hand back to his temple and rubbed at a patch of pain near his scalp. "This is how it went down. We sat around a table and listed people in each department who were too good to lose. The untouchable names. At first it was just a dozen, then a few dozen, then the numbers added up quickly. So the process was easy. It took care of itself."

I strung up a brief silence between us. "Whose idea was it to fire me?"

"You're not listening. Nobody said a thing about firing you. Nobody mentioned you once." His gaze on me tightened, then eased. "You never came up."

I said that if Diego had been there, the outcome might've been different.

"Wait, are you kidding? *He* would've saved you? After you fucked up all his accounts?" His wild eyes widened. "How do you think you got stuck with a client like Prostate? You were his grenade. And I, like a dumbass, fell on you."

I took a quiet breath to process where we were, the two of us, and the fact that this entire conversation was taking place below ground. I suppose it shouldn't have mattered that we were in the basement, except some part of me felt this exchange wasn't real, that reality belonged to the world above our heads. I sensed something in me starting to burn. I could taste the char of it, the thin scratch in my throat.

"You," I said. "What about you?"

"Me?" He chuckled. It was the first time he looked as I remembered, the laughter bulging out of him.

"You could've saved me. But you didn't."

"Different departments, my friend. You're outside my little—"

"That's bullshit," I said. "Don't make excuses."

"Excuses?"

"Maybe you wanted me gone," I continued, "because you saw me as a threat. You wanted to keep your title. *Youngest partner ever.*"

"Let's be honest, Seth." His words were clipped close to the root. "You never wanted to be partner."

I insisted that I did. I really, really did.

"No. You just cared about *making* partner. It's not the same thing." He rubbed his eyes. "Trust me, it wouldn't have suited you anyway."

"How can you say that?" My eyes, I found, were watering. "How can you possibly say—"

"Well," he said, "you tell me. Have you been enjoying the partner lifestyle?"

"What the hell are you talking about?"

"You've kinda been living like a partner, haven't you? You've been driving my big fancy car. And you had a blast using Diego's big fancy office." Moon served up a wide grin. He then raised his foot a little off the floor and employed it to stroke the inside of my calf, before I stepped back. "Josie says you were obsessed. Says it really got you off."

"Enough."

"Hey, no judgment! Everyone has their kinks, right?"

I said it wasn't like that, that he was distorting reality.

"Reality, fantasy, what's the difference?" He stretched one arm above his head to grip the top of the doorframe, its wood creaking. "It was exciting to play partner, wasn't it? And I gotta hand it to you. From what she told me, you nailed the performance. You did a great job," he continued, "in the role."

I refused to raise my voice but ordered him to be quiet, and I meant it. I wasn't going to permit this in my childhood home, and I definitely wasn't going to let myself be slandered by *him*, a man with so little respect for human dignity that he kept a skull on display like it was some object to be fondled at his whim whenever he—

"Really?" he cut in. "We're fighting over Xiang-Xiang? Over a girl?"

He might've flashed me a wink, but it was tough to see. The wall clock's flickering glow was our only light.

* * *

I prayed he'd be gone before sunrise. But there he was, sipping coffee with my dad at the kitchen table, while, in the living room, Doniyor hovered above my mother's torso. He was elevating her splayed legs while she strained on a yoga mat.

"You're up!" she cheered. "Don, give the old lady a break? Meet my son?"

I shook the hand he'd been using to support her lower body. Thick veins latticed up and down his forearms.

"Your mom," Don began, "is one tough woman."

He started listing all the strides she'd made since the start of rehab. If only, he continued, all his clients were as dedicated! I nodded politely while sneaking occasional glances into the kitchen. Moon and my father were engrossed in their own business.

"The hip," he went on, cupping one fist in another, "is a uniquely special joint. The knee? Strong, but limited mobility. The shoulder? Lots of mobility, but not very strong. The hip has the best of both!"

My father had finished his coffee and was reaching for a refill. Moon raised his empty cup, indicating he too would partake.

My mom wiped at the mat with her shirtsleeve. "Don, tell Seth what you told me. About your family."

He pinched at his dry-fit tee for a moment's separation between fabric and pecs. Then he proceeded to tell me about his grandmother, who grew up on a dairy farm near Bukhara. After she died, Don and his siblings cleaned out her attic. That's when they confirmed what they long suspected: She was a Jew.

"Can you believe?" she said, before rolling up into a cannonball with Doniyor's coaxing. "What a small world!"

I went into the kitchen to pry Moon and my dad away from each other, but they ignored me. They were busy discussing macroeconomic theory. With their cups brimming, they looked happy.

I decided to take Giles for a walk. As I urged the dog through the mist, I tried to shift my thoughts away from Moon. The person who most needed my attention, after all, was my mom. I still didn't know her prognosis or what exactly had shown up on the scan, but I was determined to spend the next few weeks dedicated to her care. Her health was my most pressing concern; my own rehab could wait.

I wasn't convinced I was a real addict anyway. I'd promised myself I wouldn't take the remaining pills, and thus far, I'd kept my word. Would a real addict demonstrate such restraint?

I was walking on Kilimanjaro when my phone buzzed. I'd learned to stop checking—my landlord's messages were relentless—but this time I did. Josie.

"Where are you?"

"Home."

"Like, New York?"

"No," I said. "The home where I grew up."

"Are you with him?"

"Who? Moon?" I paused by the curb. "Not right now, no."

"So where is he?"

Giles seized his chance to rest and flattened himself on the concrete. "I want to talk with you, Josie. I want to discuss our past."

"Forget the past," she said. "He's not picking up. I've tried a million times."

As much as I wanted to take this opportunity to disparage Moon, I decided to keep the conversation civil. That was the mature thing to do. It would prove I harbored no grudge. "How are you two?"

"I'm sorry?"

"I just mean, is it smooth sailing? Or, you know, are you and Moon going through a bit of a rough patch?"

"A *rough*—you know what? Fuck it. The two of you deserve each other. I'm done. I'm done! I'm at his dad's funeral right now, and everyone wants to know why he's not here. They're all freaking out. They're about to call the police. They're convinced something's wrong. And maybe they're right? Like, who the hell skips their own dad's—"

"He's fine," I said. "He's at my folks' house."

"What?!"

"It's my fault. If I hadn't borrowed his car, he never would've—"

"Here's the thing," she fumed. "You, Moon, sort it out. I need to get back to the office."

I felt Giles tugging on his leash. I took a moment to reorient myself. "What day is it today? Saturday?"

"Who cares? My clients don't care. Another day, another missed deadline." She went silent, and I could hear the wind hitting her receiver. "I gotta go," she muttered. "They're lowering him into the ground."

* * *

I returned to find the house all but empty. "Where is everyone?"

My mom was still lying on the yoga mat, leafing through a celebrity magazine. "Don had another appointment. Did you read about that state senator who broke both legs skiing? Don's his therapist too! Unreal." She set the magazine by her side.

"And the others?"

"Your dad and Robert went to get the window replaced."

The mere mention of his name sent a chill through me. "When'll they be back?"

She shrugged, still horizontal.

"Mom," I said, "are you able to get up?"

Fighting the mat, she raised her upper body an inch or two before buckling into a smile. "Lying down feels better anyway."

I was glad to find an outlet for my distress. "They just *left* you here?"

"Honey, really, I'm fine."

"I can't believe—"

"Look, I'm comfortable, see?" She slid both her hands under her head for a pillow, just to make her point.

I lay down on the floor beside her. Staring up at the living room ceiling, I felt the weight of our shared silence pressing on my joints.

"Dad said they found something. What did they find?" I turned toward her. "Mom?"

Her fingers picked at the mat underneath her. "When you get old, they always find things. Most are nothing!"

"So you're still waiting to hear?"

She nodded. Her fingers kept picking while she stared up and away.

I told her that, no matter the results, I intended to stay a few weeks. To look after her. To care for her.

"No need. I have your father. And I have Don."

Real great caregivers, I thought. In the event of a fire, she would've been left flat on her back, swatting at flames with a rolled-up tabloid.

"And what?" she continued. "Give up your job at the agency?"

If ever there was a time to tell her the truth, this was it. The window was open. I could feel a cool wind blowing in, gently, just before it shut.

She urged me not to worry about her, to go back to New York and enjoy my life. "And if you meet someone," she added, "that'd be nice too."

I assured her I was meeting plenty of people.

"People is different than someone." She reached a hand toward me. "Jewish, not Jewish, either way. You'll make your own decisions."

I explained that, funnily enough, I'd been spending a lot of time with my fellow Jews lately.

"Chabad is a . . . client of yours?"

"No," I said sharply. "I just go there sometimes."

"Just to go? For no reason?"

"Well, I—"

"Don't get me wrong!" she said. "It's great. I think it's really great. It's just, aren't they a bit . . . wacko?"

My eyes narrowed from the sting. "Who told you that?"

"I just mean—"

"They're believers," I cut in. "They *actually* believe."

"Good for them," she replied, after a pause.

I offered to help her up, but she said she was fine where she was. I suspected she was staying on the floor in order to shame my father upon his return.

"Hey, can I ask you something?" I pulled myself up into a seated position. "'If Judaism is terminable, Jewishness is interminable. It can survive Judaism.' What does that mean, you think?"

"They sound like empty words to me."

"Empty?"

"Too abstract." She thought for a moment. "But maybe I'm the wrong person to ask. Truthfully, I've never liked the word 'Jewish.' It sounds indecisive. I'm a *Jew*. You and your father are *Jews*. There's no point in hiding it.

"Did I ever tell you," she continued, "why we named you Seth?"

"Let me guess," I replied. "So people would know I was Jewish right off the bat? So I couldn't hide it, even if I tried?"

"No," she said, her voice thinning out. "We just liked the name."

My mom and I turned to the front door when my dad and Moon appeared. They filled the house with their twin presence, their hair damp—presumably from riding home in Moon's convertible in misty weather. My father had never looked so young; Moon, never so old. It was as if they'd agreed to split the age difference and meet in the middle, side by side in the carpeted foyer.

"Hey, Robert." I leaped up. "Can I talk to you a second?"

His shirt was drenched, and I could see the heavy chest hair underneath, unchanged since I'd gotten a glimpse at his bachelor party. He kicked off his shoes, set them politely near the door, and brushed past me into the kitchen. Pouring himself the last of the limeade, he took it in one hard gulp.

3.

Some things you shouldn't have to say. *Can't* say. For example, how do you indicate to someone that it's best practice to attend their own father's funeral? How do you express, with the utmost sensitivity, that regardless of the strain between father and son, the death of the father marks an important occasion in which—

"*Please*," Moon said, "shut up?"

He wouldn't budge. He said he felt no compulsion to leave. Besides, he was enjoying his time with my family instead. Also, he hated Irish Catholic funereal rites, specifically the days-long mourning. So morose. Jews, he said, had the right idea: dump the dead in the ground and quickly move on. I explained it was more complicated than that. There was also the process of sitting shiva.

"Perfect." He slapped our couch's middle. "I'll sit right here."

I took a seat beside him as my mother futzed in the kitchen. I felt I had no other options left. "Moon," I began, "do you know what faith means?"

"To me, it means nothing. No offense."

I could hear the tinkling of water glasses being placed in the dishwasher. I wanted to go help my mother, so she wouldn't have to strain.

I replied that faith, as I understood it, isn't tied to any one religion, or even religion at all. Then I asked if he wanted to hear something

I'd written on the subject. I warned him it was a bit corny. I promised I'd keep it short.

Moon pulled his feet up and tucked them under. He was listening.

It was what I'd started composing in my head at Chabad, the sentences I never had a chance to put down on paper but nonetheless memorized: "Most people think faith is about God and the afterlife. But if you're truly faithful, you're not focused on what comes after. You're too busy believing in what is. You look at every moment of every day as a tangible gift, something to hold in your arms. So when you die," I continued, "you die from exhaustion. It's hard to carry every moment of every day. It begins to add up, all that weight. It's much easier to be faithless. To carry nothing. To spend your days being carried along. But then, when it's all over, you realize you've wasted your life. Because you never believed in it to begin with.

"Anyway," I said. "That's it. That's faith."

I left Moon to assist my mom in the kitchen. When I returned, he'd popped to his feet. He'd thought it over and here was his proposal: he and I would drive in the Thunderbird to the wake in Connecticut; then, once the Rover's window was fixed, he'd come back to get his car. Just as I began voicing my vigorous objection—why was *I* going home with *him?*—he announced to my parents that we had to dash. My mom set about preparing snacks for our trip.

I tried explaining to Moon that there was no reason for me to join him, that my mom needed me at home. But as soon as he walked out the front door, I followed him to the Thunderbird and lowered myself in when he undid its locks. I can't say why I was so quick to follow him, only that I felt tethered. I had two choices: I could go along willingly or find myself dragged.

The ride began smoothly. We were making good time, though we would catch only the tail end of the wake. The funeral was long over.

"I've always hated funerals," he said. "Such bullshit. Someone dies and suddenly they're a saint." He cut hard to the shoulder without easing off the gas pedal. "You know what?" he said, shouting a little. "That's our whole business."

"Our business?"

"Eulogies. That's what we do." He sped up in the hunt for his next opening. "Companies give us their shitty products, and we tell everyone why they're the best." He weaved back into the nearest lane.

"In this analogy, products are dead people?"

"More or less."

I sat quietly in the passenger seat.

"That's all a funeral is," he said, loosening his grip on the wheel. "The world's most boring ad."

When we arrived at the McCloone family's driveway, it was packed with cars, so we had to park on the street. The gargantuan house towered over its neighbors, double, if not triple, the size of my family's home.

Josie was sitting on the front steps to greet us. I expected her to stand and embrace Moon, but she stayed where she was. "You left me here," she said. "Alone."

Moon reached for her, and she swatted his hand. I was thrilled to witness this little violence between them. It felt like an invitation, like a door flung wide open.

Moon sighed and exaggerated a pout. Then he wrapped an arm around my shoulders and pulled me into the frame. "Forgive us? Please?"

Given the circumstances, he did deserve a good measure of forgiveness, but Josie wasn't really focused on him. She wasn't even looking in his direction, in fact. She was too busy passing her eyes across my face, reading the lines of it. I felt assured that, in these few moments, she was gleaning all the details she needed—where I'd been, what I'd done, who I'd failed and how. I almost welcomed her scrutiny, the thoroughness of it. I couldn't remember the last time I'd been seen all the way through.

Josie extended both her arms high, one for each of us. Together, we helped pull her upright and in we went.

* * *

The grand foyer of Moon's childhood home was full of people I didn't know. As it turned out, Moon didn't know most of them either. "Who invited these vultures?" he kept muttering. It was only when we made it into a quiet room by the kitchen that his presence seemed to register. Inebriated relatives lined up to offer condolences and express relief that he'd turned up. A person I figured was his mother stood off to the side.

Moon tried to keep a close hold on Josie and me, but we both managed to slip away; she was eager to get a drink, whereas I had something else in mind. I excused myself to use the bathroom, then found a staircase that led to the house's top floors. It was empty up there, though I could hear echoes of booming voices below.

I can't explain how I knew what Moon's bedroom would look like, or even how I knew I'd found it when I stepped inside. All I knew was that I had to move quickly. I checked to make sure I was alone, then locked the door behind me.

I went to work opening drawers. Money. I needed money. I told myself I wasn't stealing from him as an act of retribution, simply economic necessity. It also struck me as equitable: I'd taken money from my own childhood bedroom, so now it was time to take from his. Besides, Moon wouldn't mind. It was pennies for him. A tiny donation for a needy cause.

But there was no money in his drawers, just socks, baseball caps, and a whole lot of trophies. It was almost funny at first. I'd open a drawer and there, lying on its side, would be another one of Moon's plastic gold karate keepsakes. He was clearly embarrassed by them all. Why else would he be stashing them away? But the more drawers I opened, the more diverse the accomplishments.

There was a trophy for speech and debate, then one for chemistry, then one for chess. I'd been a fine student, above average certainly, but I hadn't amassed a hardware collection like this. It was a form of greed, wasn't it, all this glory? Infuriatingly excessive, just like everything about Moon was excessive. And yet nothing of value to me. Nothing I could use.

I felt an urge to take out a few trophies and smash them to bits, except I feared maybe he *wanted* me to do this, that he had—as absurd as this sounds—left them in his drawers to bait me. No, I couldn't fall prey. I had to make a chess move he'd never anticipate. I had to go bigger, go bolder.

After checking again that the door was locked, I stripped from the waist down. Then I reached for one of his largest karate trophies (1ST PLACE, NEW CANAAN SHOTOKAN, 5TH GRADE NINJAS DIVISION) and readied myself into a crouch for a daring act of desecration. I was giddy to notch a victory, when I froze. Maybe I was playing right into his hand. Maybe I was still doing what he wanted me to do, doing what *he* would do, if the roles were reversed. The mirror beside Moon's bed offered a humiliating glimpse of my paleness. I fumbled my pants back on and returned all his things to their rightful place.

I found Josie more or less where I left her. She was sitting in a beige armchair, swirling a whiskey, and watching Moon from a distance as he chatted with family.

"I hate the floors," she said. At the room's center was a wooden inlay of an eight-pointed pinwheel. It looked razor-sharp, embedded beneath us. "But it can't be helped. Rich people have the worst taste."

I nodded, though I wasn't paying attention.

"Hey," she said. "Where'd you go? You were gone a long time."

I decided to try, just one time, telling the truth. I told her exactly what I'd done in Moon's bedroom without embellishment, including what I'd almost done until I stopped short.

She kept her eyes on Moon, following his movements. "I'll give you credit," she said. "You've always had a creative imagination." She offered me a sip from her glass.

We sat together for a while in silence. I considered asking why she'd felt compelled to attend both the funeral and the wake; it seemed something only a significant other would do. Though I suppose I didn't belong either. We were both, on paper, insignificant.

Some of Moon's father's friends were getting unbearably loud, so we inched our chairs away. It seemed wrong to me that everyone at the wake was drinking.

"Why?" She took in more whiskey. "What's the big deal?"

"It's just, given the circumstances . . ." I held my voice flat.

"If somebody dies in a car crash, you still drive to the funeral." The glass remained at her lower lip. "Or would you walk, Seth? Is that how you'd pay your respects?"

I wasn't sure if Josie was a step quicker than I remembered or if I'd simply lost the ability to keep pace. She'd always been like this, though, feeling for seams in a conversation and ripping right through them. She handed me her glass again as she adjusted the top part of her dress.

"Can't believe you stole his car." She laughed and snatched back the drink. "Seriously, what were you thinking?"

I tried to explain as thoroughly as I could. I laid out my reasons in a linear fashion, except that, in doing so, my logic sounded to me neither reasonable nor linear. "Basically," I concluded, "I was on a mission to help someone. But she was already getting help, so she didn't need me. And then I realized *I* needed help. So I drove home."

"You were chasing a girl?" She gave a condescending smile. "How cute."

She asked to see a picture of Ramya, so I pulled up one on my phone. I was struck by how different the photo appeared to me now. Had her eyes always looked like that, so vacant and washed out?

"Skin and bones," Josie muttered. "But I'll admit she has style."

Moon was standing on one of the pinwheel's spokes in the company of a half dozen other people. I recognized none of them except Wesley. He looked the most disheveled of the bunch; his hair, which had been spiked for Moon's bachelor party, was matted and dull. Passing a drink to Moon was a stringy blonde with a tiny mouth and panoramic forehead. I had an intuition that this was his ex-fiancée, though I couldn't say for sure. His mother, meanwhile, was nowhere to be seen.

"Let's get out of here," Josie said.

"Already? What about Moon?" He was leaning near Wesley and whispering something. I focused on the two brothers' facial expressions, straining to make sense of them.

"He won't miss us," she insisted. "Trust me."

A server spun past with a platter of sandwiches cut into triangles. I wanted one, but he was already out of reach.

"It's *fine*," she whined, pulling at my sleeve.

I tried to resist. He wasn't my friend, not at all, but I still felt an obligation not to abandon him.

"Listen." Josie's face sobered a little. "I feel stupid saying this, but I'd like your help with something. At work."

"But . . . now?" I reminded her I'd only just arrived.

"Never mind," she said. "Forget I asked." She called back that same server, so she could leave him with her empty glass. Then she stepped sharply toward the door.

Before I could tell the bereaved we were leaving, Josie had begun leading me back down the driveway. I wanted to text Moon just so he wouldn't worry about our disappearance, but she wouldn't let me. "You'd only be bothering him," she said.

As we walked in the direction of the downtown, the houses began shrinking and huddling closer together. We arrived at the train station after ten minutes. I was worried about the cost of the tickets, hesitant to dip into the little tzedakah I had. Thankfully, Josie covered it. Once we boarded, the conductor punched holes through the pair.

"Can you believe I've got to go in on a Saturday night?" She stared out the window. The setting sun was driving shadows deeper into the marsh along the tracks.

"Who's the client?"

"It's another pitch." I could tell she was weighing whether to reveal the name. We whistled through a denser strip of marsh, picking up speed. "It's KFC."

"Hey!" My voice kicked an octave higher. "As a kid, that was my favorite."

"It's the dumbest pitch," she said. "Part of me prays we don't win it."

"What's it for?"

"New brand credo." She scrunched her face in a show of disgust.

What, I asked, was a brand credo?

"It's the same as a tagline. We just charge more for it."

It wasn't all that surprising that RazorBeat was constantly refreshing its terminology. Though it did irk me a little, or at least seemed incongruous with the basic logic of branding. Hadn't we always stressed to our clients the importance of consistency? Anyway, I wasn't sure what to say. I just nodded.

"They're not rolling it out externally, just for employees. It's an attempt to boost shitty morale. They want their workforce to embody the values of Colonel Sanders. Never mind that Sanders was a racist who bankrolled the KKK."

"Really?"

She pulled on her sweater, fumbling slightly with the sleeves. "That's the rumor."

"KFC and the KKK. Perfect." The tall grass outside the window was swaying back and forth. "What could possibly be wrong with morale?"

The train kept lurching forward, unable to lock in its rhythm. Occasionally our car would bump the one in front or behind, and all the seats would clank in place.

"When I worked at Sötma, my morale was pretty low."

"No shit," she said. "You felt you were too good for the job."

"Maybe. But it wasn't the job that bothered me. What I couldn't stand was the uniform: the dumb hat, the dumb apron. It all made me want to disappear. But then I realized that was the whole point of the uniform. You disappeared in it. When customers walked in, they didn't see you. They saw the uniform, not who was in it."

She rested her feet up on the vacant seat across from her.

I stayed quiet for a bit and listened as the train slipped low into a tunnel. "But maybe it's not so bad. I could get used to it."

"Used to what?"

"Being invisible." I paused. "It might be nice, in a way."

The conductor made his final rounds and barked at us to remember our belongings. He said to check twice, since people forgot things all the time.

*　*　*

It was a Saturday night, so RazorBeat was empty. I was used to walking its corridors in the wee hours, but this experience felt different. All the color had drained from the place. The design department, once wallpapered with magazine clippings and mood boards, was barren. Josie explained that, in an effort to reduce printing costs, creatives were now told to *pull swipe* online instead. I'd never heard that phrase before. I nodded it away.

As we toured, I couldn't believe how many vacancies remained. It was a corporate graveyard, the frosted glass like an eerie fog. I went down the list.

"Camille?"

Her cubicle had been replaced by a cold-brew coffee dispenser. She'd left to found her own personal-branding agency, the kind that promises C-rate celebrities a ton of followers, bots or otherwise.

"X?"

Josie said he'd accepted an early retirement package. I tried turning the doorknob for a peek inside his old office, but whoever had taken the reins had reset the lock.

"Diego?"

"*Him?*" Josie turned. "He was the first to jump ship."

"I remember," I said. "Who took his office?"

It remained unoccupied, his seat unfilled. There'd been a protracted and ultimately fruitless search to replace him, so the head partners were finally considering promoting from within. This was RazorBeat's typical thought process: look inward only as a last resort. The best creatives, like the best clients, were presumed elsewhere.

Josie trailed me as I stepped into Diego's old office, then spun off into her own corner.

"What about you?" I said, inspecting an empty bookshelf.

"Me?"

"You could take his job."

She insisted she didn't want it. She'd rather do the work herself, not supervise others. Her sweater sagged off her shoulder and she left it alone.

Moon's office wasn't far down the hall. Hanging from his door was a circular whiteboard on which colleagues had scrawled erasable-marker messages of support: *Sorry for your loss* and *My condolences*. (One misinformed colleague had penned *Get well soon!*) With his door ajar, I could see inside. No human skulls, no karate trophies.

Just a couple of potted succulents, the kind that need almost nothing to survive.

"My desk," I said, finally. "Can we go?"

Josie led the way there, though I could've found it in my sleep. I was hopeful that seeing it might provide closure. When we arrived, I saw it too was vacant.

"So," I said, resting my hand on the desk chair's back. "They replaced me with no one?"

"Actually, they replaced you with everyone."

"Sorry?"

"This is FreeBeater Central. A new copywriter sits here every day. They're all brainless. I'm better off doing the copy myself."

I pulled out the chair to take a seat. Its gray mesh was fraying at the cushion's front edge, just as I remembered.

"Enough," Josie squealed. "You helping me or not?" With the toe of her shoe, she kicked at the chair's lever, trying to rock me backward and throw off my balance.

The truth was that I couldn't wait to help her. The sheer fact that she still believed I could be helpful was a confidence boost, even if I wasn't sure myself.

As we arrived at her desk, I felt electric with purpose. I would dive into the work and put myself to the test: I'd see what I'd retained, what I'd lost, what I'd become. I was waiting for her to power up her computer, but her hands weren't reaching in that direction. There was a moment or two when I told myself I wasn't seeing what I was seeing, that her hands were not her hands, and that they weren't undoing my belt.

* * *

I was dismayed that I got hard so abruptly. It was a damning act of insubordination: my libido had bypassed all the proper channels, ignoring my appeals for temperance. But, in my defense, I hadn't anticipated Josie would throw herself at me this way. It was a jarring, almost unnerving sensation—her hands working on me the way teeth treat an apple.

I tried to slow the pace of things, to buy myself time, to withdraw from whatever I found my person pulled into. But there was no way to extract myself from the situation, to drag out of myself the right series of words to initiate such an extraction. So I went along with it. I said nothing as she took me in, said nothing as she adjusted herself toward the difficult-to-achieve angle of her desire. The whole time I showed no emotion, blinking coolly. There were security cameras all over RazorBeat, and I feared we were being watched. I wasn't so much worried about myself (one perk of being fired was I couldn't be fired again), but what about Josie? Wasn't she taking a big risk? It was the weekend, which meant the guards were off duty, but maybe the footage was monitored at a remote location? Maybe, I wondered, Moon himself was monitoring us? I'd gotten so used to the idea of him tracking my movements that nothing I'd done lately seemed out of his view.

"Josie," I whispered. "Josie, don't you think that maybe—"

"Stop talking. Stop thinking." Her hands gripped hard at her mess of a desk and pushed against it, away, away, away. I tried to withstand the rhythm of her repulsion. It was a relentless force; it was enough.

"We shouldn't have done that," I said finally.

She unstuck her dress from the undersides of her thighs, then made a trip to the bathroom. Upon her return, she was squinting from the glare of the globe lights.

"It was a mistake," I continued, "because you're not sober." The whiskey remained sharp on her breath.

She plopped down into her desk chair. "Look in the mirror."

I struck back that I was completely sober. Hadn't drank anything at the wake, hadn't touched any pills in days. "See?" I took out the tidy handful and watched it glow.

Josie winced and curled in close. "What are those?"

"They don't belong to me," I said, tucking them back into my pocket.

"Who gave them to you? Moon?" She swiveled in her chair, raised herself a few pumps, and tapped the power button on her monitor. "You should stop trying to be him."

"I'm not," I insisted. "I'm really not."

My right hand dipped back into my pocket for the pills, for the quiet comfort of simply holding them, and I knew at that moment the real reason why I hadn't swallowed this last stash, why part of me needed to have it within reach.

I could feel the office humming silently around us. It was a smothering silence, the kind that grows heavier with each exhale.

"My mom's sick," I blurted out.

Josie spun her chair back around. She'd been retreating into her work, but now I had her attention. "What is it?"

I hesitated. "The doctors aren't sure."

She offered me a quizzical look. In my vagueness, I was giving the impression she'd contracted some unidentified pathogen. Yes, Mom had the medical community stumped! And for all I knew, maybe she did. I'd gotten no real info from my parents. I wasn't even sure what the doctors weren't sure about.

"Try to enjoy," Josie said, "whatever time you've got left." Then she smiled weakly, her monitor looming tall behind her. Maybe it was bigger than Ramya's after all.

I couldn't help but read her comment as a veiled reference to Moon. I should be thankful, in essence, my mom was still alive, not like Moon's dad. Every time I tried to escape thoughts of him, I felt bullied back into his unrelenting orbit. I was determined to forget about him entirely when Josie said, out of nowhere, "You wanna know the real difference between you and Moon?" Her gaze bored into me. "You buy into all this."

"This?"

"RazorBeat. The business of branding." She paused. "You actually believe in it."

She drew nearer. Her hand found the knob of my kneecap. "When I design a logo, I don't lie to myself. I don't pretend I'm leaving a permanent mark on the world. It's just another stupid mark, another stupid symbol. It doesn't mean anything."

I took a moment to gather myself. "Symbols mean things. That's literally what they do."

"But not everything means what it says." Her tone sweetened a little. She was in presentation mode. "Let's try a thought experiment. Say you're a car company with the best safety record in the world. You'd build your brand around safety, right? I mean, that's your competitive advantage. Now what if you're a car company with the worst safety record?"

"You determine your own competitive advantage, and you brand around that."

"Wrong," she said. "If people think your car is gonna kill them, they're never buying it, never even taking a ride in it. You need to counter the negative perception and prove you're safe. So you *also* build your brand around safety.

"Now, to the average customer, both brands look and talk exactly the same. Both offer the same message. Both run basically the same ads. Is there a meaningful difference between the two?"

"One of the brands is lying. The other isn't."

"All brands are lies," she replied sharply. "Some just happen to be true."

I looked away from Josie and stared out across the whole of the office. Almost every wall was glass, the thick kind, impossible to see a fist through.

"I know you miss it here," she said. "But the work is bullshit. There's no substance to it, none." She spun around to see if anything new had popped into her inbox.

I wished we could've stayed on the topic of my sick mother. As our conversation drifted from her, I almost sensed her condition worsening from our disregard.

A discreet clearing of throat. "Can I ask you something?"

"Give me a second." She finished composing a reply to an email, then swiveled to meet me.

"Judaism and Jewishness." I paused. "Is there a meaningful difference between them, you think? Is one more substantive than the other?"

"That," she declared, "I'm not touching."

"Why not?"

Her dress, I noticed, wasn't fully buttoned to the top. A sliver of blue bra glistened where the two cups joined.

"I don't know anything about Jews," she said. "I only know about you."

I focused on her face and the hard slopes of her cheeks. Had she cried, tears would've wasted no time plummeting to the floor. But I'd never seen her cry. Couldn't even imagine it.

"Why are you sleeping with him, Josie?" I stooped a little, bringing the two of us level. "I'm not judging, I swear. I just want to know why."

She folded her legs up and under her to sit higher. It felt like she was about to tell a story, or maybe make one up, something with a life lesson buried loosely inside it. Her breath stalled, then returned.

"Seth," she began, "remember how you and I would stay late in the office? How we'd wait until everyone was gone? How it felt, for a while, like our little secret?" There was, I'm sure of it, the hint of a smile. She was stretching the silence thin, seeing how far it would go. "Well, I'm done with secrets." Her hand reappeared on my knee. "I'm too old for them now."

Her hand lingered on me for a moment. It was the kind of gesture I'd always associated with sexual harassment, the sort of thing HR would strongly warn you against. I looked into Josie's eyes to see what was written there, if anything.

"But you're not *telling* people you're sleeping with Moon, are you?"

"Who'd even care? Besides you, obviously."

"What about Travis? I imagine he might take an interest."

Josie recalled both hands to her lap. She was sober now. Her eyes turned out a steady light. "I'll tell anyone anything," she said, "so long as they ask."

I waited for her to continue, to say more about her and Moon, or possibly even her and Travis, but it was clear this was the extent of her explanation, if you could call it that. She slumped back in her chair, and it creaked in response.

I said we should get started on KFC. It was, after all, getting late.

"Heading home," she said, with one eye on her inbox. "Need to get some rest."

"What? Are you serious?!" I'd endured all her condescension without objection, though this felt different, a slap of betrayal. "Was KFC a ploy? Was that all it was?"

I expected her to snap back at me, but she didn't. Her face rounded quietly into a gentler expression. "Seth, just tell me the words and I'll say them."

"What do you mean? What *words*?"

"Any words." She chuckled, buttoned all the way up, then put her humming computer to sleep. "I'll say whatever you want to hear."

4.

I walked home from RazorBeat. It was a long trek back to my apartment, but I wanted time to think.

What had led Josie to seduce me? No way was she attracted to me, not anymore. Probably just an effort to expose me in my degraded state, to humiliate me further. If so, it worked. The last time I'd left RazorBeat, I'd gotten to keep a cardboard box of my belongings. This time I'd been dispatched with nothing.

But the more I mulled it over, it seemed unlikely Josie's actions had much to do with me at all. It was about Moon. She wanted to punish him for one reason or another, and sleeping with me would do the trick. Though it didn't strike me as an effective method. From all I knew about Moon, he wasn't the jealous type; he'd be more hurt that we abandoned him at the wake. Based on his enigmatic ethical code, it would've been preferable had she and I stayed at his house and stolen away to his childhood bedroom, surrendered to the heat of our carnal passions, then sauntered back downstairs to gorge on crudités in the afterglow of copulation. He could've appreciated—maybe literally applauded—such behavior.

As I navigated the city sidewalks, I kept thinking about the sight of him stepping awkwardly into his grand foyer. He seemed more at ease at my parents' humble abode, sipping limeade from concentrate and squeezing into hand-me-down pajamas. He seemed more at home in my house than I did.

It was midnight when I got to my lobby. The doorman had his back turned—might've been Sergei, but I couldn't say—and was preoccupied with a stack of packages. After taking the elevator and arriving at my apartment door, I found my landlord had made good on his threat to change the locks. Fortunately, there was a fire escape at the end of the hall that extended all the way to my kitchen window. I stepped out onto the railing in pitch darkness and managed to reach the window's narrow ledge. I tried to force open the window with an upward yank, but my landlord had locked that too. Repeat attempt, repeat failure. As a breeze blew hard and steady at my side, I considered letting myself drop. No jumping, nothing as dramatic as that, simply dropping. It was seven stories. It would've done the trick.

I'd never contemplated suicide before, not seriously at least. I knew Judaism forbids it, going so far as to deny suicides burial in Jewish cemeteries. Not that I cared where I'd be buried or concerned myself with following Jewish law, just that I didn't want the Jewish people to suffer another casualty because of me. If a team's shorthanded, you don't quit midseason. You stick it out.

But I wasn't really on any team, was I? Or at least I wasn't contributing all that much. Maybe I belonged buried outside the cemetery. Maybe that's where I was destined to end up all along.

I was about to do it, truly, when I stopped. I imagined the phone ringing at my parents' house. It would be an unknown number, so my parents would assume it was somebody from the hospital calling with test results for my mom. They would take a deep breath, maybe even hold hands, before picking up, just to prepare themselves for the possibility of bad news. And then, of course, they'd have to bury me. And if I had to be buried outside the cemetery, wouldn't they want to be buried there too? So they wouldn't be separated from their only child for all eternity? I thought about what Nadav said about parenthood, how it flips your whole world upside down. But he didn't mean this. He meant in the usual way, I was pretty sure. In any case, I stopped.

Is there any quiet way to shatter a window? I don't believe so. After failing to crack through the glass with the fleshy part of my fist, I tried stabbing at it with my key. If I woke the entire apartment build-ing, so be it. Eventually: breakthrough. Glass rang out in splinters, misting the air below. I plucked out big shards from the casing until I cleared a space large enough to swing one leg through. Using the top rail for leverage, I birthed myself clumsily into my own kitchen.

The smell hit me first: my electricity had been cut off, which meant everything in my refrigerator had soured. I lit a candle from a drawer and, holding my breath, surveyed the place. My bed had been stripped, sheets left in a pile, just as I'd asked Yael to do. Countless notices from my landlord near the front door. Mouse droppings on the jute rug.

It was a horror of a home, though no worse than I could've expected. The only surprise was the placement of my beloved note-book. While it warmed my heart to see it again, I was confused to find it in the bathroom—more specifically, perched on the edge of my toilet seat. Then I opened it and discovered Moon had scribbled a letter inside. Though it wasn't a letter, really. It was a poem.

<u>My Sweet Fuckface</u>
I miss you like a river misses the peak of a snowy mountain.
I miss you like a branch misses blackbirds in a blue sky.
I miss you like a parking spot misses its Land Rover.
I miss your sweet laugh. I miss your sweet smile.
But most of all, I miss your sweet throat.
Thank you for taking all 12 inches of my fat hairy cock.
Thank you for kissing me and cuddling with me after.
Thank you for being mine, always ♥

I read it, read it again, then a few more times. This is how I'd been taught to analyze poems: to weigh each line thoughtfully and unpack its meaning. Though this wasn't, I reminded myself, some Edna St. Vincent Millay sonnet on an AP exam. It was filth and deeply disturbing to read. I was disturbed. Deeply.

The poem was clearly meant to shock me; it was a gag gift left on the shitter. I tried to remind myself of the state in which Moon wrote it: his father had just died, and I'd taken his car. Of course he'd been upset. But it wasn't the vulgarity that threw me. It was the tonal shift in the last two lines, the tenderness of them. Each time I read through the poem again, I wanted to believe the lines didn't say what they said, that they weren't so sincere sounding. I also would've preferred had the poem been sloppily written; a slew of typos and clichés would've been easier to dismiss. But I had to admit, as much as it pained me, the poem wasn't without quality. The similes? The anaphora? This wasn't jotted down in two seconds. He'd put in thought. He'd taken care.

I thought about ripping out the poem and tossing it in the trash, but I couldn't shake the notion it carried inside it a hidden message, that it was speaking with intent. My dad had mentioned the possibility that Moon and I were more than friends, and I'd been quick to set him straight. What if he'd picked up something about Moon I missed? My dad wasn't blessed with sharp powers of intuition; he could comment only on what he could see.

The most unsettling part was Moon's poem was getting me hard. I could sense him observing the bathroom scene from afar, taunting me, squealing with delicious delight at the unignorable impact of his little prank. I slammed the notebook shut and attempted to turn my attention to other things, but to no avail. The harder I tried to bury Moon's words in my subconscious, the more they fought for the surface, seeking air.

I suddenly felt more grateful for my tryst with Josie. He could mock me all he wanted—I'd taken his woman right back from him! Never mind that the experience had been emasculating, a prank of its own.

I knew I wouldn't be able to sleep. The stench in the apartment was horrible, but even worse was the knowledge that Moon had recently been inside, that a trace of his presence lingered within my walls. I needed fresh air. Given how late it was, I figured no one would see me if I simply took the elevator down to the street.

As I passed back out into the lobby, the doorman (clearly not Sergei) glared at me, now wide-awake. I worried he might dial the landlord or the police or possibly both; instead, he swiveled.

"Package from your friend," he said, retrieving a tiny cardboard box.

What new prank was Moon playing now? I moved to the side of the lobby and crouched low so the doorman wouldn't see as I opened it. But why open it at all? Why endure yet another humiliation? After a fitful deliberation, I tore through the packing tape with my teeth.

Dear Seth,

Thank you again for letting us stay. We hope you and your pretty artist girlfriend are having fun. (Her name is???)

We bought this at the Yad Vashem gift shop. It says Lizkor—"to remember." Now you will never forget the Holocaust. Or your keys.

Yael and Dalit

I lifted the key chain from its tidy bedding of crumpled tissue, putting my thumb through the silver loop.

* * *

For the next week, I lived like a squatter in my own home. Each morning, I passed unseen from kitchen window to fire escape to elevator to lobby and back out into the street. I kept waiting for someone to notice me, but it never happened.

I spent my days like a thrifty tourist. With no job and my tzedakah running low, I made no suggested donations while stopping by many of the sites Yael and Dalit had visited. At the Statue of Liberty, I scaled the helix staircase and stared out from the crown into fog. At the Guggenheim, I rode the elevator to the top, then spiraled down over the course of an afternoon. I aimed to avoid tour groups and locate individuals who were alone like me. Sometimes, when I was convinced of another person's solitude, I'd shadow him or her for a few minutes, only to feel slighted when a companion would appear and deliver the finishing blow of a kiss. Then there were those who were in fact alone. I thought about approaching them, but I didn't wish to disturb their peace. So I kept my distance. I'd reach for my pills and count them, one by one, to keep myself company.

As for Moon, I told him to drive to my parents' house when his car was finished being repaired and pick it up himself. I had no desire to see him again, and whatever sympathy I might have mustered following the funeral flittered away after reading his poem in my notebook. But he insisted he needed the second driver. Or was I willing to pay to have the Rover towed across state lines? Eventually I gave in. I wanted to check in on my mom anyway. One last trip with him, then I'd separate myself for good.

The day before we left, I decided to visit Sötma. I figured it had to be closed by now, and, sure enough, I was greeted by an active construction site where the building once stood. A plywood barricade was painted army-tank green and stapled with posters featuring an architectural rendering of a luxury high-rise. It was populated with computer-generated sketches of tenants standing stiffly in glistening kitchens. GIVE YOUR NEW NEIGHBORS, the posters ordered, A WARM WELCOME!

Looking through a crack in the plywood, I could see what had been the foundation. Leveled. That was the word Odette used, and I could confirm now that it was fitting. No sign of the original storefront. No coffee cups or holiday ribbon or partridges. And no Ramya.

As I turned to go back to my apartment, I noticed a nearby storefront with balloons, blue and yellow, like fists shaking hotly in the breeze. I stopped and read out loud the writing on the sandwich board: Sötma was having its grand opening.

* * *

"Odette?"

"Well, if it isn't the great war hero, Eddie Slovik."

"Who?"

"So," she said, "you came crawling back." Her lips drew tight and thin.

"This place," I said. "It looks great." I recognized remnants from the old location, many of which I'd packed in boxes myself. But now everything looked reborn. The old Sötma had only one window; here, there was glass on all sides. One set of gray curtains rested on a sill, waiting to be hung.

I told her I was sorry. For abandoning her.

"Think you're the first?" she cackled. "I've been through hundreds like you. You're all kids and you act like it."

Her rebuke was oddly refreshing. I was a kid again.

"Not to worry." She began stacking coffee cups on the top rack of the espresso machine. "I've had help."

Travis appeared at the opposite end of the store. He looked different from how he had at his RazorBeat interview, not nearly as angular. Though it was possible the Sötma hat and apron were only reshaping his appearance and he was the same underneath.

I flinched at first, then I decided to approach with my hand outstretched. I wanted to make clear I didn't consider him my enemy, that I even felt remorse for how I treated him. Maybe he'd delight in hearing about the indignities I'd suffered in the interim. Maybe he'd relish rubbing them in my face.

Travis saw my hand and rejected it outright. "I know," he said, "who you are."

As I struggled to formulate a reply, he cocked back his head and steamed.

"You're not Xavier from HR. You're the one she's fucking at work." He cut his voice low to a whisper, so Odette wouldn't overhear from the counter. "You're Robert McCloone."

The words wheeled through the air, dove hard at my ear. I swore to him he had things mixed up. He seemed skeptical, so I produced my driver's license as proof; I was relieved to confirm that, according to the state, I was still Seth and not Moon.

Two customers walked in, and Odette dashed off to greet them. Travis remained upright in his apron, perhaps the same one I'd once worn.

"So you're not . . . Robert?" He appeared disoriented, blinking erratically, a goldfish straining to make sense of its bowl. "You never slept with her? Really?"

I considered making a full disclosure, but I didn't wish to upset him, not at his place of work. I assured him, unequivocally, that I wasn't Moon and left it at that.

After the customers exited, Odette beckoned Travis to help her with the curtains, but the avowed Marxist wasn't listening. He locked his glare on me, screwed it in tight. "She would never fuck you anyway. Wanna know why?"

"Curtains! Chop-chop!"

"Because," he continued, "you're a mess. Just look at yourself." He gestured at my hand. It had, unbeknownst to me, scooped the pills out of my pocket and begun worrying them between thumb and forefinger like found bits of sea glass.

I hurried the pills away and drifted toward the door.

"Come again!" Odette cried in mock farewell, her voice brittle. I wondered who'd die first—my mom or her—and pushed myself out into the street.

Upon exiting, I noticed the awning above. Replacing the old Sötma logo was a version uncannily similar to Ramya's: the typography and color palette were a clear knockoff. I took photos as evidence. Maybe she'd want to sue for unauthorized use of her intellectual property. Or maybe, I thought, she'd be happy. Her art was out in the world.

5.

On the drive, we'd said little, done the limit. I planned it all out. Moon would stay in the driveway. I'd sprint inside the house, grab the keys from my parents, and then he'd shove off in his Rover. It would be a clean and easy handoff—no chitchat. But my mom had other intentions.

"We missed you two!" she cheered. She was holding open the front door for us while steadying herself on her walker.

I insisted Moon couldn't come inside, that he was in a big hurry, though she insisted otherwise. Just a few minutes, she said. Moon and I took seats opposite each other at the kitchen table.

As she peppered us with questions, I set my gaze on his broad face, how it appeared to absorb the room's brightness, a light fixture in reverse. Ever since reading his poem in my notebook, I detected a change. Or at least he looked different to me. I'd always considered him a straightforward case—ridiculously simple, in fact—but the outline I'd drawn in my mind had blurred, no longer a crisp border between who he was and wasn't.

"Much traffic?" my mom asked.

"Not too bad."

"Only at the bridge," Moon added.

"Don't get me started! If you time it wrong, it's backed up through Delaware. It's a small state, but you'd be surprised how—"

"The traffic wasn't bad," I reiterated.

Moon reached to stroke Giles's ears while my mom started on a new batch of limeade. "You boys are lucky. You get so much vacation!"

"His dad died," I said, "so he's on leave."

She shot me a barbed look. "That's *terrible*," she exclaimed, part empathy, part reprimand. Hadn't she raised me to be more compassionate? One of her walker wheels was caught in the rut between the tile and floorboard; I thought about helping, but it rolled free on its own. "Were you two close?"

Moon took in a deep breath with theatrical intensity. "Inseparable."

"Was it . . . expected?"

"That's the thing that gets me." He shook his head and leaned back in his chair, his huge hands interlocked behind his head, elbows high as pennants. "Pops was fit as a fiddle!"

I could see Moon felt no compulsion to tell my mother the truth. He was just entertaining her questions. It was all entertainment, even if his loss was real.

"I'm sure," she said, reaching for a pitcher, "you'll meet him again. Someday."

I looked at her with total bewilderment. *I* was the wacko one for going to Chabad? Here she was, predicting a heavenly reunion between Moon and his buried father. Wasn't that counter to what we believed as Jews? As rational humans? Maybe she was just trying to comfort Moon using what she knew about Christian dogma. Or maybe illness really was changing her. I wanted to ask if she'd received any update from her doctors, though I didn't want to broach the subject with Moon present.

Moon stood and helped my mom retrieve the pitcher. He did it exactly as a loving son would, setting its weight gently in her hands.

* * *

"For the last time, just tell me. What the fuck's in Allentown?"

Moon and I were stocking up on snacks at a highway rest stop. My mom had offered to make us lunch, and Moon had been eager to accept, but I insisted we get on the road. I said I had time-sensitive work to finish at RazorBeat, which I knew would pass muster with her. To his credit, Moon held his tongue regarding my unemployment. We each permitted the other his respective deceptions.

Before leaving my parents' house, I'd made one last demand of Moon: a brief detour. It wouldn't take long, I promised. And he didn't even have to join me. He could drive the Rover back to New York, and I'd return his rental later that same day. He rejected my proposal and opted to follow instead. A hundred miles later, I'd taken him wildly off course, and he'd intuited where we were going.

"Just drive home," I said, facing him in the rest stop parking lot. "Please?"

He shook his head. "You've pulled this shit before."

"What shit?" The drone of passing traffic was an electric razor nearing the ear.

"Your whole . . . disappearing act."

"Fine. So keep following me then," I said, throwing back an aggressive handful of trail mix.

For the rest of the drive, I could sense Moon driving too closely on my rear (*"Thank you for being mine, always ♥"*). I made sure to periodically tap the brake and then push hard on the gas, padding the little distance between us.

I pulled up a block shy of BrookeHaven, careful not to give away my destination. Moon parked his Rover behind me and rolled down his window.

"Hey, what's this all about? Seriously."

"I'll be back soon." I estimated less than an hour.

"One HOUR?" He dropped his forehead to the wheel in exasperation. "And what should I do in the meantime? Jerk off in the

car? On my cowhide leather?" He ran a palm over his hard swoop
of armrest.

"Just drive home," I repeated. I was stoic in my delivery, though
I did find some pleasure in the situation. Moon couldn't risk leaving
behind either car, so he was chained to me. I wanted to abuse this
power, to yank viciously on the studded leash.

"Nothing in this shithole!" he yelled, as I walked down the street.
"*Nothing!*"

Due to the lack of traffic noise, his voice carried far. It kept carrying
and carrying, long after it died out.

* * *

I suppose it was foolish to expect Ramya would've dressed up for
my visit. She greeted me in the same bland uniform she'd worn in
the ice cream shop; if there was any difference between now and
then, it was that her polo had lost its biting whiteness. I considered
giving her a hug, then refrained. Even the lightest touch, I worried,
might throw off the trajectory of her recovery.

Standing at the doorway where I'd formerly been turned away, I
was excited to enter and see what I'd been denied, see perhaps how
I might fit into such a world. It was not to be. Ramya insisted we
leave BrookeHaven—she'd earned open-campus privileges two weeks
ago—and go to a coffee shop nearby.

The walk there was awkward. I rambled about the weather,
about rain that had been in the forecast but never materialized.
Ramya said little, nodding in step. I worried, strangely, she might
evaporate.

As I strode alongside her, I felt I was walking with a whole new
Ramya, while I was, unfortunately, the same old Seth. When we
arrived at the coffee shop, I was reminded of Sötma. I rushed to
take out my phone.

"I've got to show you something. You won't believe this . . ."

But somehow the photos of the new Sötma awning had gotten deleted. I even scrolled back as far as my Birthright album, just to double-check. Gone.

With only twenty tzedakah dollars remaining, I bought an iced coffee for myself and a green tea for her. She broke off to stake out a table near the window.

"So." I set down our drinks between us. "How are you doing?"

She lifted her dark mug to where the rising steam could touch her chin. "Let's start somewhere else."

"Fine." I breathed her in. "Come here often?"

"Five days a week, actually."

I rested my elbows on the unsteady table. "You work here?"

That made sense, I supposed. BrookeHaven was a rehab center, not a prison.

"Is it better than Sötma?"

"Meh," she said. "About the same."

The same? How could it be the same? Odette treated her terribly! She was constantly teasing or tugging or prying or pulling at every aspect of Ramya's being.

"Can I be honest?" She dragged the tea bag to the mug's lip and performed compressions with the back of a spoon. "I barely remember her."

"You're joking."

She shrugged. Scooping out the tea bag, she laid it to rest in the saucer.

I felt increasingly desperate to learn more about the path that led Ramya to rehab. I needed to know which drugs were responsible, not only out of concern for her, but for my own well-being. If indeed I'd developed my own dependency, it seemed important to know what I was depending on. I placed the last of the pills on the table.

Ramya skimmed her eyes over them, perplexed. She asked, calmly, what I was doing.

"They're yours," I said. "I'm giving them back."

I explained that I wanted to make things right. I didn't intend for her to take the pills, not in the least; I was glad to throw them in the trash immediately, with her consent. I simply felt an obligation to return them to her. These pills—I'd taken to thinking of them as survivors—were all that remained from that final stash in her locker. I promised that, as soon as I paid off my other debts, I'd compensate her for the rest. I was good for it, really.

"These?" She used the butt end of her spoon to inspect the lot, inching them back and forth along the table's surface. I worried she was contemplating swallowing one or two—why had I offered drugs to a recovering addict?!—when she announced, flatly, "These are worthless."

I paused. "They must be worth something."

"No. They're counterfeit. That's why I left them behind." She handed me her spoon, as if it had served its purpose. "Or maybe not counterfeit. Just very low dose. They didn't do a thing for me."

I stared at the pills, baffled.

"Duds," she declared, her lips thinning out the sudden heft of the word. "You're hooked on duds."

It seemed impossible. If the pills were fake, what about everything I'd experienced while taking them? The sporadic clenching, the unstoppable twitching, the boring of all those holes through the soft middle of my mind—was that all fake too? I wanted to ask Ramya if this was possible, if people got *hooked on duds* in this way. But I worried it would sound trivial to her. She'd gone through the real thing.

After trashing the pills, Ramya sat back down. She quietly sipped her green tea, hunching to meet it.

"Either way," I said, "I'm sorry for stealing."

"Don't be."

"Sure, except—"

"I'm the one who's sorry."

I gave my iced coffee a shake, a fresh roll of the dice. "Ramya, you don't have anything to apologize for."

"I do, actually." She adjusted the collar of her polo. "It's one of the steps."

I knew about the steps from watching TV and movies. Or rather, I knew of them. I couldn't say what they were.

"I have to apologize to everyone. Friends, family."

I swallowed hard and thought of my phone calls with her father. She sat upright, giving me a better look at her face. It shed a cast of shadows.

"How's your family doing?"

"My dad, you mean? Overbearing as usual. He downloaded an app for tracking addicts in recovery. It's very Big Brother. Or Big Father, I guess."

"Does he know we're . . . together right now?"

"He'll just see I'm here and assume I picked up an extra shift. Anyway, I'm sorry." She added, "It's not personal."

I nodded, though I didn't understand. How could an apology *not* be personal? Wasn't the personal aspect what made it sincere? Still, I accepted, if for no other reason than to help her progress to her next step, wherever that might take her. I felt fairly certain it was leading far away from me.

"So you remember nothing?" I studied her for some brief glimmer of a response. "Do you remember us?" It came out more sentimental sounding than I'd hoped. I hid behind another loud rattle of my coffee.

"It's not amnesia," she answered. "You just kinda let go. It's like training your mind to pack light." She said hi to one of the passing busboys, clearly her coworker.

"I was pretty gone most of the time anyway," she added. "See this?" She laid her wrist on the table, flipping it so the lighter side shone. "I have no memory of getting it."

"None?"

"None."

I stared at the Chinese character I'd stared at many times before, though I pretended it held novelty, like something dug out of deep soil. "What does it mean?"

"No idea." She leaned in, as if gossiping about a friend. "So *ugly*, isn't it?"

I looked at her tattoo more closely now, the top stroke pitched like a roof and two vertical lines like stilts underneath. It reminded me of the Hebrew letterforms I studied growing up, the ones I was taught to sketch on loose-leaf paper and pronounce haltingly for anyone who cared to listen.

I asked if she'd considered getting the tattoo removed. Immediately, her arm flipped over.

"I *like* having it," she said. "It's a reminder of all my fuckups, in case I forget."

A smile emerged, then dipped back under the still surface of the moment. She gazed out the window. A long pause followed.

"There's this video game," she began.

"The infinity one?"

She shook her head no. "This one's older. It's called *Braid*."

"Oh."

"To save the princess, you go backward. At first you jump clouds and cross bridges, but the only way to beat all the levels is rewinding time. That's how you advance."

I nodded, so she could see I was with her.

"But there are these green things that aren't affected by the time switch. Like, if you blow up a green bridge, then rewind, it's still destroyed. After a while, nothing's synchronized anymore. It's like time gets all chopped up, and you feel totally scattered. Like there are little pieces of you everywhere. I guess I can't explain it." She sighed long and deep. "My brain's not what it was."

I wanted to reassure her, to tell her she sounded exactly as she always did, but I stopped myself. Because I'd known her only during her addiction, I feared sending the wrong message. Better to say she was unrecognizable to me? A stranger?

"Anyway," she said, taking in the mug's warmth. "Those green things. You can't change them back."

I nodded and waited for her to go on, but she didn't. I steeled myself with a healthy sip and then set my drink back down. "Ramya, there was a night at your apartment. I pinched you in front of all your roommates. I hurt you, I think. I'm sorry. I'm really sorry. I want you to know . . ." I dug my thumb into the side of the plastic cup, leaving a concavity. "Do you remember that night?"

"Honestly?" She shook back her hair. "No."

"Really?"

"Yes," she said. "Really."

The clouds outside were rearranging themselves, fresh cuts of sunlight streaming in through the coffee shop's windows. The thin laminate of our tabletop glistened.

"I'm relieved," I said. "I've been feeling so guilty."

"Your lucky day, I guess." She raised her mug again as sunlight hit her eyes.

*　*　*

Walking back to our cars, I expected Moon to have driven off. It seemed like the Moon thing to do: get bored after playing with the Rover's many dashboard gadgets, then speed away like a bullet in hot pursuit of some new target. But this I did not expect: both cars parked and him gone.

Where the hell was he? He couldn't have gone far on foot. My time with Ramya hadn't lasted the hour; she'd emptied the rest of her tea into a to-go cup. I called out his name, trying not to expose myself to attack. It would've been typical of him to hide—possibly behind that mailbox, or those two dumpsters?—then leap out and sweep my legs. After some tentative searching, I tried his cell. No answer.

There was nothing keeping me there. With his rental's keys in my pocket, I could've driven back to New York alone. But what did I have to rush home to? Another eviction notice? A fresh serving of mouse droppings? Plus, I did feel some responsibility. I was the reason he was in Allentown in the first place.

I began checking storefronts. There was an upscale Italian bistro with a historical plaque and a wicker window box of pansies. No Moon. Next door was a dive bar, even more run-down than the one near Chabad. And that's where I found him, sipping on bourbon, slumped in front of two TVs airing the same basketball game. One set was a half second behind the other.

"Game's almost over," he slurred.

A player was gathering himself at the line. He missed a free throw, then missed again.

"Come on," I said, pulling the back of his sleeve.

"Hey, hey, relax, MOM."

A couple of hulking oafs at the bar were enjoying our little charade. It was clear that, in practically no time, Moon had befriended the town he'd been maligning.

I'd seen him drunk in the past, but never this sloshed. One eye kept falling out of focus, as if half his brain's circuitry had come unplugged.

"Can you even stand?"

"Can I *stand*?" Moon tuned his voice to a nagging pitch, mocking me before his adoring audience. "How about"—he looped his heavy arm around my neck to drag me down with force—"I bend you over right here . . ."

The oafs were in hysterics, raising their glasses to toast his antics. I managed to slip from his hold, then headed toward the exit.

"Wait!" Moon slapped a fifty on the counter and stumbled off the barstool. The two of us rushed our disagreement outside.

"I left you for less than an hour!" I raised a finger for him to count.

"You left me for *weeks*," he hit back. He wiped his mouth on his blue cuff and smoothed the sleeve where I'd pulled at him. "I think I might be a little tipsy."

"You're hammered," I corrected.

"I'm also starving."

With Moon clearly too drunk to drive, I begrudgingly proposed we get food somewhere nearby. An elderly couple was walking past us en route to the bistro; the man seemed less stable than his wife, holding her arm for support.

"Looks romantic," Moon belched. We followed them in.

6.

After a few bites of pasta, Moon sobered up. This seemed typical of the speed and ease with which his body operated. He was an efficient beast—swallowing, digesting, and discharging at a frightful clip. By the time our water glasses were refilled, we could hold a normal conversation, or at least normal for Moon.

"She broke the car window," he said, trucking another ricotta-stuffed shell into his mouth.

"What? Who?"

"You met a lonely Pennsylvania girl online. Traded nudes, jerked off for a few weeks, then decided to close the deal, so to speak. But you overstayed your welcome. She took a crowbar to my Rover as a parting gift. End of story."

"No!" he revised, almost choking on his enthusiasm. "She already *had* a boyfriend. You were her sidepiece, for fun. Somehow the cuck catches on and takes his frustration out on my defenseless SUV." He put down another shell. "Am I getting warmer?"

I was barely paying attention. My hand kept returning to my pants pocket in search of the pills. Duds or not, they'd given me something to hold.

"And now we're eating noodles in Allentown. Why? To win her back? Teach the hothead cuck a lesson?" The would-be detective placed his fork on the edge of his plate, its tines angled ominously up. "I'll confess something right now, Seth. I'm no fighter."

I bit into some bread. "Karate?"

He didn't ask how I knew, didn't even flinch. "Martial arts more closely resembles dance than fighting. Though it is true that—"

"Look, it doesn't matter. No one's fighting anyone." I picked at a bed of wilted broccolini. "And why do you care, anyway? What does my personal life have to do with you?"

Moon said nothing, digging into another shell. After a hard swallow, he rubbed at his throat. Was it a loaded gesture? Was he signaling something? His poem, I remembered, made mention of my throat. But he wasn't signaling anything; the food had gone down the wrong way.

I told him not to concern himself with my affairs, though I did need one more hour. Alone.

"Knew it!" he exclaimed. "What's the girl's name? Or is it the cuck?" His baseline exuberance made it tough to gauge how inebriated he was. He insisted he was fine to drive, but I wasn't sure. Best to give it another hour, to be safe. Which was perfect timing, as far as I was concerned.

"I'll explain later. Please, just wait here. Order more pasta or something." I looked at him sternly. "And no more drinking."

"But . . . I like drinking." He said it plainly, without slant.

I was tempted to point out his father's alcoholism, but I refrained. I simply made him promise he'd abstain for the next hour. I took both sets of car keys, just in case.

The sprint to Chabad didn't take me long, even though I stopped for flowers on the way. The last of my tzedakah went toward a dozen tulips.

It was a surprise when one of the triplets opened the door.

"Hi," I said. "Mom or Dad home?"

She asked me to hold on, then charged up the stairs. Standing alone on the Chabad porch, I remembered the first time I visited, how anxious I felt waiting for Nadav to greet me. But then, with each visit, I grew more comfortable. It might not have been my ideal place to go, but it was a home when I needed one. I had to express my gratitude in person. I hoped the flowers would show I meant it.

After a moment or two, I heard the plodding rhythm of an adult descending.

"Hana!" I extended the bouquet to her. The already-browning tips of the tulips grazed her cheek as she found her grip.

"Shalom, Seth." She stepped to the side and cleared a path for me to enter, which wasn't the same as inviting me in.

Had I come too late in the day? Should I have announced myself in advance? I'd always felt welcome walking in through the door (*Where Every Jew Is Family!*), but now I had the distinct impression of intruding.

Asher rushed toward me in recognition. I knelt down, giving him my palm for a high five, but he misunderstood the gesture, expecting I would hoist him up. Fragile as he was, I didn't lift him. Instead I tousled his hair, careful not to disturb his yarmulke.

"Where's Nadav?" I asked Hana. "Wait, let me guess: *business in Bethlehem.*" I meant to signal I remembered them, that I still bore the stamp of our time together, that I really was, in a way, family.

I wasn't prepared for her to start sobbing. She gave Asher the flowers to take into the kitchen, and he hopped a few paces away.

"Hana? Are you all right?" I leaned forward. "Did something happen to Nadav?"

She sat and hid her face at her inner elbow. "Nothing happened," she said, her high voice muffled.

"Has he been . . . physical with you?"

She began sobbing again. I could hear Asher in the kitchen filling a vase.

"He's unfaithful. Is that it?"

She shook, an illegible yes or no.

Entering an Orthodox man's home—a rabbi's, no less—and asking such questions was surely forbidden. But despite all prohibitions, I sensed this was the only way I could help her, and clearly she was in need of help. It was intoxicating, that need.

I kept grilling Hana, but she wouldn't volunteer anything more. I started begging, explaining I was desperate for her to confide in me. After a while, my desperation became too much. It was time to go.

I took slow strides toward the door in the hope of drawing her out. Only when I turned the knob did she speak up.

"We're broke."

I turned back to Hana. Her hands were smoothing wrinkles from her dress.

"He keeps losing and losing. He can't stop."

Asher returned with the heavy vase in his hands. He was balancing the desire to show off his handiwork with the strain of holding the flowers upright above his head. I gave him an approving look, which I hoped he'd take as a suggestion to leave the room. Instead he rested the tulips on the highest shelf he could reach and plopped down beside me on a chair.

"Gamblers aren't good men," she said. "They leave things to chance instead of trusting in God." She explained that she'd been studying the Talmud; she would read Nadav's books late at night, slinking down to his study after he fell asleep. Then, having made this admission, she shrunk back into herself.

I tried to get more out of her, but she'd said enough. Having finished sobbing, she began the work of attending to her tears—where they'd fallen, where they'd dried, where they'd left a touch of salt.

"Anyway," she added, sitting upright, "it doesn't matter. I can't stop him."

Asher got up from his chair and went to sit beside his mother. He took a toy pony out of his pocket and plucked out its legs, one by one. Each left its socket with a pop.

"Where is he now?" I asked. How dare he do this to his family? *Our* family.

"The casino. As usual."

My hands were starting to clench. They were ready to grab Nadav by his throat and drag him back to his house, back to the person I needed him to be.

I was about to leave Chabad when I heard a voice that shook the whole length of my spine.

"Seth? Sethhhhhhhhhh?????"

I hurried—*ran*, in fact—to get ahead of the situation, but it was already too late: there was Moon standing at the doorframe, one foot already making its way in, rubber sole soon to squeak on the hardwood floor.

Hana took to her feet, stepped toward the entrance, and welcomed yet another uninvited guest. "Shalom," she greeted.

"Sla-lom," he slurred, grabbing my shoulder to hold himself up.

Since I'd last seen Moon, he'd managed to get even drunker. He looked like a wreck, but at least Hana had experience when it came to such things. There were wrecks stumbling in and out of her home constantly.

"This is . . . Robert," I explained. I wondered if she might recoil, given Chabad protocol (*Where Every Non-Jew Is an Outsider!*), but she didn't refuse him. Asher took an interest, hurrying toward Moon much as Giles had. I swooped in to intercept. It mattered to me that the two not come into contact, that I hold some line between them.

Moon extended his arm to shake Hana's hand, but I grabbed his sleeve and pulled it back. "Really," I insisted, "we should get going. *Now.*"

He consented with a grunt and waved goodbye to Asher. The boy
looked at Moon, then looked at me, then placed the legless pony at
the lip of the brick fireplace.

Hana showed no signs of her earlier dismay as she escorted us out.
Before shutting the door, she said, "Please give our best to Yael," not
even waiting for a reply.

On our walk back to the cars, Moon struggled to keep pace with
me, staggering wildly from one intersection to the next.

"How the fuck did you find that place?" I finally exploded, turning
to face him. "Did you follow me?"

"GPS," he answered, proud and breathless.

"But I never took the car there. I never even parked there!"

"You took the keys, though." He pulled out his phone to show
me his tracker app, but it slipped from his hand. The hardware fell
on the curb, an easy kick into a sewer grate, had I felt bold enough.
He bent over, lurching to rescue it.

"So that was her?" he said, bracing himself on a yield sign. He
swept back some hair that fell just above his eyes. "Fuckable. A little
matronly, but fuckable, for sure."

"Stop."

"And who's Yael? Is that a second girl?"

"You're really—"

"Pretty hot name. Ya-el! Like being named for an orgasm."

"Shut the fuck up."

Before long, we were back at the Rover. I claimed the driver's seat
while he slumped into the passenger side.

"Where are we going?" he asked, eyes straining against the weight
of their lids.

"Shut the fuck up," I repeated, then put his girl in drive.

* * *

As soon as we pulled onto the highway, Moon passed out cold. I didn't trust he was asleep, so I tried talking to him, just to test it. I said outrageous stuff, anything that I knew would expose whether he was listening. "I'm your fuckface," I whispered. "I am your sweetest fuckface." He didn't stir, not even an eyebrow twitch. Then a tractor trailer behind us honked, and he jolted awake. He took a confused glance out the window.

"Hey, man, seriously, where are you taking me?"

We were only a few minutes away, so I spilled the beans.

"Gambling?" He stretched his neck and adjusted his headrest. "Not a fan."

I said something to appease him, something about casinos being fun. Though I too had no interest in gambling, nor any money to gamble with, nothing even to pawn. My landlord had probably begun dispatching all my belongings down the trash chute. My furniture, my clothes—gone. Everything but my notebook, which I'd kept on my person for safekeeping.

"It's for losers," he asserted. "You ever heard of gambler's ruin?"

I shook my head and kept speeding.

"It's nothing advanced. Basic stuff, Stats 101." He cleared his throat and rolled up his sleeves. Josie likely enjoyed this about him, how he could take the reins and keep a conversation humming along. "If you play against somebody with better odds than you, and you play infinite times, you lose. If you play against somebody with more money than you, and you play infinite times, you lose." He was waiting for a reaction, but my gaze was on the highway. "The casino has *both* better odds and more money!"

"Right," I said, maneuvering toward the exit lane. "But we're not playing infinite times. That's working in our favor."

"Huh?"

"Infinite times would take forever. But we can't play forever. We're mortal."

He paused to process. "So being human gives us a fighting chance?"

"Sure."

Moon slapped me on the chest so hard, I nearly swerved into an oncoming bus.

"DEATH! DEATH is on our side!" Moon stared up through the open roof for a moment, his eyes straining against an immeasurable distance. After a span of silence, he went back to Hana and Yael. "You're really banging *both* of them? At the same time?" He whistled a little something through his teeth.

I pulled into the first parking spot I could find. We were about to leave the car and head inside together, but first I decided to level with Moon. To be honest with him, for a change of pace.

"This isn't some fun excursion," I said. "It's a rescue mission."

"I'll need a cape! I'll need—"

"Just *listen*. It's very straightforward." My eyes glared with impatience. "Someone's in the casino who doesn't belong in there, and we need to get him out."

Moon was still drunk, though he was starting to come out of it. "This person, he owes you money or something?"

I said it wasn't like that.

"So why," he said, unbuckling himself, "do you care?"

I wasn't sure how much to reveal, so I revealed everything. I explained that, while living in Allentown, there was a rabbi who took me in. And that it turned out he had a serious gambling problem.

Moon saw the seriousness in my face and chuckled. "A rabbi? Really?"

I nodded.

He pushed open his car door and stepped haltingly out onto the pavement. "*A rabbi walks into a casino*," he said. "How do I know this isn't a joke?"

I outlined our strategy on our way inside. First, we needed to split up, so we could cover more ground. Then, as soon as either of us spotted him, we'd call the other one. Together, we'd descend on Nadav—peacefully, of course—and that's when I'd lay into him. I'd berate him for hurting his loved ones. It might be a tough intervention, but it was critical to be firm with him, emphasizing the depth of pain he caused. It was for his own good. This was the start of him turning his life around. This was the first step.

I started to give Moon a physical description of the rabbi, but he said it wasn't necessary. "How many rabbis am I gonna see?" With that, we stepped toward the gaming floor. I reminded Moon one last time to call me the instant he saw him. Then we went our separate ways.

I hadn't been in a casino in years. I felt transported by the sounds—the electric chirps, the euphonic cries, the bells chasing bells. From all the commotion, it sounded like everyone was winning big all around me, but I could see that wasn't true when I caught the dead glare of their eyes.

I hurried through busy sections of roulette, blackjack, craps, poker, and the rest. As I walked, I thought more about what I'd say to Nadav when I found him and the tone with which I'd say it. Perhaps a gentler approach might serve me best. I'd start by establishing common ground. I'd explain that I too had experience with addiction, so I knew a little about what he was going through. No, I wasn't quite an addict in the way he was, though I'd still felt that same pull, the impulse to keep reaching again and again toward something that already has you in its grasp. And I could help him. I'd be there for him, like he'd been there for me.

I'd finished two full loops of the gaming floor and still no sight of Nadav. I was about to embark on a third when I heard a buzz. Rushing the phone out of my pocket, I saw that, to my surprise, it wasn't Moon. It was my mother. I let the phone squirm in my palm a few more times, then resumed my search.

As I was making my way past the row of cashiers, I stopped myself. This was my mother calling. My *sick* mother. I still hadn't gotten an update on her health, and yet here I was, ignoring her call. If she had news to share—good or bad or very, very bad—I needed to hear it.

I staked out a quiet area. Just as I was bracing myself to meet her voice, I felt someone smack me violently hard on my backside. When I spun around, there they stood—the two of them, one larger than the other. Moon was out in front, while Nadav held a few feet behind. He was nearly hiding in Moon's shadow.

I could faintly hear Nadav making overtures, how it was a nice coincidence bumping into me here, how he and Hana had grown concerned after I left, how Asher missed me most of all. But only faintly, since I wasn't paying attention. I was focused on Moon. I asked why he hadn't called me, since that was the plan.

"Too busy." Moon sipped long at a drink he was holding.

"You were too *busy?*"

"Listen, when you're rolling hot, what do you do? You keep rolling! Isn't that right, Rabbi?" Moon wrapped one of his heavy arms around the top of Nadav's frame, the same gesture he'd done with me countless times before. It was a pretty epic night. That was the exact word he used, *epic.* "Now, if you'll excuse us," he continued, bowing his large head toward his companion, "we need to go cash out." And with that, the two left for the cashier booth to collect what was won.

7.

When the casino's doors sighed shut behind the three of us, I let loose.

"What the fuck is wrong with you?" I pushed Moon hard in the shoulder. Because of his size, he didn't budge, or maybe he didn't feel it. He'd gotten drunker again, courtesy of the casino's free drinks. "You think it's funny to enable an addicted gambler?"

Nadav slipped in between us. "Seth, I think it's important to take a deep breath and—"

"You're a fucking addict. That's what you are." I spun back toward Moon. "How did you even find him?"

"He was standing at the roulette table."

"Which roulette table? I checked them all."

"The high-stakes one. In the VIP area."

It hadn't occurred to me there might be a VIP area, though of course there would be and of course Moon would find it. Unthinkable for it to have gone any other way, just like it was unthinkable that he might step into a casino and not leave a winner.

Nadav was itching for an opportunity to scurry away, but I wouldn't let that happen, not yet. "You," I said, pivoting toward him. "You're a phony. You're a fraud."

He tried placating me. He visited the casino only occasionally, hardly at all. And besides, he continued, people make mistakes, right? Everyone sins sometimes. He started pulling out quotes from

Kabbalah, but I could tell he was nervous from how he kept fumbling his words. As he spoke, he stiffened his arms and held his palms open to me, like I was the sky, like I was rain.

Rage was still pulsing through me. I'd believed in this man, and now I felt ashamed for believing. I could tell I was about to cry, so I did something to stop the tears in their tracks. Stepping close, I reached for his yarmulke and, in one swift and sudden motion, threw it to the ground. Then I dropped my foot down upon it.

As Nadav bent low to retrieve his trampled skullcap, I continued raining insults upon him. Finally, Moon told me to knock it off. He said it was "too much." Said I was "acting like a child."

Ordinarily I might've responded to Moon with a few choice words of my own, but I had had it with words; what I needed to wield was something as hard and literal as my person, specifically my fists. I spun toward my former colleague and, finding him smiling, reared back and slugged him right in the lower half of his gut, the thick part that bulged out over the borderline of his belt. He let out a big exhale, almost like a laugh. It *was* a laugh. So I aimed higher. I took my time to size him up and punched him squarely in the jaw. I was surprised to find how much it hurt my hand, though I supposed this hurt meant something good, meant he was hurting too. I looked up and confirmed as much. He wasn't laughing anymore.

I knew I had to hurry to land another blow, though my right hand was still throbbing from its first tour of duty. I decided to wind up with my left and hope for the best, but I never had a chance to see it through. Moon had anticipated the attack and, midswing, intercepted me.

Power, I was expecting that from Moon. But it was his velocity that proved most astonishing, how the full force of him swept in like a riptide and stole me off my feet. With my whole body in a bear hug, he took me hard against a lamppost, the light beam shuddering down on us. I tried using my one free arm to punch his back, but it wasn't free for long; he reached up and locked the arm behind me, trapping it against my own weight. Then it contorted at an unfortunate angle, and I heard a small tear opening in the stitched fabric of my person, like a dinner napkin ripped at the trim. His grip was strong, stronger even than I imagined. I continued to fight with all I had. I knew if I stopped, he'd let go, so I kept thrashing, if only to see how thoroughly he could crush me, how broken I could become. Maybe the pills were fake, but this—*this*—was real.

Nadav was making an effort to pull the two of us apart, or really talk the two of us apart; he kept saying things intended to defuse the situation and convince me to stand down. I wasn't listening. Even if I had been, it wouldn't have mattered. His words no longer carried weight with me. They were all sound and no substance. They were like my words, but from his mouth.

I waited for Nadav to draw a little closer, then I kicked out my leg. I couldn't see exactly what I hit, though I was encouraged when I heard a yelp of pain that I attributed to him. Buoyed by this success, I began thrashing with even greater intensity, but Moon's grip on me only tightened, then tightened further. Eventually we were no longer separate beings. When he yelled, my throat trembled. When he inhaled, my lungs filled. We were two skydivers strapped together for our lives and plunging fast, falling deeper and deeper into each other as much as the atmosphere itself.

Then I couldn't breathe. Moon's forearm had inched higher, and I was now in a full-on chokehold. It occurred to me that, if things went on like this, I might die. No, I *would* die. With each passing second, the possibility was compressing into hard fact. I tried to signal I needed air, but I couldn't get out the words. Nadav, meanwhile, wasn't even focused on us anymore. He'd taken a seat on the curb.

The balloons in my brain were deflating. With the world slipping away, and his forearm locked in place, I homed in on a patch of skin. I bit down. *Hard.* I wanted to take a chunk out of Moon. I'd disappear him, piece by piece.

He cried out, in either pain or surprise or both, and hurled me down onto the pavement. Whatever was holding my shoulder together had had enough; I heard a sharp and much deeper tear, indicating I was no longer intact, that my left arm had parted ways with the rest of me, even if technically it remained attached. I was still reeling from the impact of this injury when Moon began kicking me in the ribs. I wasn't expecting this added brutality, but there he was, drawing his right leg as far back as it went, then snapping it home repeatedly into my side. I wished I'd been lighter, light enough for him to punt me far away and out of range, but instead I lay flat and inert, a throw pillow filled with gravel instead of goose feathers. In between kicks, I mustered what little oxygen I could to call out his name. Not "Moon," but "Robert, please, Robert." He wound up for one final kick and then, at the last second, relented. I could see blood was trickling down his forearm, and Nadav rushed in to hold him steady and inspect the bite mark. "Son of a bitch," Moon kept repeating. "Son of a *fucking* bitch."

I watched one tend to the injuries of the other. Something about the way Nadav reached for Moon and helplessly took his injured arm in his grasp, I started to imagine that the two were chimpanzees and that Nadav might start licking Moon's wound. Absurd, yes, but don't animals do that, and aren't we animals? I attempted to get up off the ground, but the pain was incapacitating. They ignored me, even when I let out a long whimper at their feet. I felt invisible lying there and remembered how it felt when I was punched in Ramya's apartment. I was grateful for that memory. I wrapped myself in the heavy shroud of it.

My vision was blurry, so I wasn't sure I was seeing correctly when I noticed Moon—the larger chimp of the two—reaching into his side pocket and producing a Swiss army knife. But it was undeniable: there he was, stepping toward me with a blade. Remaining quite composed, I wondered how he'd attack. Would he stab or slash? Would he stick the blade *in* me or slice *through* me? It seemed a philosophical question: Was I a destination or a way to somewhere else? As I prepared to learn the answer and accept what I figured was the end, he bent down and cut off a long strip of my pant leg. A tourniquet. He was fashioning a tourniquet for his arm. After some maneuvering, he made a double knot and pulled it tight with his teeth. Then he turned his attention to more pressing matters.

"Come on," he bellowed. "Let's go celebrate!" Tucking his knife away, he took out his wallet and held it with two hands, exaggerating its weight. It was fat with payout. "You know places around here, right?" He was looking at Nadav.

I drew a breath, and the air was all blades. Cries of insects from the nearby river flecked the silence. The sky was dark and full. Lights from the casino's facade were sparkling in Moon's eyes, so it looked like he was blinking back tears.

"*Please*," Moon said, still blinking. "Please?"

I couldn't respond. I was too busy coughing up blood.

* * *

Allentown did have a hospital—a relatively decent one, actually— so if in fact I had had a fiancée who'd required serious treatment, I could've done a lot worse than this facility. It comforted me, the idea of my fictional beloved getting good care.

Moon and I were seated beside each other in the ER's cramped waiting room. Despite his initial desire to go out on the town, he changed course when it became clear I might not survive until morning in the absence of medical attention. The rabbi had nodded and said goodbye, promising to pray for me. He then got into his car and shut the door, though we never saw him pull out of the casino's parking lot. He was probably just waiting for us to leave.

"So," Moon said. "How'd I taste?" He peeled off the strip of pant to study more closely where I'd gotten him.

"Salty? I don't remember."

"Sorry the meal wasn't to your liking." He wrapped it back up again.

Each time I took a breath, I wanted to die. The punch to my eye at Ramya's had been equally acute, but that pain was localized. My whole body now felt out of order, each part broken in a broken sum.

The ER was packed, so it wasn't clear when I'd be seen. Sitting across from us was a couple, roughly our age, who appeared worryingly high; their eyes kept floating up to the ceiling and snowflaking back down. Oh, and the woman was pregnant.

"You *bit* me, man. Really, what's wrong with you?" Moon threw back his head, as if an answer might fall from above.

"Not sure," I wheezed.

"Sorry about the kicking, though. Something came over me."

I said I wasn't mad. I probably deserved it.

The woman attempted to lie down, resting her feet on the chair beside her, but one of the nurses tapped her and cautioned against it. Despite her dazed state of mind, she took instruction well. She wore a baseball cap with the brim off-center while her partner—husband? boyfriend?—slumped deeper into sleep.

"So that was a real rabbi? Seemed like a regular guy to me."

I shrugged. More pain shot through me—the sharpest I'd ever experienced in my life, like a sunbeam through the thick of a magnifying glass.

He picked at the area around the bite. I could tell it was bothering him. "You know, I've been where you are now. Got the living crap kicked out of me once. Was in the hospital for a week. Sipped all my meals through a tiny plastic straw."

The woman pulled down her cap's brim to shield her eyes from the fluorescent lighting overhead. Still unsatisfied, she removed the cap entirely and buried her face into her shoulder.

"The Attack of the Wes."

"Huh?"

"My baby bro. I used to push him all the damn time when we were kids. I mean literally push him, like off the swing set and stuff. My dad would slap me across the head and tell me to stop it, but it was so easy, you know? Like it was totally natural, because he was so much smaller. Then one day he's getting off the school bus, and I push him down the steps. Not all the steps, just the last one, so he falls on the curb and busts open his lip. And everyone on the bus is watching, right?"

The woman began to moan. It occurred to me she might be in labor.

"So Wesley gets up, and his mouth is all blood. He's furious. Like, I finally snapped him. He grabs me, pushes me against the side of the bus. Choking me! And I'm not fighting back. In fact, I'm letting him do it, to build the little guy's confidence, you know? But it's no good, because the kids on the bus can't see. They can *hear* us fighting, but we're way too close, even with their faces pressed up against the windows. So I throw myself WWF style onto our front lawn, just to give them a show. And Wesley pounces on me! Man, it was glorious."

"*Glorious?*"

"Yes. Fucking glorious." He sat upright. "He'd never stood up to me before, not once. Way too soft. And I was worried as hell, because I knew the bullies at school would eat his ass alive, just like they did to me. Or used to, until I learned self-defense."

As Moon got deeper into his story, his hands began to dance with each other in the air. There's no other way to say it: They were dancing.

"Anyway, we're rolling around on that lawn, and Wes keeps wailing on me—in the face, in the throat. The whole bus is going crazy, right? Because no one expected this, not from Wes. The driver is shouting at us to quit it, but he can't unbuckle himself. Like, legally, because of safety regulations, he's *got* to stay on that bus.

"So I'm eating this up! My baby bro, becoming a man and shit. I could've cried, I felt so proud, like a proud coach. But then he lands this one punch, and I can't breathe. And he keeps punching and punching that same spot, like he knows he hit gold or something. So I stare directly at him"—Moon stared directly at me—"like, *Hey, come on, that's enough. You've done enough.* And the scary part is he stares right back at me, and he's like, *Yeah, I know, I'm sorry.* His face is sympathetic. He's sobbing even. But his arms keep swinging! Like the rest of his body didn't get the memo. And now I know I'm fucked, because it's like I'm fighting *two* of him. There's the one who's my bro, the one who loves me. And then this . . . stranger."

Moon smoothed his hair to the side, every strand in agreement. With his story complete, his hands settled down to rest. I studied him closely, looking for any scars from Wesley's assault, but of course they were long gone. And the bite mark I left, it would soon fade too. It would be easy to look at Moon in a week's time and not see he was as wounded as anyone else.

Then the woman erupted with a shriek. Her man was still dead asleep, and she was all alone, waking up from something horrid. She tried shaking him to help her, but nothing. She took a magazine from the coffee table, rolled it tight, and smacked his face. Nothing. Then, in that instant, I understood. He was the reason she was shrieking. He was, by the look of it, completely gone.

Moon stood up to approach them, and I seized with worry. What if another fight broke out? I would've pulled him back, but I lacked the strength.

The woman looked up at Moon with swollen pleading eyes. She reached for his arm, the bitten one, but he withdrew it just in time. She begged him to help, to get the doctor, to do *something*. He took out his wallet and handed her his fat stack of winnings. "All of it," he later explained, "just to shut her up."

8.

As it turned out, my mom did not have nothing. I spent the next few weeks at home, chauffeuring her around Maryland as she received treatment for a tumor in her pelvis the size of a kumquat. In between her oncology appointments, I tended to my own medical needs: I was rehabbing a torn rotator cuff and three broken ribs.

During one of the first visits to her oncologist, I learned that the tumor would be excised with the help of an old friend: IQBlade360.

"But that's for prostate," I piped up.

"Not exclusively," the doctor answered. "Are you in med school or something?"

"No. I've just heard about the technology."

She swiveled back to her desktop monitor. "Oh?"

I explained that one of my former clients invented it. My mom took a proud shine, sitting upright under the doctor's dense wall of diplomas.

During one visit, my mom had to undergo a particularly lengthy procedure, so I had extra time. I decided to head to the main floor of the monolithic medical center where walk-ins were processed and ask the receptionist about scheduling a drug test.

"For which drugs, specifically?"

"All of them."

She looked at me quizzically.

"I want to know what drugs I took. If they were real or not." I explained that I'd swallowed a whole bunch of pills, nearly three hundred in total.

The young woman with long curls straightened in her seat, reached for a phone mounted on the wall. "When did you take them, sir?"

"Months ago," I answered. Her hand eased from the phone.

"Whatever it was," she said, "it's out of your system by now."

"But how do I know if I'm addicted?"

"Addicted? To what?"

A line of prospective patients was forming behind me.

"If you were addicted to something, sir, you'd know it."

I tried my best to level with her. I admitted, in no uncertain terms, that I really did believe I *was* an addict. I'd demonstrated all the classic warning signs, the trademark behaviors, the typical symptoms.

"But this was . . . months ago?"

"Yes."

"And you've been clean ever since?"

I nodded.

She stood and snapped at the line to bend back on itself, so nurses could pass more easily through the hall. When she returned to her seat, her face had stiffened, forcing the slack out of the air between us. "Listen," she said. "Do you need to be seen or not?" The question made me step away for a bit. I needed to think it over.

While I was busy ferrying my mom back and forth from doctors' offices, my dad devoted himself to her recovery at home. He cared for her in a measured way, providing the exact amount of whatever she needed. Four hundred milligrams of ibuprofen, three episodes of *Seinfeld*. He approached it like assembling a model battleship: the directions printed and laid out on the table, the pieces labeled in clear plastic baggies.

I was home alone with my dad one afternoon when I decided to confess. I told him about all that had happened—how I'd lost my copywriting job and then everything spiraled thereafter. Or rather, *I* spiraled it. The blame lay with me.

I worried, though, about telling my mom. Wasn't it selfish, I asked him, to unburden myself of this stuff? Would it be better to wait until she was healed?

My dad was loading dirty plates into the dishwasher. "Do you think your mother and I are fools?"

I wasn't sure I followed.

"We've known about all this for months." He hesitated. "Well, not *all* of it."

"Was it Moon? Did he tell you?" I remembered how chummy the two had been, how they'd chatted at the kitchen table like old pals.

"Your landlord must've called us a hundred times alone." My dad ran a sponge over a wooden salad spoon.

"But you never said anything? The whole time?"

"Believe me, *I* wanted to." He shot me a fiery look. "Your mom said absolutely not. She was too afraid."

"Afraid? Of what?"

"Of pushing you away." He gave the dish soap bottle a squirt. "She thought that, if we tried talking to you about all this, you'd feel ambushed and leave. And then where would you go?

"There had to be a good reason for all your lying. That's what she kept telling me, telling herself." He glared at me with suspicion. "Was she right?"

I tried to answer honestly. I said I wasn't sure. Maybe I had no reason, and I lied just because I could.

"Well, before you talk to her tonight, you should come up with one." Foam formed as he scrubbed hard at a spatula, which he set firmly on the top rack. Then he turned toward me and exploded:

"Will you please spare me with the woe-is-me bullshit? It's *obvious* why you lied to us. Why you kept lying over and over."

My father never cursed, especially not at home. I stiffened in place.

"You were trying to protect us. You were trying to protect your mom especially. Because you didn't want to hurt her. Isn't that true?" He was still shouting, though not at the same level. He'd softened, tiny soap bubbles still clinging to his hands. "Or, at least, *partially* true?"

I thought it over. Yes. It was true.

"Perfect." He wiped his hands dry on a rag. "So tell her."

After he left the kitchen, I stayed put for a while, listening to the dishwasher do its work—how it lightly knocked the plates and glasses and silverware back and forth, jostling them, getting them just clean enough.

*   *   *

I took a job at the Starbucks near my former high school. Ordinarily I might've felt ashamed, except my mom's cancer steeled me against all that. Every espresso shot I pulled, I pulled for her. I recognized very few of the customers; most of my peers had left Columbia and never come back. Then, one day, a woman walked in whose voice I knew instantly. It was Mrs. Beiselman, along with her grown-up daughter, Abby (I got her name when taking her order). She had Beezy's same build—short and stocky—though her face was quite different, almost enough to miss the resemblance. When the mother tried to pay, I said their drinks were on the house. Special promotion, I told them, and that was that.

My barista wages mostly went to help with my mom's medical bills, and the rest I used to settle with my landlord. He agreed not to press charges but demanded double the security deposit. Which, honestly, was fair. My kitchen, with its shattered window, had gained a reputation as a popular nesting spot among pigeons.

In the spare time I had, I wrote. Mostly I worked on my ventriloquism essay. I was pleased with its closing flourish:

Every ventriloquist act presents us with a moral decision: we must identify with either the ventriloquist or the dummy, the subject or the subjected, the voice or the instrument through which it's heard. And yet the hierarchies of power are perhaps not always so clear. When the ventriloquist steps onto the stage, is his dummy not dragging him? The two are inextricably bound, and thus both are subjugated. Each becomes the dummy of the other.

I also wrote letters. I composed one to Hana and was surprised when she replied later that week with a detailed update. Nadav had packed up all his things and moved out, leaving everyone behind. Chabad was letting her stay temporarily in the house, but the situation was untenable. She described feeling stuck. She knew she could work something out, if only she had time to think.

On a humid Sunday, I drove my parents' car to Allentown to take Asher off her hands, just for a few hours. I found him in one of his less communicative moods, his high chirp barely audible over the shush of the AC.

"Want to see a Pigs game today?" I'd made sure to check the schedule beforehand.

"Not really."

I stole a glance at him between stoplights. "But . . . Woo?"

"Gone," he said, flicking his vent, aiming the air away from his face.

"Too bad. Where is he now?"

He said he wasn't sure. Probably he was traded.

"Okay," I said. "What should we do instead?"

Asher had never been to the local zoo. Within the hour, we were standing very still and staring at an albino ball python coiled behind terrarium glass.

"It's not moving," he said.

I replied that it was probably resting.

"Maybe. Or maybe it's hunting." He looked up at me, then back at the coil.

I told him the glass was thick. We didn't need to worry.

"Sometimes I do that."

"Do what?"

"Pretend I'm asleep."

"Why?"

"So I can hear the buzzwuzzies."

"Fuzzy what?"

"The buzzwuzzies live under my bed. They come out when I'm sleeping. So sometimes I have to trick them." He sounded resentful that he had to stoop to such deceit.

"What do they sound like? These buzzwuzzies."

"They cry. A lot."

Without realizing it, I was kneeling beside him. We were alone; the zoo's livelier attractions garnered greater attention. "And why are they crying? Asher?"

He touched his thumb to the clear edge of the glass.

"Are they lonely?" I turned him away from the snake to face me. "Is that why?"

"It's because they're imaginary. And they want to be real. Like us."

I could feel the eyes of other reptiles in the room.

"The buzzwuzzies are *never* lonely," he said, turning back to the knot of python, pressing both palms against its enclosure. "They're always together. They're a family."

He was, I feared, about to start coughing, but this time I was more prepared. I was fully present.

"Asher," I said, "your family loves you." I uttered it quietly at first, then again with added force. I gave him a hug, and he hugged me back, until suddenly he broke away: the snake had drawn his attention when it raised its smooth wedge of a head.

* * *

Before driving back home, I made sure to do two things. First, I asked Hana for Nadav's new address. I wasn't sure when I'd feel ready to write him a letter or what I'd say in it, but I felt it was important to reach out. I'd been holding off because of lingering anger; his failings seemed like failings of Judaism overall, an indictment of the entire faith, and hadn't I been trying to believe? But it wasn't fair to conflate the two. If I'd made the mistake of putting too much faith in him, that was on me. Next time I'd put faith in something larger.

Second, I decided to get coffee. Ramya's shop was nearby, and I was eager to discuss *Braid* with her. She hadn't explained that, on the video game's fourth level, even small movements influence the flow of time—step right, and time advances; step left, it goes backward. I'd find myself simultaneously fighting battles from the past and future.

"Is Ramya working today?"

The teenager behind the counter was busy tamping a portafilter. "Quit."

"What? When?"

"Last week. Last month maybe."

"Where'd she go?"

He shook his head without looking up.

"Is she still in Allentown?" I leaned in. "Is she out of rehab?"

He slotted the filter into the mouth of the machine, then bent low for milk. "Maybe she's traveling." It wasn't clear if he was offering me a precious nugget of intelligence or just expediting my exit. I left without buying a thing.

I tried putting myself in Ramya's shoes. If I were her, where would I travel? But it didn't matter. Even if I knew where she was—and

even if I believed she wanted to see me—I couldn't afford to go
there. I'd need to work for at least another year as a barista before
considering any travel. There was, however, one other way for me
to make money. The opportunity fell into my lap.

*   *   *

"Moon?"

"Who else!" he replied, his baritone booming out of the phone.
I could imagine the sound ricocheting off the interior walls of his
office and onto the slick finish of his desk.

I asked how things were going.

"Insane. I'm like a chicken running around with its dick cut off."

"Head?"

"All of my budgets. Fucked!" The tenor of his discontent suggested everything had returned to normal. He was even cursing
like himself again. "How are you feeling? Your front teeth still
sharp as ever?"

"They're fine, thanks."

"And your folks? Mom still obsessed with that margarita mix?"

"Huh?"

"The lime stuff."

"She's fine," I reported. "And how's Josie?"

"No idea." He gave a flat chuckle. "I'm back with Meghan now."

"Oh, wow."

"Don't act surprised. It always had to end this way."

"What way?"

"Me and her." He sounded resigned. His voice grew small and
cold as a coil. "You can only sling it loose for so long."

It occurred to me that I'd never gotten a full accounting of what
led to their broken engagement in the first place. I'd taken Moon's
explanation at his word, but that was before I really knew him.

"Listen, this is a business call," he continued. "Want to earn some easy cash? Think of it like Christmas spending money. Never mind, you're Jewish. Well, Jews love money, so maybe—"

"Stop. Just stop."

"I signed a pharma client in Baltimore. They need a brand philosophy."

I hesitated. "Brand *philosophy*?"

"Same as a brand credo," he said. "You've done a bunch of those, right?"

I held the phone to my right ear lightly, like an ice pack.

"Anyway, they're launching a new antidepressant. Should be a load of fun!"

"What kind of antidepressant? An SSRI or something else?" I'd recently done a bit of reading into the subject.

"I can email you the research if you wanna sift through it. Better yet, do your own research. Pop a few happy pills yourself. Look, the client wants a writer on the ground: full-time, eight weeks. And I'm not fucking up another budget, flying a senior copywriter to the Murder Capital, putting him up in an overpriced Murder Marriott, while the—"

"So it's just freelance?"

"Yup." He added: "But maybe, with time, who knows?"

I took a moment. "When do you need an answer?"

"Today."

I would've declined out of hand, had I not needed the money. My reluctance to involve myself with RazorBeat again had nothing to do with Josie; I hadn't thought about her in months, hadn't even talked to her, except to extend my congrats when I heard she made partner. And I'd stopped harboring resentments toward the agency long ago, so it wasn't about wounded pride either.

"Well?"

"Moon, let me ask you something. My notebook." I reached for a paper clip, thinking of how I might bend it, break it. I gave the sharp end to the callused part of my palm and saw the skin pale under pressure. "Why'd you write all that stuff?

"What I mean is," I continued, "what was the point?"

Since being home, I'd spent hours with the notebook, leafing through its entries. I returned to Moon's poem with frequency. It didn't help that he'd taken the middle spread, so the journal instinctively opened to it. I still hadn't ripped out the page.

"Oh, you know. Just a joke."

"A joke?"

"Yeah. Like a funny story."

"But it wasn't a story."

"Sure it was! It was totally a story."

No, I wanted to say. *It was a poem. And poems aren't like stories. Stories you can just make up. But poems are something different altogether.*

Moon paused, which was unusual for him. He typically expelled all his words in one go, though now his delivery took a different turn. "What do you think?" he said finally, his mouth at my ear. "Am I a writer?"

* * *

At three in the morning, I beat *Braid*'s final level and got to the princess. I'd spent many long nights in my parents' basement trying to reach her, but ultimately my victory proved anticlimactic: the screen went blank, a mushroom-cloud white. I looked online to read up on explanations. Some players theorized it was intended to represent a doomsday scenario. The seductive princess, they said, was a metaphor for the atomic bomb. Others offered different interpretations. Was the princess a femme fatale? Perhaps she'd misled the hero from the start.

I had the urge to call Ramya. I'd texted her a few times recently, but I hadn't heard her voice in forever. Calling this late seemed like a safe bet, since it would go straight to voicemail. She answered after the first ring.

"You're up?" I said. "It's three in the morning."

"Not for me, Seth. For you."

The disparity threw me. "Where are you?"

"Los Angeles." She hastened to clarify: "I'm out here now. For school."

"Oh."

"I had to go wherever they'd let me in." A note of helplessness entered her voice, like she'd been boxed up and shipped west.

"You like it out there?"

"My hair does. Low humidity."

"How much are flights to L.A. these days?"

She insisted I'd hate it there, so there was no point to me visiting. I understood what she was really saying.

"Just finished *Braid*," I said. "What'd you think of the ending?"

"Didn't make it that far."

I was incredulous. "You gave up?!"

"Got bored halfway through. What happens?"

I slumped back on the bed. If the game hadn't held her attention, my retelling wouldn't either. "Screen goes white," I said. "Everything just explodes."

"Weird."

"The princess symbolizes an atomic bomb." I waited for her to respond, but she stayed silent. "You spend all this time trying to rescue her, and when you finally do, she blows up in your face."

"It's a trap?"

"Yeah."

"Weird," she repeated. "Are you sure she wants to be rescued?"

"She's always crying out for help."

"But when you reach the princess, she . . . dies?"

"Right."

"So you kill her."

"Well, we *both* die. It's not fair to—"

"You kill her." She paused and, quite possibly, brushed back her hair. It was a gesture I'd seen her perform many times in Sötma's basement, just after removing her hat and setting it in her locker. "Maybe she never wanted your help. Maybe she wanted someone else to save her. From you."

I sat with it for a moment. I said I wasn't sure about her theory.

"If only she wasn't dead," she said. "We could ask her."

Ramya and I spoke for a bit longer, until she said she had to go to sleep. In those waning moments, my cell phone grew hot against my ear. Ordinarily I'd switch to headphones, but not this time. I liked the hard kiss of the metal, its humanlike warmth.

It was almost sunrise when we hung up, but I still wasn't tired. I felt energized, in fact. I reached for my notebook and turned to a blank page. It was time to get to work.

I hadn't been briefed yet by Moon, but already I had ideas about how to approach the new pharma project. It would be important for me, I felt, to gain the client's trust early. So perhaps I'd try something unconventional. At our first meeting, I'd confess that I suffered from depression. I'd explain to the client, without going into much detail, that I'd struggled with it all my life and that the past year had been the biggest struggle of all. In short, I understood deeply why their product mattered, because I knew firsthand what antidepressants meant for depressives like myself. Then I'd have the room's full attention. I could begin.

I was about to start scribbling when I paused. The notebook looked raggedy. Its binding had frayed, and most of the pages were filled up. Clearly, it was time for a new one. I thought it over for a moment, then knew exactly what I'd use.

The basement closet was filled with bins of school supplies that my parents had saved from my childhood. There were pencils, crayons, markers, and, yes, countless notebooks. Though mine were all in horrendous shape—torn and bent and scribbled to death. Totally inappropriate to bring to a client meeting. There was one, however, that had never been used at all.

It wasn't hard to find the bin with Mishaal's ninth grade English notebook, since I'd been the one to put it there in the first place. I'd saved it, along with a few other mementos: his soccer jersey, his yearbook photo, random stuff like that. In any case, the notebook was in pristine condition. All it had was his name written in tiny letters on the inside cover, and that didn't bother me. Like I said, tiny. Nobody would notice.

I tucked the notebook under my arm and headed upstairs to make coffee—nothing fancy, just drip. I poured myself a large cup, no milk or sugar, and sipped slowly while standing by the kitchen window. Out of habit, I reached into my pocket, just for something extra, though those days were behind me. Then, in no time, the sun came up. And I could see everything clearly again.

Acknowledgments

First, an author's note: the Derrida passages are quoted from *Archive Fever*, translated by Eric Prenowitz, and published in 1996 by The University of Chicago Press.

This book owes a lot to the care and devotion of many, as do I. Deep gratitude to the following: my agent, Alia Hanna Habib, for being a tireless advocate and believing in books with her whole heart. My editor, Zachary Knoll, for giving me permission to add when my impulse was to cut. My publicists, Kathleen Carter and Taryn Roeder, for helping these characters find their way into the world. Thank you to everyone at The Overlook Press, Abrams, and the Gernert Company.

I'm indebted to friends, early readers, and fellow writers who offered invaluable feedback and support: Hanif Abdurraqib, Kaveh Akbar, Emily Cunningham, Adam Dalva, Jay Deshpande, Andrew Eisenman, Lizzie Harris, Ruth Madievsky, Alex Reubert, Susan Epstein Rogers, Jessi Stevens, and Erica Wright. Thanks to Clint Smith, Vivian Lee, and the entire L&L family. Thanks to Peter Wolf, rest in peace.

I'm grateful to my former colleagues at the branding agencies where I worked as a copywriter, including Interbrand, Siegel+Gale, R/GA, and VSA. I hope I captured even a fraction of what it was like. It was something, wasn't it?

I'm grateful to the communities that made space for me and this book: Vermont Studio Center, Paragraph, the Rutgers Writers House, the libraries at Columbia and Pratt, and the coffee shops that looked the other way when I lingered for far too long.

I write because of my teachers. Thank you in particular to Joseph Borlo, Jorie Graham, Garth Greenwell, Betsy LaPadula, Avi Matalon, and my eleventh grade English teacher, Mario Costa, who once told me: "The only thing more tragic than tragedy is comedy."

Lastly and most importantly, my family. V, thank you for believing in the book I would write, not just the book I'd written. And to my mother, for being the one whose edits meant the most, because I knew they were true. And finally, to my father and to my son: You both inspire me to be a better person and a better man.

About the Author

BEN PURKERT is the author of the poetry collection *For the Love of Endings*. His work appears in the *New Yorker*, the *Nation*, and elsewhere. He is the founder of Back Draft, a *Guernica* interview series focused on revision and the creative process. He holds degrees from Harvard and NYU and currently teaches at Rutgers.